The Deep End of the Sea

Heather Lyons

Cerulean Books
ISBN: 978-0-9858653-1-3
First Edition

Cover design by Carly Stevens
Cover art by Kelsey Patton
Book formatting by Champagne Formats

The Fate Series

A Matter of Fate (#1)
Beyond Fate (#1.5)
A Matter of Heart (#2)
A Matter of Truth (#3)
A Matter of Forever (#4)

Praise for The Deep End of the Sea

"Heather Lyons's **The Deep End of the Sea** is a radiant, imaginative romance that breathes new life into popular mythology while successfully tackling the issue of sexual assault. Lyons is a deft storyteller whose engaging prose will surprise readers at every turn. Readers will have no trouble sympathizing with Medusa, who is funny, endearing and courageous all at once. The romance between her and Hermes is passionate, sweet and utterly engrossing. This is a must read!" –RT Book Reviews

"One of my top reads for 2014. Heather Lyons weaves an incredibly creative and addictive story. This is more than a must read, it's a must buy. Immediately." –Rachel Van Dyken, #1 New York Times Bestselling Author of The Bet

"Fascinating mythology + Imaginative plot + Sexy Greek god = YES PLEASE." –New York Times best selling author Cora Carmack

"A unique twist on Greek mythology that will have you rooting for Medusa from the very start." –Kelly Hashway, author of the Touch of Death series

"This novel honestly captivated me from the start like no other I have read thus far this year. Greek Mythology has always been something of interest to me, but this novel made that grow to new levels. Lyons has a way with words, I first learned of this in her Fate Series, but this novel...it blew me out of the water. Everything about it was so eloquently executed and beautifully written. It has left me eagerly anticipating what comes next from this author!" –Jennifer Snyder, author of the Tethered series

To my grandmother,
who I spent countless hours stargazing with,
and from whom my love of mythology stems
from,
I miss you.
This one's for you.

gorgóna

Chapter One

I let it happen again.

The temple settles into that stagnant silence I've long since learned to loathe, and these are the most cohesive series of words I can string together for many desolate minutes. *I let it happen again.* Resolutions apparently mean nothing, even if crafted under the best of intentions. Had I not, just this very morning, recited a daily pledge held dear to my heart: *I shall not let myself be used for death?*

And yet, a man is dead, and I was the weapon that slayed him.

I move closer to where he now stands, forever frozen in terror, and press my shaking hand against his outstretched stone one. "I'm sorry," I whisper, though he cannot and never will be able to hear my words. "So, so sorry."

His eyes, wide and mercifully detail free, offer me nothing in return. Once I commit his features to memory, I construct a life history with a name worthy of his sacrifice. Walt was single (I can't bear the thought of spouses and children, thus my collection of singletons) and a bit of a daredevil when he wasn't volunteering to teach literacy to adults in poverty stricken urban areas. He'd gone spelunking at least a half-dozen times, sky diving twice, and bungee cord diving off some crazy bridge in Colorado just once, on his thirtieth birthday. Walt liked to write poetry; how could he not, when his now-deceased parents had named him after one of the greats?

Walt liked to talk about poetry, too, which means he needs to be with others like him. I strip my flannel work shirt down to a tank top and get to work. Shoving stones around when half of one's body is reptilian isn't the easiest of tasks, and it requires a great deal of precision and care.

As I always tend to do when placing a new statue, I flash back to the one and only time I'd broken one of my victims. I'd been tired—he'd snuck upon me when I'd been sleeping—and an overestimated shove sent poor Nikolaos face first against the temple floor. I'd spent most of that night collecting the pieces which once made a whole man, blubbering in misery. As penance, his head, missing an ear and part of his nose, still sits on a shelf in my bedroom. *Treat us gently*, I like to imagine him telling me nightly before I sleep. *We deserve your care.*

I have not failed Nikolaos since. Over the ages, to transfer the statues around the island, I've developed a routine that includes wrapping the bodies in a thick quilt before putting them up on casters. It takes a painstaking amount of time to shift them short or long distances, but each person deserves nothing less from me.

Walt's group sits just outside the temple. They are the philosophers of our island; it only seems natural they would find much to appreciate in both the sun and the stars. I struggle with his body over the stairs—they are tricky to maneuver for me even without hauling a two hundred pound statue—but eventually, I get him exactly where he'll fit in best.

"Ladies and gentlemen, this is Walt," I tell the still faces forming a cluster near a non-functioning fountain. "His poetry is as beautiful as his namesake's."

I angle Walt so his eyes face theirs. It's late afternoon, and there is soft orange light filtering down upon their features. It's a

2

beautiful sight, which only saddens me, because all of that talk about death and beauty being intertwined is one of the biggest loads of crap I've ever heard. Death isn't beautiful. Too often than not, it's messy and brutal; even when done in sleep, there's still that theft of breath, that failure of a heart. Death is an act of violence.

I should know. I am one of the most prolific murderers in history. And I think about death constantly.

I often wonder what my own death will be like, if I am ever blessed to embrace it. I'm not too picky in my imaginings; I'll take any sort by this point. Logically, I'd prefer a less painful exit, but, knowing my luck, it'll be as ruthless as the one once reported and still widely believed.

It ought to be noted I have some of the most wretched luck to ever be doled out, so there is that.

The sound of waves crashing against the shore sends my eyes to the horizon. I've tried to drown myself in those waters more times than I ought to admit over the years, but the sea always spits me back out. I've also tried overdosing on pharmaceuticals, stabbing myself in the chest and eyes (which was just as painful as you'd imagine), and throwing myself off a cliff. Melodramatic, yes, and all ineffective for an immortal cursed with impenetrable skin and a digestive system apparently filled with acid.

Death is not my friend. At least, not yet.

I greet Nikolaos when I bolt my bedroom door shut. I had the locks installed after one too many people suffered poor Niki's fate after stumbling upon me at night. Even still, I sleep fitfully, terrified of being caught unaware. "We have a new resident," I explain to him, throwing my flannel shirt in a nearby hamper. "His name is Walt. He's kind of cute."

Niki sneers a bit over that. He's a bit of a xenophobe and dislikes anyone who isn't of Greek descent. And Walt is most definitely not Greek. Or, at least, the kind of Greek Niki and I grew up with.

"It was stupid," I tell the bust. "I was planting seeds at my potting table in the outer temple—the new hybrid dahlias that Mikkos brought me a couple of weeks ago? And I had my gloves on and there was dirt everywhere, and I'd taken off my sunglasses to wipe the sweat off my brow. The Girls tried to warn me, but it was too late."

Niki's flat eyes hint at disappointment.

"I know. Believe me, nobody hates me more than I hate myself at this moment."

The snakes on my head hiss in sympathy; a couple stroke my cheeks lovingly. They aren't Nikki's biggest fans, but they tolerate his presence in our bedroom for my sake.

I wish they could talk. Just to answer me, to let me know my words aren't useless. That the vestiges of humanity I desperately cling to aren't in vain.

As I shower later, I watch the lingering dirt from gardening swirl around the drain. Just that morning, I'd been planting seeds to cultivate new life. By the end of the day, I'd taken yet another that no amount of seeds could make up for.

I am a monster. The worst kind of monster. The kind that people have told stories about for thousands of years. The kind that daredevils like poor Walt seek out, even though many believe I'm nothing more than a myth.

I am the Gorgon Medusa. And my eyes can turn anything living to stone.

Chapter Two

Once upon a time, there was a girl who lived in Athens. She didn't excel at anything; in fact, she was rather average in every way except one: she was beautiful. The old saying is that beauty is in the eye of the beholder, but it was universally acknowledged that this girl's beauty was nearly unparalleled. If anyone had ever bothered to ask the girl if she treasured her beauty, she would have told them no—she would have much preferred a more useful attribute, such as weaving or singing or the possession of an artist's hand. Determined to be more than just a pretty face surrounded by coveted hair, though, she persuaded her parents to allow her to become a handmaiden at the goddess Athena's temple. It was here that the girl truly flourished, as the other handmaidens cared not a whit about her looks. Duty and intelligence were prized, and these were qualities the girl felt she could cultivate in such an environment.

One day, a sickly stranger appeared at the temple, begging for mercy. The girl was assigned to care for him; over the next few weeks, they grew to know one another. He was charming and handsome, and the girl and the stranger would converse for hours about any topic under Apollo's sun that suited their fancies. He was the perfect foil for her in debates, always weathering her arguments good-naturedly while maintaining his own firm convictions. But the thing she grew to value most about the stranger was that he never fawned over her looks. If he paid her a compliment, it was for her character or mind, and this pandering to her secret sensibilities made her weak to his charisma.

"Come away with me," he'd begged after his health had improved. "Let us be together forever from this moment on." And while she was tempted to agree as her heart had grown soft to his presence, she had also made a vow to serve Athena.

"I cannot," she told him. They then parted: the stranger off to where it was he once came from and the girl to her responsibilities as a handmaiden. She mourned this loss egregiously, doubting herself and her commitments deep into the night.

She was heartbroken until the stranger came back, five nights after he'd left. "I cannot stop thinking of you," he'd whispered to her in Athena's temple. "You have stolen my heart." He'd taken her hands then, the first time they'd ever dared to touch, and the girl noticed his fingers were wrinkled, as if they'd spent much time in water.

"Come away with me," he told her once more, and in the dim lamp light she saw storms brewing in his eyes. "You will be my queen. Anything you want, anything—it will be yours as long as you agree to be mine, pretty girl."

Taken aback by his sudden reference to her looks, she insisted, "I cannot. I am sworn to Athena."

This was not good enough for the stranger. His touch grew rough, his temperament irate. He was so close she could smell salt water in his hair. "She cannot have you. I claim you as mine. Do you hear that, pretty girl? *Mine.*"

The soft feelings she'd harbored for the stranger quickly transitioned to fear and disgust. She beseeched him to let her go, yet he refused. His hands grew rougher still until they turned to violence. Her clothes were ripped, her body thrown to the ground. "Do not make a sound," he grunted as he tore her innocence away.

"I promise I'll gift you an experience you'll never forget. One that will endear you to me for the rest of time."

As she lay weeping afterward, the stranger pressed hot kisses against her wet face. "We must part tonight, I'm afraid; there is work for me to do to ensure our future. But be assured, by this time tomorrow, we will never be parted again. You'll never need to fear for your future again." And then he left her, broken and bloody on the floor.

The goddess Athena was livid to discover one of her hand-maidens was no longer chaste. "You dared to defile my temple," the goddess of Wisdom had seethed. "You must pay the price for your foolish, unclean ways." No matter how much the girl pleaded with the goddess to understand she had not willingly given herself to the stranger, in the end, there was nothing she could do to stop the curse.

The girl whose beauty was once fabled became a horrifying monster.

Her legs twisted together into a reptilian beast. Her hair, so envied by women and the subject of many an ode by men, transformed into a nest of vipers. And her eyes became weapons that offered any beings who looked into them certain and quick death. Coupled with the trauma from her experience with the stranger just hours before, the girl quickly prayed for death from the gods above.

"Poseidon will never touch you again, not when you personify monstrosity," Athena had sneered to her as she writhed on the ground, sobbing. Even the goddess would not look at her now, as her eyes could slay the immortal.

Wrecked and alone, the beastly girl was banished to a tiny, enchanted isle off the coast of her beloved Greece, aptly named Gorgóna. Surrounded by her tormentor's waters and left with a heavy heart and a steadily growing collection of statues, she'd long since given up on salvation.

This is my fairy tale. It's definitely not a happy one, much like those the Brothers Grimm wrote a few hundred years back. And for a long time, I had a hard time accepting it all, like any sane person would. I am a normal girl. Normal girls do not become monsters who kill dozens of poor souls. It just wasn't done. Even in Ancient Greece, when the gods and goddesses were active and meddlesome, it just didn't happen to normal girls like me.

Or, I guess it did. If I'm being honest, I've heard way too many stories of people getting the short end of the stick simply due to the fickle nature of the gods. I don't personally know these fellow victims, being trapped on my little isle and all, but I do think of them often and pray that they managed to escape their fates better than I did.

But there's no way around it. I am, in fact, a monster. A hideous one, to be precise, but as I don't have any mirrors on Gorgóna, I can't verify that one for certain. I rely on the fact that every single person I've frozen over the ages boasts abject fear on their face, which makes me believe they find me pretty horrifying. And it sucks. It genuinely, truly, absolutely, unequivocally sucks. I hate stealing lives.

Thus, not only am I a monster, I'm a really lousy one. A lonely, classic Five Stages of Grief following, insecure, shut-in of a pathetic beast who talks to the snakes on her head and the statues on her island.

I sometimes wonder if this is what Athena meant for me to be. After I'd spent years being her handmaiden, she must have known my character to some degree. I wasn't an aggressive sort, nor was I a leader. I was a docile girl who thrived on routine. I loved helping people. I was not one to yell at others. I had trouble killing insects or rodents that infiltrated her temple. I cried when my father butchered sheep for us to eat. Maybe this is why she chose to mold me into a killer; maybe she knew that my heart, too often called soft by those who knew me well back when I was human, would not be able to handle the actions I had no control over.

Obviously, I no longer worship Athena. I prayed faithfully to her for the first dozen years of my exile, begging her to reconsider her decision, to understand I'd not willingly defiled her temple, yet an answer never came. To make matters worse, I could never escape from Poseidon, either, as his waves batter my island constantly. So here I am, stuck in a never-ending nightmare, thanks to the gods, and no matter how many times I ask myself, "Why me?" I am never given an answer.

Chapter Three

Gorgóna, which can be traversed from one end to the other in approximately ten minutes, is enchanted, but I am not cut off entirely from the rest of the planet. Parts of my temple have been upgraded, such as the bathroom and kitchen. I have books and magazines delivered regularly. I have a laptop (sans webcam), WiFi, and a smartphone that keep me abreast of anything I want to know, ranging from politics to fashions to music and trends. I have taught myself countless languages over the years alongside mastering accents, and I am a sucker for absorbing any and all slang that weaves in and out of popularity. It makes me feel connected to the world, like it hasn't kept spinning while I stand still. I order clothes (well, mostly shirts, tunics, and dresses, as pants and serpentine bodies do not go well together) and jewelry (you'd be surprised how pretty jewelry can soothe a girl when she's feeling down in the dumps about her looks) often.

I know it is shocking, but I even have a couple of friends, ones who provide me these upgrades that maintain my sanity. One of them, Mikkos, is an eighty-seven-year-old blind Greek sailor who discovered my island in his teenage years. I'd found him before he saw me, and it'd given me a chance to warn him off. He'd left that first day, dutifully following my command to not gaze at me, not if he wanted to live, but came back ten years later after a hereditary disease robbed him of his eyesight. "Figured it'd be alright for us to meet formally," he'd said to me, and later I cried because I could look at his face and know that there was no way for my eyes to deprive him of his breath. Since then, he comes to visit me once a month, bringing with him a plethora of items, including food, toiletries, and packages from a post office box he'd set up for me on the mainland years before. In return, I send with him various items from the temple, such as urns and art, so he can sell them and deposit the funds in my bank accounts. Since I am an instrument of death, I try to balance my karma by donating money to worthy causes across the globe. My current favorites are Doctors Without Borders, shelters for the abused and poor, disaster relief funds, rape survivor networks, and animal and nature conservancy funds. Mikkos teases me about how I waste so much of the money I've amassed over the years, but he's put some of his money in the pot more times than not.

He and I are friends, dear friends.

I worry about him. He's so frail nowadays, his skin like tissue paper, and each time I see him, there are fresh bruises. He tells me he doesn't heal like he used to. I ask if he ought to be making these trips at sea to visit me, yet he always maintains that he's fine. Says he likes my company, likes that I laugh at his jokes and don't consider him an addled old fool like so many of the girls back home. I contend that I do believe that, and then he and I laugh together, but I secretly worry. There will come a day when Mikkos will not come to my island anymore, and I will not know if it's because he can't or if it's because he's died. And if he dies, there is no way for me to go to his funeral and pay respects to one of the kindest souls I've ever been blessed to know.

I love that old fool.

I broached the subject with him during his last visit. We were sitting on a mosaic-laden patio overlooking my garden; even though he can't see the view, Mikkos always insists we enjoy our wine al fresco. "Is your son still in Thessaloniki?" I'd asked, pouring him only a little more Cabernet Sauvignon. It's his favorite, and he'd been the one to bring it to me, but he also needs to be able to steer his boat home—and being blind, his senses must stay sharp, not muddied. Interestingly enough, Poseidon never rages when Mikkos travels to Gorgóna, not like he does when other travellers seek out my isle, often fighting punishing storms and waves just to find me. The waters stay calm for Mikkos' journeys to and fro, almost like the god knows I need my friend.

While appreciated, this confusing act of kindness does not endear me to the Lord of the Seas.

Mikkos laughed at my question about his son, like I'd said something of great amusement. "He will never come home. He's met a girl, you know."

Mikkos' son was always meeting girls, and that was a problem. He was thrice divorced, with seven children. Seven grandchildren that Mikkos hardly knew. It was a horrible shame, one that left me simmering in sympathetic, righteous fury far too often; but then, my feelings on such matters were hardly relevant. Nobody involved would ever ask for my opinion, no one except for Mikkos. What did I know about having a family, after mine had died so very long ago?

"You should call him, ask him to come for a visit," I urged gently.

His eyes, cloudy yet still beautiful, dulled for the smallest of moments, and I wished I had legs to kick myself. But then he found my hand and laid his brittle one over it. "You are a good girl, *matakia mou*. The world would be a better place if there were more people like you in it."

I'd forced back the maelstrom of emotions threatening to overtake me and answered with a light voice. "If there were more people like me around, the world would have a tiny population. Be glad there's just me, and that I'm confined to this island."

His dear face scrunched in irritation. "You do not give yourself enough credit. Were you the monster they say you are, I would not be sitting here with you, drinking wine and reflecting

12

upon my failures as a father. Instead, I would be at the entrance to the grotto, with all of the other laymen."

"They are not laymen," I protested, and he hushed me, like he tended to do.

"Fishermen, then. You could have easily killed me, *matakia mou*. But you didn't."

He calls me his eyes, which is so lovely of him, and yet bittersweet at the same time. Because his eyes are gone and mine are still here, and I wish, oh-wish so much, that I could say the situation were reversed.

The Girls love Mikkos. He is the only other person allowed to touch them, especially since he brings them little treats every time he visits. Legend claims my snakes are just as deadly as my eyes, but the actual truth of the matter is: I don't know if they are.

It's weird, right? That we've been together for over two thousand years, and I've murdered far too many people, and I can't say, one way or another, that the dozen snakes on my head are equally responsible?

They are gentle creatures, individually named by me but normally referred to as a whole, since they intertwine together more often than not. More importantly, they abhor death just as avidly as I do. I know this not because they tell me in words, but because they get depressed. A strong sense of malaise infects them, rendering them listless owners of poor appetites. So we do not risk anything, not when it comes to anyone except Mikkos. And even then, it took a good decade before they let him touch them.

But it isn't only Mikkos they like. There is one more person who the snakes adore, only it's always done under the cover of a thick wrap. And that's Hermes. Yes, the god Hermes, Athena's brother and Poseidon's nephew. And while I do not think too favorably of the gods and goddesses in general now, I will admit I am also quite fond of the messenger god.

Okay, more than fond. He is, to be precise, my best friend.

13

Hermes began visiting me shortly after I became a monster. In addition to being a messenger for the mighty Zeus, he also ferries the souls of the dead for his uncle Hades. I, being a newly minted murderess, had souls for Hermes to ferry. I loathed and feared him at first, convinced he would abuse me like his relatives had, but he is a persistent thing. It took years—literally, hundreds of years—but he chipped away at my shell with acts of kindness small and large.

Once, early on in our relationship, I awoke to sounds just outside my inner sanctum. As this was before actual locks were installed, when a heavy urn served as a doorstop, my heart nearly jumped out of my chest. I lowered my voice to what I hoped sounded monstrous and shouted, "Depart forever if you know what's good for you!" But a knock sounded in the darkness as a response, rattling me and the Girls. I attempted one more warning, "You must wish for death. Leave this island and never return!"

And yet, it wasn't a wayward stranger who answered. It was a god. "I've brought you something."

Hermes had brought me something.

I didn't know what to do. So far, he'd been kind in his brief visits, but the gods are, at best, temperamental, so one never knows whether the wind will blow in his or her favor. I left the door firmly shut, and after what seemed like an hour, and the silence around me punctured only by Poseidon's angry waves against the shores of my tiny isle, I arose to ensure his departure. The moment my hand touched the door, he called out, "I'm leaving now. If you need more, let me know. Sweet dreams, Dusa." A rush of wings followed, signaling his true departure.

He'd called me Dusa, a name my youngest sister bestowed upon me back when her hand had to hold one of my fingers, it was so small. I'd not heard the name for years, and here it was, coming from a god.

I ended up crying. The Girls were soft and loving, peppering my face with tiny licks that served as kisses, but I wept long and hard for so very many things. I cried for my sister, who I surely would never see again. For the life robbed from me, and for the situation I was trapped within. And I cried for the sweetness of a name I'd never thought I'd hear again.

When I finally got up and dusted myself off, I decided to open the door. For all I knew, I could be stepping into another of the gods' traps. And yet there was no trick awaiting me, just a pile of thick, beautiful blankets. Until that moment, I didn't have such luxuries, and I, being partially reptilian, chilled easily. Winter was miserable—drafts flowing off the Aegean made sleep bitterly elusive and days stretched out in front of me forever. Warming myself out in the sun helped somewhat, but at night, all bets were off. I was wretched.

But that pile of blankets ... it was a turning point for me.

Over the next hundred years, more gifts came, alongside improvements for my temple. During festival times, when I would drown in melancholy over what once was, he would bring me sweet treats, wine when I wanted to indulge in my sorrows. When my family passed from this land to the next, he let me know in the gentlest ways. Books appeared when he somehow knew I was bored to tears, and then lessons to learn how to read languages other than Greek. He was the one to bring me a lock for my door, and furniture for me to sit and lay on.

Even still, I forced him to keep his distance—I could kill the gods, after all, and was leery of his intentions toward me—but slowly, oh so slowly, he and I began to talk. I resented it at first, compared him to his louse of an uncle who charmed me with words before violating me, but Hermes persevered when others surely would have given up. On the days I refused to open up about myself, he told me of the outside world. I heard of places I never knew existed, learned the world was round and that there were peoples across vast expanses of water. He told me of scientific discoveries, of stories both true and imaginary. He allowed me to ask him—*a god*—any questions I wished, and in return he answered me honestly and thoroughly.

It took a good couple of centuries before I allowed him within ten feet of me, and only after we devised a plan to keep him safe. In those early days, I relied exclusively on scarves (which he brought or had sent to me) to wrap around my eyes and my snakes. It was terrifying, going blind in the presence of a god who had the ability to transform or maim me at his whim, but Hermes treated me kindly. Respectfully.

After a thousand years, I had to admit that Hermes was someone I could trust. Today, I cannot imagine my life without him. And there is a comfort in that, unlike the fear I harbor over Mikkos' fragile existence.

Chapter Four

"Dusa?" calls a voice, and I scramble to find my glasses.

"Hold on a minute!" I slap on a pair of deep black, mirrored wrap-around shades and then quickly bind the Girls up in their scarf. They hiss in protest, but it's only half-hearted, as they would never risk hurting Hermes.

I whip my head back and forth to ensure no parts of my eyes are visible. Then I do a double, triple check of pat downs before heading into the cella and calling out for him to come in.

My favorite god strolls into this main room of the temple, a warm smile gracing his divinely gorgeous face. "Greetings! And how are you on this wonderful day?"

I wait until he's a few steps away before putting a hand out. The fool would hug me if I let him. Has he no sense of self-preservation? Even though he must already know it, I tell him, "I killed somebody yesterday."

His well-loved Vans sneakers squeak against the worn tiles as he comes to a halt, my outstretched hand half an inch away from his chest. I drop it as he says, "It's not your fault."

"Really? I think Walt would disagree."

I know it sounds foolish and typical, especially since he's a god and all, but when Hermes smiles, it's really breathtaking. My breath catches as he says, "Ah. A poet, then?"

He knows me too well. "I'd been reading Whitman this last week. It seems fitting."

He attempts to move closer, so I shift backwards and motion him towards his chair. Hermes is here enough that I've designated a chair to be his exclusively; Mikkos has one, too. But then, it's not like I have a ton of visitors who clamor for my company, so giving my closest friends their own seats in my home wasn't a huge burden. Plus, as Hermes was responsible for bringing me the furniture in the first place, I figure he has every right to find comfort here. "He knew the risks," Hermes tells me. "Plus, if you want to blame anybody for that man's death, go ahead and blame my sister."

It's a common saying from Hermes, and one I secretly cling to in the dark of night, when my life and deeds press heavily against my heart. Isn't it always easier to blame somebody else for our actions? But no, that's not fair, because it was my responsibility to be more careful.

"Or," Hermes says, his dazzling smile now bittersweet and wry, "my bastard of an uncle."

I push my glasses closer to my face. Paranoia over losing him due to any carelessness on my behalf is a constant companion during his visits. "I don't want to talk about that." And I don't. I may tell Hermes nearly everything, but this is not a subject I wade into voluntarily.

"Dusa, it's been two thousand years—"

Nice way to butter me up, reminding me how old I am and all. "Your point?"

"My point being that after such a lengthy amount of time, I don't think you've ever come to terms with what has happened to you."

I laugh. I mean, really. How can he say such a thing with a straight face? "Don't be ridiculous. Of course I have."

The snakes under my wrap hiss loudly; I tap on the mass to

quiet them down.

"If that is the case, then you surely won't mind if I talk to the Assembly about the matter."

"No!" The word echoes throughout my statue-filled yet unbearably empty home.

Hermes studies me for a long moment. I try not to squirm under his gaze, but it's difficult. His eyes, a beautiful blue-green that alters with his moods, are piercing, like they can see straight through skin and into cells that make a person whole. Today, they are a happy medium of the two shades. I have to look away, though. It's too easy to get lost in such eyes.

"Give me a good enough reason not to."

We've had this conversation more times than I can count. "You know why."

He runs a hand through his sandy hair, a bit longer lately than he's worn it for years. I rather like it this way, all askew and artful at the same time. "While I can understand your hesitation—"

I know him well enough to not fear disagreeing. "You most certainly do not."

He sighs in quiet frustration.

"Hermes." I lower myself onto a chaise, as it's the only kind of furniture suitable for reptilian bodies, and pick at a worn spot near the seam. I've put off reupholstering it far too long. "We've gone over this."

I sneak a quick peek over at him as he leans forward, arms against his knees. He's wearing one of my favorite t-shirts of his, a thin and fraying red one whose picture of a surfer has faded to the point of obscurity. The first time I saw him in it, I thought him to be exactly what a beach bum traversing the Mediterranean ought to look like—all gorgeous and golden in skin and hair. As I find him to be the most beautiful person I've ever met, inside and out, I can only imagine how the ladies in the outside world must fall at his feet.

I often imagine what his life—and everyone else's—must be like nowadays. What it'd be like to walk in a city with buildings as high as the sky and transportation as fast as the wind. And I wonder, as I have for the bulk of our relationship, just what it is he gets out of these visits, and from me. Because he is a god, a beautiful one who's charming and intelligent and witty, and I am a monster that kills unsuspecting adventurers.

In all these years we have been friends, I've been too afraid to ask why he keeps coming back. Because there's always the fear that, one day, he'll choose not to.

"Do you trust me?"

His quiet question snaps me to attention. I blink from behind my dark glasses and offer a smile. A far cry from fangs, but at least there is no need to hide my teeth. "Of course."

"Then trust me with this."

As much as I do wholly trust him with my life, I do not feel the same toward the rest of the Greek Assembly. To face the gods and come away with a potentially worse punishment? Thank you, but no. "Hermes—"

"You cannot possibly tell me you are content living in isolation on an enchanted isle for the rest of eternity." He stands up, his gray slip-on Vans squeaking again. It's a soothing sound, despite his words. "Don't lie to me."

Well, of course I don't enjoy being a cursed monster, but it's not like I have a lot of options right now. If I go to the mainland, the opportunities for murdering innocents skyrocket. Plus, there's always the excellent chance that I'll be captured and a) be experimented on, b) locked away in an even more restrictive place, or c) outright killed (although I've actually debated whether the risks for that one are worth it or not). If I face the gods, something even worse than what has already happened may be forced upon me. What if they make it so I lose the vestiges of who I am and I turn insane and rampage against innocents? It's a prospect too terrifying to risk. "You know I am not. But—"

"There are no buts." He squats down in front of me, far too close to where my tail is, which shames me even to this day. I have a tail. *I slither around on a tail.* You'd think by now I'd be okay with this, but I'm not.

I hold a hand out so he doesn't come any closer and ask

something I've long wondered. "Why won't you let this go?"

His head tilts to the side as he studies me. "Because a wrong has occurred."

Over the years, I've learned that Hermes has a bit of a knight in shining armor complex. He is always trying to right wrongs, save people, and make the world a better place, which is one of the things I love best about him. His goodness is a beacon I can't resist navigating toward, especially when I commit such atrocities myself. Even still, I tell him softly, "You can't save everyone."

He stands up and looks away for a long moment. It gives me a chance to get up and put proper space between us. I can't risk anything happening to him, either. I would find a way to kill myself before I ever allowed that to occur. So I pretend to examine a few pots of recently seeded plants over by a window, like they'd somehow managed to burst out of their casings in their effort to reach for freedom in less than a day.

I've been trying to do it for over two thousand years.

From behind me, Hermes murmurs, "You're right. I can't save everyone; that much is true." He pauses. "Dusa, I've respected your wishes over the years, even though it's been hard for me."

I turn to find him a couple feet away. His shoes didn't even squeak against the polished floor. I jerk back, knocking into one of the pots; thankfully, he's quick enough to catch it before it hits the ground. I gingerly take it from him, careful to maintain no skin-to-skin contact.

"I find that I cannot sit back and allow for this to happen anymore," he continues quietly. "The simple fact is, my uncle raped you, and somehow my bat-shit insane sister blamed and cursed you for it happening in one of her temples. In no way did you deserve what happened to you." He shakes his head slowly as he closes in on me. "You've born it better than any other person I could ever imagine. It's time for it to end, though. I sorely regret not doing anything earlier."

As with any recollection of those events, I close my eyes and focus on my breathing. But really, it does not help. In my mind's eye, that series of catastrophes is still crystal clear to the most minute of details. The smell of Poseidon's salted hair; the feel of his rough yet water wrinkled hands against my skin; the sound of his voice, so bloody reasonable and soothing, as he rationalized why I ought to feel privileged he'd taken notice of me. The sounds of my screams. The sight of Athena's eyes, crazed and bloodshot. The feel of my body twisting into a monstrosity. Every last, horrible action is right here in my mind like it happened earlier today. I shove at the memories, plead with them to stay away.

Time doesn't heal; or, at least, it hasn't healed such wounds for me, no matter what I told him earlier. Time is just another captor of mine.

"She is the goddess of wisdom," I whisper. "She must have had good reason to do as she did."

His voice matches mine. "No. It's like I said—she's *insane*. Her being named the purveyor of wisdom is one of the greatest of cosmic jokes."

I open my eyes and suck in my breath, as I always do, at the sight of him. "She is your sister."

His lips tilt up at the corners. "Which is the unfortunate reason why I know her character so well."

The fear of the unknown is too much, though. I just can't give in, not when I can't weigh the variables fairly beforehand.

"Dusa." We're now mere inches apart; sunlight glints in his golden hair, spilling out in a dazzling array that highlights his divinity. "I've already submitted my petition for the next meeting in two weeks. I'd hoped for your blessing, but I cannot idly stand by anymore. Not when you hurt every single day."

What? My head snaps up and the glasses shift. Both hands slap against them in horror. "Personal space, Hermes," I croak.

But instead, he places a hand against my arm. It feels alien ... yet wonderful. It's warm and so *real*. Despite wanting to sink into the foreign sensations seeping through my body, I try to shake him off, but it's no good. He's so close to me now—close enough that I can smell the wind on him. Stars above, it's intoxicating. I squeeze my eyes shut and send a prayer to the Girls, begging them to not move a muscle.

They must sense my fear, because they do as I wish. And then the unthinkable happens: Hermes' arms go around my thin, misshapen body, pulling me into the warmth of his chest. I resist, my own limbs as stiff as those inhabiting the island with us, but my friend will not let common sense stop him.

And I am too weak to do what I should do, because, instead of shoving him hard and fleeing, I give into the impulse overtaking my sanity and rest my head against his shoulder. The Girls do not move, but I get the sense they are in a fragile state of relieved joy to be touching him. Touching anyone, really.

Much like I am.

"You are not alone," he murmurs, his face much too close to my glasses. I'm sure to develop a headache later, my eyes squeeze shut so tightly. But the words on his breath feel too good against my skin to let me do anything other than stay where I am.

When was the last time somebody held me like this? I can't recall the last instance. Mikkos is never allowed this close. He may be able to touch the Girls, and occasionally hold my hand, but I've otherwise kept him at a distance. This is the first time I've ever broken down and allowed Hermes to touch me, and it's stupid, I'm stupid, because if he was to die, to become one of my statues ...

How would I survive?

"My father will listen to me," he tells me, a strong hand gently rubbing my back. He believes in me, and this realization—while assumed before, now solidifies into assured truth. It's a glorious feeling, knowing somebody out there is willing to do this for me; but he's risking so much, going to Olympus to argue against judgments made by his sister and uncle. I shouldn't let him do this. Over the years, he's conveyed to me of the epic showdowns that rage amongst the assembly—and the gods and goddesses of Olympus are just as vindictive and unforgiving toward their own as they are toward mortals. I cannot let him risk himself for me.

"Athena—" I'm horrified my voice is so broken.

"Don't think about her. She's—what she did to you is unforgiveable. She's not worth a single one of your thoughts."

I shiver as his words trace my neck. "Your uncle—"

"Him neither," he tells me.

What would life be like, outside this temple? I know the basics, thanks to computers and smartphones Hermes and Mikkos have provided me over the years, but I've never actually set foot off of my isle of exile in ages. It would be ... terrifying, I think.

But, here in the circle of his embrace, I allow myself to imagine how it could be a blessing, too, especially if there was no fear of harming innocents. He has already petitioned the Assembly. Come next month, it will be discussed with or without my blessing or participation. And the more I think about it, the more I realize that maybe he has a point. Before—I had no say in my punishment. I've born it quietly.

Maybe it's time I finally take a chance.

When I tell Hermes this, he lets out a relieved exhale of a laugh, like he was holding his breath, not truly believing I'd agree so easily after years of fighting otherwise. Gooseflesh breaks out up and down my neck as his breath once more caresses my skin.

His head tilts down so his forehead presses against my temple, rendering me into a facsimile of the statues surrounding us. I can't help but pray silently, *Zeus above, if I ever had the smallest bit of luck, let me experience it now and ensure my glasses do not shift. Keep your son safe.* "I knew you'd eventually see reason."

The laugh that comes from me is tiny, but inside, joy begins to bubble.

A hand presses against my cheek, and then I am flying and falling and freezing and all over the place, because his lips press gently against my temple for a delicious moment. Surely I must have drunk too much wine, because all of this—his touch, his concern, his friendship—it's left me heady and hopeful. I marvel at how easily he can touch me right now—me, a monster, and he's as steady as always.

My eyes remain closed until he lets go and steps away. Irrationally, the hint of tears taunt me by this loss. When he's in the entryway, I find the courage to ask, "Why are you willing to risk your brethren's wrath, Hermes?"

"You're worth it," is all he tells me, his face illuminated by a grin that Apollo's sun would envy. And then I hear the rush of wings, and my friend is gone.

Chapter Five

They're hidden behind my dark glasses, but thanks to the bright light reflecting off of the Aegean's vivid blue waters, I have to shade my sun-sensitive eyes as I watch Mikkos' boat angle toward Gorgóna's small landing and dock. This is an unexpected visit; Mikkos told me during his last trip he had a series of doctor's appointments this week, ones he'd put off far too often in the past but meant to finally fulfill as the ache of age in his bones became too much. His fear of the unknown must have matched my own, though, because here he is coming to my isle rather than visiting with a doctor.

I head down to the edge of the wooden dock and call out, "Yassou, Mikkos!" The Girls hiss in excitement around me, waving their bodies in the air.

I am greeted in kind as the boat slows down in its approach. He is used to navigating toward my voice, which still dumbfounds me. How he has become so adept at sailing without his eyes is a true mystery; all Mikkos will say is that boats and the sea are in his blood, and that not even a loss of sight could keep him away from what he was born to do. I catch the line he throws me and loop it around one of the dock's pillars. "What brings you out here?"

He grins up at me, his teeth gapped in a way that only endears one to him even more. "Do I need an excuse to visit my favorite girl?"

Sweet talker. "Of course not. It's just, you said you had some doctor's appointments, so I expected you to be there rather than here."

He lifts up a box. "Yes, well, I realized it was a much better use of my time to come out to this comfortable island and share wine with a dear friend than sit and listen to all the things wrong with me." I take his elbow and help him up onto the dock. "But, we can discuss that later. I have a treat for you that is time sensitive."

I lead him up to the temple, to the patio he loves, especially now that hot sun graces our table. While he sets the box down, I head inside to gather a bottle of Cabernet he'd brought a few years back and a pair of tumblers. "Are you hungry?" I call out, a hand going to a plate of cheese and crackers I'd prepared earlier for a snack.

He is, so I stack everything on a tray and return outside, only to find him sitting with a tiny white kitten. I instantly rear back, terrified of turning a helpless creature such as this to stone, but Mikkos calls out, "It is blind, like me! Come, come—meet Mátia. My neighbor, she had kittens and this one was close to being put to death for what he was born with and could not help. I said to myself, 'I know the perfect owner for this creature.' And so here I am, with a friend for you."

He holds out the tiny beast, and I stare at it in wonder. Its eyes are blue as the sea surrounding us, but their glassy stare settles nowhere in particular. I come closer, my hands trembling as they reach toward what has only been a dream in the past. The Girls whip around my head, frenzied—if I had to pinpoint an exact emotion they're feeling, I'd say it was delight.

Excitement tingles across my skin. "Are you sure?"

"Quite." Mikkos passes the kitten to me, and I hold it up,

marveling at its softness as a large purr builds through its lungs. "Just as I thought," comes my friend's satisfied response. "He needs you just as much as you need him."

I'd never had a pet before—not when I was younger, living with my family, and certainly not when I was a handmaiden for Athena. As animals are just as susceptible to my curse as humans, I'd shied away from them over the years, especially after a number of birds had frozen mid-flight and shattered as they freefell toward oblivion. Their deaths had been just as devastating, so I've obviously had a strict no animal policy for the isle (snakes on my head notwithstanding). And yet, here I am, holding a tiny kitten, and it is still alive as it snuggles closer to me. The Girls are enraptured, yanking my head down so they can take turns rubbing their small faces up against the soft fur.

As I stroke its tummy, I ask wryly, "Mátia, huh?"

He feels around until he finds the plates of crackers and cheese. "It seemed fitting."

I can't help but laugh at the irony of him naming this sweet creature *eyes* when its own are defunct.

He wipes cracker crumbs from his beard. "You can change it, if you like."

I stare into the glazed orbs and smile; my heart fills with joy. He's still here, still alive. Today is a day of most generous miracles. "I most certainly will not. I love this name."

Mikkos grunts and pours us wine. I let him talk about inconsequential matters as I stroke my new pet until it falls asleep, sated and purring in my arms. And then I ask, because I love him so very dearly, "While I appreciate this little guy more than you will know, I am also concerned that you are here instead of being at the doctor's. Has something happened?"

His blank eyes swivel toward me, like he can see me when I know it to be impossible. "What is it that they can tell me that I do not already know? I am old, and when you are old, things tend to fall apart in your body. I am no different than any of the people who have aged before me. My time is coming."

I watch him sip his wine, tiny bits of panic lacing each breath

I pull in and out. The Girls go still on my head. "What does that mean?"

His thin lips curl upwards, but I am not graced with the gap between his teeth. "It means that I choose to spend the time I've left doing things that make me happy. Coming here to visit an old friend makes me happy." He sets his glass down on the table. "I wanted to bring you someone to remind you of me for when I'm gone."

My voice is as fragile as my emotions when it leaves my lips. "I will always remember you, kitten or no."

This pleases him, even though he acts like I'm being ridiculous. We stay on the patio and drink wine and eat cheese and crackers for hours more, and when the sun sets and Mikkos is too sleepy to captain his boat, I lead him to my bed and tuck him in. It is the first time in all our years together that he stays the night, but now, more than ever, I will not fight for him to leave.

When I come back out to the terrace to clean up, I find Hermes lounging in Mikkos' chair, rubbing his nose to Mátia's pink one. It's a lovely sight, one that acts like a fist around my heart, but it's also unwelcomed thanks to the element of surprise. Luckily, his back is to me, so I can rush back inside to find my sunglasses. I want to rail at him for being so reckless, but it would wake Mikkos. So I wait until I've got the Girls under wraps and the glasses firmly in place before I head back outside. "Are you crazy?"

He turns to face me, his smile nearly blinding me in the candle and starlight around us. "When did you get a kitten?"

The Girls hiss in excitement, waving around underneath my scarf like they want to share the story. I hush them and tell Hermes, "Mikkos brought it to me today." I reach down to scratch Mátia's head in his arms. "It's blind, so it is forever safe from my curse."

As annoyed as I am for his blatant disregard for his own safety, stars above, it is good to see Hermes tonight.

"I am inordinately annoyed with myself for never considering such a thing prior to tonight. To be bested by an old mortal!"

He chuckles, passing the kitten over to me. "Is that him I hear snoring in your chambers?"

I laugh ruefully. "I'm afraid we had too much wine, and I didn't think it safe for him to travel by himself at night."

"You realize that, day or night, it is no difference to him, right?" He selects a scrap of cheese off the plate. "His remaining senses, honed by the loss of sight, exceed your own. Mikkos could steer his boat in a tempest and still make it back to the mainland in one perfect piece."

Mikkos and Hermes have never met one another, but it does not mean Hermes does not know all about my friend. "I realize that, it's just ..." I allow myself the luxury of pressing a kiss on the kitten's head; I'm rewarded with a contented squeak. "I'm worried about him."

Hermes says nothing, but he doesn't have to. The understanding and sympathy in his eyes lets me know what he thinks of this. I can't help but wonder if he knows when Mikkos' time will be up, but I will never ask.

He pops the last bit of cheese into his mouth. "You will never have to worry about such a matter with me."

And yet, I do, each time he is with me. It's a bitter conundrum I'm faced with—do I selfishly continue to put Hermes at risk so I may have him in my life, or do I force him away for his own good yet lose the person that means the most to me? I focus on the kitten's paw, now batting haphazardly at one of my fingers. "I suppose that is a perk of having a friend who is an immortal." But as I do not want to think of Hermes ferrying Mikkos' soul anytime soon, let alone lose Hermes, I ask, "Are you hungry? I can get you something to eat."

He doesn't have to eat—none of the gods do—but, as he told me once, it's a social pleasure he enjoys partaking in.

"I'm fine, thanks." He motions to the freshly empty plate in front of him. "I've stolen the rest of the crackers you left behind."

I pretend outrage. "You are a thief, sir."

He laughs, and I swear, his laughter is infectious. "Fine. I will bring you more crackers on my next visit."

Speaking of ... "What brings you here tonight?"

The ease so noticeable moments before slides off his face. And I know—just know. Something awful happened in the world today, and, as expected, Hermes would have been on the ground helping ferry souls to the Underworld. While this is not an un-common occurrence, it's not his favorite activity, either. I ask gently, "What happened?"

He runs his long fingers through his hair. "Bombings."

It surprises me that an overwhelming yearning to reach out and touch his hand strikes me fast and hard, especially as just a few days ago we'd never touched. I ache to offer this comfort, but insecurity is a terrible fiend. I snuggle closer with the kitten; lucky little creature, to be so immune to the travesties of the world around it. "I am sorry to hear of this. I have not yet read up on the news of the world today. Did many people die?"

He nods gravely. "But let us not talk about such a tragedy—at least, not in this moment. You asked why I am here; the truth is, I wanted a distraction from the day's events. So I thought to myself, it is time to attempt an experiment I've longed to try. Are you game?"

Awake now, Mátia escapes my arms and skitters across the table, sniffing out a bowl of cat food I laid out for it earlier. Mik-kos was wise enough to come prepared with not only kibble and a collar with a bell on it, but a small bed for the kitten to sleep in. I reach out to keep him from going headfirst over the table. "What kind of experiment?" I ask warily.

I'm given a half-smile. "It's time I meet the Girls in person."

I sputter out my laughter. "Most definitely not."

He pulls my wine glass over and drains it. "Why not?"

"Are you serious?" How could he even thinking of such a thing? I lean forward, a hand used as a wall, safely barricading Mátia. "Hermes. We have no idea if the Girls are just as cursed as I am."

"There's a chance they aren't."

They like this idea, as they twist in frenzy, hissing atop my head. I tap on the mass with my free hand. *Sorry, Girls. As much as you may want this, there is no way I am risking him.* "There's a chance they are."

The hissing turns most decidedly toward disapproval.

"Thus, the experiment. I'd like to see them." He flashes me that smile of his that I swear must charm the entirety of Olympus. It's nearly impossible to resist it myself, but the image of his stone body in my temple knocks me back to reality. "I think they'd like to see me, too. It's not fair that Mikkos gets to pet them when I can't."

One of the Girls sneaks her little head toward the edge of the scarf. I poke her back before she gets too far. "If I didn't know better, I'd say you sound jealous over this."

He leans forward, tracing the bottom of the wine glass with a finger. "Maybe I am."

I outright laugh now. A god, jealous of a blind mortal? Impossible. "Don't be ridiculous. Didn't you just say I had no reason to worry about your death? And here you are, tempting it to happen simply because you want to *pet* my snakes?"

Much hissing escapes my scarf.

He chuckles. "Okay, perhaps not pet—but I certainly would like to meet them."

I reclaim Mátia and snuggle him closer. If he's unable to see to reason, then I must be the one to put my foot down. "You've met them already. You just want to see them. My answer is no."

He's incredulous. "No?"

I'm firm. "No." The Girls go limp against my skull.

He pours himself more wine in my glass and sips it slowly. I fully realize that he could force me to show him what's on my head—I'm painfully aware of just how at the mercy of the gods I am—but I do not fear this from him.

From any of the rest of Olympus, yes. But not Hermes.

"Would you mind explaining why?" he asks me once he's drunk half the glass.

I tell him the truth. "I won't risk you."

As disappointed as he looks, I think deep down he is pleased by this answer, too.

Chapter Six

I did not tell Mikkos about Hermes' petition for the Assembly to review my case before he left Gorgóna. It wasn't that I didn't trust my old friend—after all, he's kept my presence a secret for years now—it was just ... I wasn't ready to verbalize the possibility that Hermes has dangled in front of me.

But I think about it, constantly.

Over the next few days, I do my best to keep busy. I give my temple a thorough scrub down, making sure I dust each and every single statue on the isle. I attempt to train Mátia to use a litter box, although he is ferociously stubborn and prefers the small patch of grass just outside the south edge of the terrace. I graft several roses together in an effort to create a particular shade I've been dreaming of for years, a light maroon tinged with yellow. Mikkos is always able to easily sell my plants. I give myself a challenge and tackle yet another dialect; I practice Khoisan, the language of the Bushmen in Africa. The clicking sounds are difficult to form, but I am determined. Poor Mátia and the Girls are beside themselves as I converse in nothing but Khoisan for a solid two days. I bake like a madwoman, tweaking my recipe for chocolate chip cookies until I'm positive they could stand their ground in a baking competition. I give myself a new manicure every day. I rework a section of the garden on the north end of the temple, rearranging the plants and flowers until I'm satisfied.

I do not allow myself to consider just how horribly awry all this could go.

Hermes comes to see me two days before the Assembly is to meet. As he kneels to slip Mátia's new nametag on his collar (which amuses me greatly, as nobody would ever be able to find his home if he got lost), I tell him, "If we are going through with this madness—"

He glances up at me. "Of course we are."

"—then I have a few requests."

Mátia scrabbles away, his bell jingling merrily against the new tag. Hermes stands up, smacking his hands together to loosen the white fur so freshly deposited on him. I can't help but delight in watching this god treat my kitten like he were his own. "Let's hear them."

I rub the back of my neck; all this cleaning has left me sore. "I am concerned about what will happen to Mátia if things do not go my way."

"Things will not—"

I hold a hand up. "I would prefer you to take care of him, but I realize you have quite a busy life. So, if you are unable to do so, will you assure me that you'll find a proper home with people who will spoil him outrageously?"

Hermes' eyes—greenish-blue today—track over to where Mátia is, now climbing into his bed for what must be his fourth nap of the early day. "You have my word that he will live the very best of lives."

Relief swamps me. He's only been in my life a short time, but that little kitten and his welfare have become crucial to me. "As we discussed before, Mikkos isn't in the best of health." I bite my lower lip, hating that I even need to broach this subject. "I did not inform him of what is happening this week. He texted me yesterday that he is heading to Corinth for the next month or so with some friends. If—" I stop, as the words are too difficult to get out.

So Hermes gently finishes what I started. "I will do as I've done for years; I will continue to watch over Mikkos and assure he is well taken care of."

My eyes widen behind my glasses. "You have?"

"Of course I have. He is your friend, and I will be forever grateful for all he has done for you."

I'm not sure how to process that, even as something tightens and swells all at the same time in my chest. So I busy myself with straightening a pile of books on a nearby table. "I've left him a recording, just in case. It's in my room, next to Niki."

His smile is tempered. "Duly noted."

I take a deep breath. "That brings me to my last request. Gorgóna is home to more than just Mátia and me. I would ask you to ensure the isle's inhabitants will be taken care of, as well."

Most people, I think, would roll their eyes at such a request. But not Hermes. His response is just as steady as the god I know him to be. "Of course." He takes a step closer to me. "I know you are worried, Dusa, but I promised you before—I will fix this."

He cannot make such a promise, not when it comes to the whims of his father and the rest of the Assembly.

"Now, as for Mátia, I'd already planned on taking him to Olympus with us. The stars above know what trouble the little dude can get into while we're gone. He'll stay with a favorite aunt until we're done with the Assembly. Is this all right with you?"

It is more than all right.

His sunny smile reemerges; if I'd been wearing pants, he'd be charming me right out of them with just such a sight. "I would have assumed you'd already have the place fully packed up. Did I not send enough boxes?"

I'd woken up to a stack of boxes, bubble wrap, and tape in the entryway at the beginning of the week with a note urging me to pack up, but the more I considered doing so, the less certain I became of its necessity. Chances are, I will be back right here in a week, having to unpack all of these boxes anyway.

I move past him to readjust the direction a nearby urn faces.

"I am sure you did. Also, thank whoever it is you sent this time for not coming past the entryway. I appreciate it." Most of the people Hermes sends with my items remain unseen to me under cloak of darkness and sleep. As curious as I've been to their identities, I've never built up enough courage to meet them face-to-face.

He stops me—another hand on my arm, and I am paralyzed by this. It's the second time now he's touched me, and I long to melt in the sensations of his warm skin against mine. He acts as if he's not disgusted by this act, although I figure he must be. The skin on my arms, a mixture of both human and reptilian textures, disgusts even me, and I have to live with it. "Dusa, please be assured I am prepared to go as far as needed to ensure that justice is yours. I've already discussed your case in depth with a number of the Assembly members who have agreed to side with me—not as a favor," he adds, no doubt seeing disbelief crease my forehead, "but because they, too, believe it to be the right course of action. My sister and uncle are not nearly as popular within the Assembly as you might assume."

I stare down at his hand, so strong and beautiful and smooth against my slightly scaled and hideous skin. My heart races until I'm dizzy. He's not even shuddering. His hand is still there.

"If your inclination is to leave everything behind, then that is your right; I will support you in this. But I know many things are of great sentimental value to you, collected over the ages. If you wish to take them with you, I will happily ensure they safely reach you, wherever you choose to live."

A knot forms in my throat, forcing me to cough a few times to clear it. "And ... Gorgóna?"

He still hasn't removed his hand from my arm—in fact, his thumb is now tenderly moving back and forth, leaving me even more light-headed. No wonder people in books and movies crave this; the mere gentle act of skin on skin nourishes the soul like no words or thoughts ever could. "I will leave that decision up to you. It can stay here, hidden—a retreat, if you ever do wish to come back, or it'll never to grace the earth again."

Part of me wants nothing better than to see this bloody isle as scorched earth, but another knows this is home. It's been both my haven and prison.

"I'm not ready to make that decision yet," I whisper.

"You do not need to." He steps closer still, and I can smell the detergent used for his clothes, lingering traces of soap on his skin, and a hint of plain old Hermes. It is my favorite smell in the entire world, more so than any of the flowers I've ever grown. "Would you like help packing?"

I know his eyes can't meet mine, not like I can with his, but, as always, I get the feeling like his pierce right through the dark plastic, straight into me as I stare up at him. "You seem so confident."

The smile gracing his lips grows until it nearly blinds me. "Is that a yes?"

It is hard to wade into the unknown, but I do so for my friend. "Since when do the gods do such mundane things as pack up a monster's temple?"

He finally lets go of me, so he can stride over to where I'd left the boxes. I try to ignore just how bereft this loss of skin against skin makes me feel. "Since right now." And then, over his shoulder, "Don't you dare call yourself that again."

I don't know how it happens, but between the two of us, the temple gets packed up in a matter of five hours. While there are things I'm more than happy to leave behind, I decide to box them up to donate to shelters in Athens. Who knows? Maybe somebody unpacking them will realize their value and make a tidy profit for their organization after auctioning them off. At least, this is what I hope will happen. I offer to make Hermes my special spaghetti, which I know him to love, but he informs me he's late to a previously scheduled appointment. I tap down the disappointment toward his leaving, making sure he sees nothing but my gratitude over a job well done. But when we reach the entrance to the temple, I do the unthinkable: I reach out and touch him for the first time ever. Just a few fingers against his shoulder, but suddenly I've just stepped off a cliff and am soaring through the air, into the unknown after drowning in the deep sea for so long.

"You are the best kind of friend," I tell him.

He doesn't say anything, just studies me with those chameleon eyes of his. They're green right now, a beautiful light green that I lose myself in. Before I know it, he leans down and kisses my cheek. It isn't a quick one like before, when his lips pressed quickly against my temple. No, this one lingers for a several heartbeats, rendering me dizzy and elated all at the same time. "Sweet dreams, Dusa," he murmurs. "I'll be back for you and Mátia early Saturday morning. Dress warm—we'll be flying to Olympus, and the air can be chilly up high."

He's gone in a rush of wind that sends the gauzy tunic I'm wearing fluttering around me. Angrier-than-normal waves crash against my shores, sending sharp sprays of water inland, but I don't care that I've possibly infuriated the bastard trapping me out here once more.

Because, for the first time in a long time, hope floods throughout my soul.

Chapter Seven

"Are you ready?" Hermes holds his hand out for mine to take. He says we'll fly to Olympus, but from how he's described it to me in the past, I know we'll be travelling there through a portal he opens in the air above us.

My fingers tighten around the handle to Mátia's carrier. I'd lain awake all night, pondering just this question. Am I ready? I've had over two thousand years to be ready. Yet, here I am, about to head to Olympus and face my fate, and I still don't know if I can offer an honest response to that question. I'm numb and excited and scared and hopeful all at the same time.

No matter what, though, I trust him. He has yet to lead me astray.

So, I put my hand in his and let him take me away from here, from all that I've known for the majority of my life, praying there will be time soon enough for answers.

I think my heart is going to burst right out of my chest and onto the exquisite tile floor below me.

I am in the waiting room outside of the Great Assembly Hall, and the receptionist sitting at a behemoth of a desk is studying me with what I can best describe as trepidation. I get it. I really do. But I've done my best; I'm wearing my wrap-around sunglasses and the Girls are firmly ensconced in their favorite silk scarf, one Hermes brought us back from Paris in the 1950s. We had a talk this morning about them being on their best behavior, and even though they're snakes, I am confident that they understand the importance of helping me out. I have two extra pairs of sunglasses in a satchel I've brought, alongside another scarf. Currently, nobody nearby has anything to fear from me.

I can only hope that this remains the case. And that the same is offered in return.

I've been in the waiting room for nearly seven hours as the Assembly discusses my case. You'd think there'd be swank, comfy furniture here in Mt. Olympus, and maybe there is elsewhere, but in here, there's nothing I can relax upon. Regular, narrow chairs are worthless when half your body is snake-like. I wish for a chaise, but then I scold myself for unnecessary greed. The Assembly is already permitting me to be here to witness their decision; this is rarity and privilege enough. It's not often they reconsider the actions of their members.

The receptionist, a stern-looking satyr, clears his throat. "Do you mind if I ask a question?"

This startles me, even though I'm the only other person in the room. Even still, I offer him what I hope is a friendly smile. "Go for it."

"How many people have you killed?"

My thundering heart sinks; the Girls hiss angrily. I find my hands instantly go to my glasses, to check if the strap holding them in place is still firmly attached. "I don't know." The words stumble out of my mouth; I am the world's worst liar, or so Hermes often tells me. Because I do know how many people have perished because of me: sixty-three souls over two thousand years. And I know each and every one of their faces better than I

40

know my own.

The Girls press soothingly against my skull; I soak up their sympathy, even if I know it's misplaced. Because I am a killer. And even though I wish desperately I could undo each and every one of those deaths, and none of them came about from purpose, there is no two ways about what I've become.

"Huh," the satyr grunts, clearly skeptical. But then the intercom on his desk beeps. "The Assembly has finished reviewing your case. You may go in for judgment now."

I pat my scarf again and check the knots. Even though it's been less than a minute since inspecting my glasses, I confirm they're not budging, either. Then I head to the door that the satyr is holding open.

"Good luck," he says before disappearing behind the closing door.

In front of me is a long hallway resplendent with mosaicked scenes. Predictably, it showcases the greatest hits of the Assembly's achievements. I find myself smiling at the ones that show Hermes—even in tile and glass, he is as wonderful and heroic as always. A few feet later, I flinch when I see Poseidon with his trident. I beat myself up over how he still has that power over me. I'd thought ... two thousand years have passed. I shouldn't react so, should I? Stars, what will it be like when I'm to stand before him in moments, face to face? I haven't seen his face in person in millennia, yet he has been a thorn in my side every single day. His waters, churning around my isle, remind me how he's trapped me; his rejection of any suicide attempts in the seas proves lingering control. Every single day, his presence has tormented me in one way or another.

I'm ready to be done with him.

The Pantheon opens up before me, and it is a good thing I'm wearing sunglasses, because it's so dazzlingly white it threatens to blind me. A semi-circle of raised thrones rings the room, each seat tailored specifically to the god or goddess who reigns over it. Instinctively, I seek out Hermes first, who sits three down on the left of the front and center Zeus. My friend gives me a supportive smile, like he knows my eyes are upon him even though the glass-es are so dark nobody could see beyond the carefully constructed mirrored plastic.

I quickly do a mental checklist of what I'm allowed to do in here: 1) stay silent, unless spoken to; 2) show no outward emo-tions; 3) keep any answers brief and to the point; and most impor-tantly, 4) tell only the truth. Zeus can always pinpoint liars, and he is notorious for denying mercy to those who set out to deceive him.

"So," Zeus booms, and my attention snaps back to him. He is lounging in his throne, dressed in a t-shirt, torn shorts, and flip-flops. There is no beard, no mustache—just sandy hair and weathered, tan skin. I can see where Hermes gets his good looks. "Medusa, is it?"

I will my hands to remain at my sides, rather than go to the Girls or my glasses. My little snakes press tightly against my skull, shaking in the aftermath of the Lord of the Skies mighty voice. I want to shake right alongside them, but I force myself to stand still. "Yes, sir."

Zeus's fingers drum against the arm of his throne. "My son is most insistent that you've been unfairly punished for too long."

Do I agree? Is that okay? I have no idea if this is something that requires an actual answer, so I incline my head just enough to let anyone know that I concur with Hermes' assessment.

"We've just had a very interesting discussion about your cir-cumstances."

Somebody coughs pointedly; from Hermes' descriptions of his family over the years, I think the perpetrator is Ares. And then, more loudly, he mutters his vehement disagreement with the use of *discussion* to describe what just went down.

Zeus doesn't look away from me when he says, "Enough of that, son."

It's then that I finally allow myself to acknowledge Posei-don's presence, sitting to Zeus' right. He is exactly as I remem-ber him: stunning, with hair so black it shines, and shrewd eyes whose color changes in waves as the blues in the ocean do. My stomach clenches so hard I feel like throwing up.

The bastard is staring at me, concern etched in his eyes. Full on, blatant *staring*. Face entirely passive, but I get the impression that a bomb could go off and he'd still be looking exactly where he is now.

His hands, on me. His voice, in my ear. The bile shoots up my throat.

Don't make a sound. I promise I'll gift you an experience you'll never forget.

"Athena," Zeus says, and I rip my attention away from Lord of the Seas. My skin crawls with anxiety as I continue to feel the pressure of his undivided attention. "Before I lay final judgment, is there anything further you want to add to counter the frankly disturbing claims your brother just presented us with?"

A god I believe to be Apollo says, "Athena? Father, we've heard more than we'll ever need from that bitch."

Zeus says, his voice tempered with what surely must be exaggerated patience, "As with any case presented to me in which you are concerned, you are also given opportunity for a final comment or argument. Athena is due hers in this case."

Athena is sitting next to Poseidon. Her hair is in a tight bun, her expression sour as she peers down at me. There is disdain there, and something else—something I can't quite pinpoint. But whatever it is, I am more than aware of her revulsion, and it saddens me. I worshipped her. Served her. "How many times do I need to say it? The little whore got what she deserved."

I literally have to swallow back the vomit. It burns as it slides back down. Athena gets her say? What about mine? When do I get my say?

"Horseshit," comes another voice, and my focus swivels to the left of Zeus. It's Hades, the Lord of the Underworld. He is dark and handsome, but what has my attention is that his own eyes are filled with anger. I must admit I am surprised to see the emotion there.

"Uncle," Athena says, but he holds out a finger towards her and her lips immediately shut in a way that tells me she's probably not in control of her mouth at this moment.

"Niece," he stresses, mimicking her formality, "this isn't the first time you've overstepped your bounds by punishing innocents; this one just so happens to be the last remaining victim. If you even try to spew that victim blaming crap again, I'll take you down to the Underworld with me for a spell. Maybe then you can understand what true justice entails."

She gasps in outrage. I can't help but stare up at Hades in amazement. I've never had any contact with him before, except for sending far too many souls his way over the years. Is he one of Hermes' supporters?

"For somebody who is supposedly the bastion of wisdom," Hades continues darkly, "you do a piss-poor job of exhibiting it yourself."

A goddess I assume to be Aphrodite bursts into laughter; the sounds of wind chimes fill the hall. She's sitting on the other side of Hermes, looking every inch of what the Goddess of Love ought to look like. And I am struck with a small sliver of jealousy, that she possesses her beauty and I a face that can literally lead to death.

The irony of this is not lost on me.

"Cease your frivolity, *cow*," Athena hisses at her sister.

"How delightful. Your daughter strives to show example of my words," Hades says, this time to Zeus.

"Athena, close your mouth or have it shut for you." Zeus snaps. An exasperated sigh escapes from his lips as he kneads his forehead. Hermes was certainly right on this account—the Assembly loves to bicker.

"I agree with our Brother," Hestia pipes up from her seat next to Poseidon. "Athena's punitive play at a snit-fit has gone on long enough. Goodness," the Goddess of Hearth and Home tut-tuts. "If she were my daughter, this nonsense would have ended long ago."

Athena's eyes bulge, but she prudently stays silent.

"You coddle her," Hestia continues, shifting in her seat until she's facing Zeus.

"Don't start this again," he warns, and then there is an explosion of arguing within the Assembly. Bewildered, I seek out my friend, but he's focused on Poseidon, who, in turn, is focused on me. I stay silent, as still as the statues back on my isle.

"Enough," Zeus eventually booms. "I've had enough of this. Hermes, you were right to bring our attention to this matter. With our influence waning in the modern age, we cannot condone such petty actions of our past. Athena, revoke the curse. The Gorgon Medusa has been punished long enough."

Athena lurches to her feet. "She desecrated the sanctity of my temple with her overzealous, whorish libido!"

An imaginary fist punches my stomach. Before I break the rules and start shrieking, Hermes also stands up, visibly shaking. "You think she *chose* that? She was *raped*, you idiot!"

His words echo across the room. I cannot bring myself to look at Poseidon, but I know, just know, he is still staring at me.

His hands, on me. Blood, on the floor.

"If you want to be angry at somebody for defiling your holy ground, then take it up with our bastard of an uncle," Hermes continues, his voice low and angry. "But you know that none of this was Medusa's fault. You are acting beneath yourself to continue to punish her for something *that was not her fault.*"

Yet another reason, in a huge laundry list of many, as to why my gratitude toward my friend is boundless.

"Here, here!" Aphrodite fist pumps in the air. I glance over at her and she offers me a smile that's a surprising mixture of sympathy and support. But then I remember, Hermes has always said that he and this sister are thick as thieves.

Zeus is clearly weary. "It's done. We've voted, and I've decided. Daughter, reverse the curse now or your Uncle will be more than welcome to take you to the Underworld as he wishes."

Athena is still not swayed. "But—"

I hold my breath. Hades rises and takes a step towards her. She slams herself back into her seat. "Fine. The beast may seek me out this week when there is time—"

Hades steps down from his throne. "Now or never, niece."

"FINE!" the goddess of wisdom yells, and something strikes me so hard that I topple backwards. Pain, excruciating and sharp, coils around me tighter than any snake could. Hands grab me before I slam into the ground, but I can't even see whom they belong to, the agony is so intense. I want to scream, want to claw at something, but I am incapacitated. My insides are shredding, my skin is on fire. All I can do is pray that the death I've yearned for for so long will be swift before I black out.

olympus

Chapter Eight

"Here. Drink this." A soft voice tickles my ears. "It will help."

I go to open my eyes and then I remember who I am. I am Medusa. My eyes offer death. I weakly root around for my glasses, but they are nowhere nearby. "Glasses," I croak.

"Open your eyes, Dusa." I know this voice, and it hurts to hear so much worry in it.

"Glasses," I try again.

"No need." His promise is gentle. "The curse has been removed."

A hand instantly goes to my head. The Girls ...? But there is no movement, no soft hissing. There is only what feels to be hair, soft and matted.

"Snakes?" I mumble. A hand joins mine to tug through the strands; foreign shudders of mixed pleasure and comfort take hold in my muscles.

"Don't tell me you miss them," a female says, the very voice that woke me up. It's kind. And I am ... panicky. The Girls, gone?

"Oh, stop," a deep voice admonishes from further away. But it's not in exasperation; it's laced with amusement.

"Eyes?"

"You are no longer an instrument of death," the female says. My throat is so dry. "Swear?"

"I swear," Hermes answers. Fingers interlace in mine; for such a recent occurrence, his hand in mine feels like it's always belonged there. "Open your eyes, Dusa."

My heart runs a marathon, and fear invades my body, but he has yet to ever lie to me. So I do as he asks, and open my eyes voluntarily, without a shield, in the face of others for the first time in ages.

I am in an ornate bedroom, in a canopied bed that could fit twenty people. Hermes is sitting next to me, his own blue-green eyes filled with concern. Behind him is a stunning woman holding a cup. Sitting a few feet away is Hades, perusing something on an iPad.

"They're hazel," Hermes says, and he sounds awed.

"Beautiful hazel." The woman, surely a goddess, glances back at Hades. "The perfect mix of green and brown. Don't you think?"

He puts down his iPad and grunts. But he doesn't look fearsome, not like I once imagined him. At least, not in this moment.

"Drink this." She nudges me with a cup.

I don't take it. Not just yet. "You're all alive," I whisper.

"Of course we are." Hermes lifts our conjoined hands and presses a quick kiss against my skin. A roar of heat streaks up my neck. "I told you we would prevail. The curse was reversed." With his free hand, he pats me on my legs—

LEGS.

I have legs! I attempt to sit up, but the woman pushes me back down. *No longer is half of my body reptilian.* A few experimental wiggles of my toes promptly send me into a fit of tears.

"What is it?" Hermes exclaims. He grips my hand harder. "Do you hurt? Did she do something to you we didn't catch yet?"

"No, no." Bending my knees produces a fresh set of tears. "It's just, I have legs, and ..."

My friend laughs the same relieved exhale I've come to know

over the years. "Stars above, Dusa. You scared me."

"I wouldn't have put such a trick past Athena," Hades mutters in the background.

I need to see these legs. *My* legs. I go to rip the sheet off, but the woman stops me.

"File out boys." She motions with her free hand toward Hermes and Hades. "Let's let Medusa get dressed and fed before we do anything else, hmm?"

It's then I realize I am completely naked under the sheet. If I'd thought I was overly warm a minute ago, I was quite mistaken, because now I am completely enflamed.

"Persephone, be nice to her," Hermes warns. He squeezes my hand and reluctantly gets up.

She blows him a kiss. "I will pretend you didn't just say that." And then, amazingly, both gods exit the room.

I wipe away the lingering tears. "You're ... Persephone?"

She smooths back some of my hair; her touch is tender against my sensitive skin. "Yes, darling. You're currently in my home in Olympus. Hermes thought it best you recuperate somewhere comfortable."

And this is where he chose? I think, but I lick my dry lips and promptly thank her for taking me in anyway.

"I am delighted to do so. Oh! Hold on a second; there is someone who wants to visit." She goes into a sitting room just off the bedroom and returns with Mátia. "This little man has missed his mama."

I take my kitten and press kisses all over his soft face. So, Persephone is the favorite aunt Hermes trusted with my baby. "Thank you," I tell her once more, letting gratitude coat my words.

She presses the cup she'd been offering earlier into my hand. "We've wanted to meet you for some time. Obviously, Hades and I have ... intimate knowledge ... of your characters over the years. Outside of what our beloved nephew tells us."

I nearly choke on my drink. "You mean, from all the poor souls I've sent to you."

"Yes, that," she says with a wry smile. She is her husband's opposite—light where he is dark. "Do not be ashamed, darling girl. Death comes for a person when it is exactly their time. Be rest assured, we are fully cognizant of the details of your situation." She smooths my hair once more. "Besides, how could we dislike anyone who has so thoroughly earned Hermes' trust?"

It is odd to hear her refer to Hermes as her nephew, or me as a girl, as Persephone barely looks a day over twenty-five herself.

She goes to an armoire nearby. "Come. Let's get you up on your feet and dressed." She motions to what appears to be a depthless array of clothing. "Would you like modern or traditional?"

Over the years, I've developed a secret love for fashion despite the lack of ability to truly indulge in it. I poured over magazines and websites, marveling over just how artful clothing has become. But now, faced with a choice of practically anything I could ever desire, and legs and a body to fit into such luxuries, I have no idea what I want.

If Persephone is bothered by my lack of answer, she doesn't show it. She extracts a billowy pale gray dress from the closet and holds it out. "How about this one? It's a little of both. Greek styling," she fingers a threaded silvery pattern on the waist, "with modern sensibilities. Let us see if those legs are working yet."

My legs tremble like a newborn foal's, but I manage to get out of the bed. She has to help me immediately, as outside of the sheets, I am exposed, raw: new, pale, pink flesh shivering weakly in cool air. But Persephone acts as if this—me—is nothing out of the ordinary. She holds onto me as I pull the oh-so-soft to the touch silk dress over my head; it floats around me like a cloud. Something in my memory, deep and long repressed, stirs—an image, a sensation, of me in a dress not quite so fine, running through a golden field.

"Perfect," Persephone murmurs. She carefully leads me a short distance over to a vanity and helps me sit before a modest sized mirror that looks out of place in such an opulent room. "Your hair is lovely." She lifts the matted mess up in her hands. "An auburn I haven't seen before, and with a natural curl to boot. No wonder Athena thought to replace it with snakes. She must have been out of her mind with envy when she saw how exquisite you were."

I stare into the mirror and see nothing but a stranger. The girl before me is pale; her face is thin but unblemished. Her hair is tangled and wild, her eyes an unstable cross between brown and green. I lean closer and stare harder. I ought to recognize this face, shouldn't I? Didn't I wear it before, even if it was for a tiny sliver of my life?

But I don't. And it's unnerving, because if I can remember running through a field, wearing a dress, I ought to be able to remember my face.

Persephone holds up a brush. "Do you mind?"

A goddess asking me if she can brush my hair? How has the impossible become so possible lately? She goes to work once I agree, methodically yet carefully brushing my hair free of tangles. I continue to stare in the mirror, searching for clues or memories, but they are worse than elusive.

They simply do not exist.

Persephone's touch is gentle, and I can't help but greedily hold onto the pleasure a simple gesture such as having one's hair brushed brings. When she's done, she brandishes the brush above my head like a magic wand in a fairy tale book. "What do you think?"

There are perfect, barrel-sized curls circling the girl in the mirror's head. Not snakes. And for a moment, sorrow and loneliness press against my heart so strongly that it's hard to breathe. The snakes—my Girls—were constant companions. It's not like I chose them; in fact, I'd resented them more often than not during times such as sleep (they rightfully hated when I leaned my head down at certain angles and squashed them) or when I had headaches and they buzzed about me with minds of their owns. But they'd been there with and for me more years than not. And now ... they're gone. And it wasn't like they'd died, and I had their bodies to grieve over.

They simply didn't exist anymore.

It's incredibly messed up how much I already mourn their

presence. "The curls are lovely."

Persephone leans down until her strawberry-golden hair presses against my darker curls. "Hermes is so right about you. You are a wretched liar." She hugs me tightly; once more, I revel in her touch. Two embraces from two gods in less than two weeks.

It's yet another miracle sprung into my existence.

Even still, I'm dismayed she might have taken offense at my words. I quickly correct, "I do like them; they're beautiful, and I appreciate your help ..."

"I know you do." She gives me another squeeze before standing up. "Believe it or not, I can well imagine how overwhelmed you are in this moment, and we three have been hovering over you for days when all you probably want to do is take a moment just to breathe."

My eyes jerk away from the mirror, up to hers. "Days?"

Persephone sighs and puts the brush into a drawer. "Athena is not always the kindest of souls. She did as Zeus requested, but she ..." Her full lips purse together. "Well, I think she wanted to ensure everyone knew she was displeased with being reprimanded." She pats my shoulder. "We'll talk more about it later, but let me encourage you to keep your distance from that one from now on."

Like I ever plan on interacting with Athena again. I am no longer her disciple. "As she and I will no longer have any reason to cross paths again, I cannot see how that'll be a problem."

I try not to squirm as Persephone studies me. I am a Gorgon, the most feared in history. I froze men and women by simply, albeit unwillingly, looking at them. But when this goddess looks at me with her green eyes, so pale they are nearly colorless, I am the one to freeze in utter anxiety. She murmurs, "That may be difficult, considering ..." But then she doesn't finish the thought. "Let's go meet the boys. There is much to discuss."

"About?" No matter how nice she's been to me, Persephone is still a goddess, and I've learned the hard way that goddesses are temperamental creatures that need to be handled delicately.

She holds out her hand and helps me up. "You, of course."

Hades is an enigma to me. On one hand, he resembles what many people think the so-called devil ought to be like: a magnificent temptation of a man, all dark brown hair and dark brown eyes. On the other, he doesn't appear nearly as fearsome as the stories I've heard of him over the ages. I suppose I expected someone as hideous as I had been, but Hades is the opposite of that. While he certainly has the propensity toward the visage of a brooding hero from some Gothic mystery, he also has a kindhearted smile. Plus, his eyes crinkle at the corners when he shares that smile, so—even though he scares me, I also can't help but feel there's something more to him than legends claim.

It is obvious he and Persephone are deeply in love, which is yet another surprise. Like most everyone, I've read the stories of how he'd kidnapped her and held her against her will half the year in the Underworld. Only, Persephone doesn't act like a kidnapped victim ought to act; that, or she's an excellent actress who suffers heavily from Stockholm syndrome. She dotes on his words, as he does to hers. They are constantly near each other, if not actively (or, perhaps, unconsciously) touching.

"Are you truly all right?" Hermes asks, pulling my attention away from the couple. I've been unabashedly staring, which is embarrassing, indeed. Clearly, I need a crash course in social niceties now that I'm around more than one person at a time.

"Yes. I'm ... it's just a lot to take in. Forgive me for not being better company."

He smiles and sits down next to me on a chaise lounge. We are on a sun porch, and the warmth on my legs is delightful. Although Persephone had said we'd discuss my situation, so far, they've treated me warily, not rushing into anything other than ordering an early dinner—linner, she called it—since "such conversations are best suited to full-bellies."

I'm not going to be the one to argue with the Queen of the Underworld.

Hermes' head tilts toward mine. "Don't be ridiculous. You are always perfect company for me." My chest swells in pleasure before he adds, more seriously, "Dusa, I wanted to—"

"Thank you," I blurt out. I hate interrupting him, but it demands to be to be said.

His eyes widen in surprise. "There's no need to—"

"Stop," I tell him, and I place my hand over his lips. It feels sinfully good to be able to touch him like this, touch him in any capacity now that I have no fear for disgust over my skin. Do people get addicted to touching one another? I think I could, easily. And just the thought of that causes heat to rise once more up my neck, forcing my fingers to drop away. "Let me finish, please?"

I swear, true twinkles appear in the green parts of his eyes. "By all means. Who am I to prevent one such as you if you wish to offer me gratitude?"

"Stop," I repeat, giggling at the feigned innocence he attempts to tease me with. "It's just ..." My laughter fades away. "You don't understand how indebted I'll always be to you. I was terrified to even give this a chance, but you—you took a huge risk for me when you didn't have to. And, it worked out. All those years, all those fears ..." I shake my head; my hair, still so foreign upon my head, swings around me. "I can't believe ..." I motion up and down my body, then run my hands across the length of my thighs to knees. "I never thought I'd ever be anything other than a monster again."

The mock innocence melts away into seriousness. "I didn't do this for your gratitude or to wish to hold you in some kind of debt. I did it because it was the right thing to do."

The way he's looking at me is too intense, so I focus on a striking fountain nearby depicting what I believe to be Persephone eating a pomegranate. Is there truth to the story? "Some would disagree, especially in light of my actions over the ages."

One of his hands comes to lightly trace the same line I'd just drawn, from mid-thigh to knee. I shiver in the warm air; confusion and pleasure swirl around my head just as surely as my curls. "We've gone over this. You didn't have a choice."

"I am a murderer," I whisper, and sadness once more threatens to crush my heart. This dream has finally come true, but how I wish I could erase all of the pain I've caused over the ages.

"Not by choice. And never purposely."

"Still."

"I would know, remember? I've ferried enough souls to the Underworld to be something of an expert."

This makes me laugh, even if just a little. Even if undeserved, his faith in me has never waivered. "Shall I forget that history pegs you as a trickster, too? As one who deceives?"

"You as well as I know what a pile of lies"—he flashes air quotes—"*history* can be. Let us not forget that history also has you, as the mortal sister of a trio, suffering an ignominious death at the hands of that twat Perseus, and that your severed head was carted around the better part of Greece for the sole purpose of slaying a Titan."

"If only," I joke, and he tenses besides me. But he knows how I'd longed for death, how I would pray daily for it. How I would curse the fact that I was immortal, thanks to Athena's fury. He always tried to talk me out of such wishes, to remind me of the good that life could and does offer, but it was habitually difficult to accept his rationalizations when a growing collection of statues populated my island.

But now ... now is my chance to do so. And it's all due to him.

"Enough of that talk," he says curtly. "It's irrelevant anyway. You are no longer a monster—not that I think you ever were in the first place—and there will be no further fear of murder if you do not so plan it intentionally."

It's my turn to tense. "I would never—"

"My point made." And then, more gently, "I don't want us to argue. Not today. Not when we have this victory to savor."

Like a moth to a flame, I cannot resist the pull to meet my eyes to his. He's looking at me like I'm the only thing in this villa, as if there weren't sights surrounding us that would make poets and artists weep and wish they had even a tenth of the ability needed to describe it in detail. No, his attention is on me, his eyes, so wonderfully green, firmly gazing into mine, and after over two thousands years of friendship, I no longer know what to say to him.

Something stirs deep inside me. When I say his name, it comes out as a whisper. He slowly leans into me, whispering my name in return. My heart slams around my chest in chaotic anticipation, making the simple act of pulling air into my lungs difficult.

"Ah, there's the food," Persephone calls, and I snap back, my cheeks flaming. Hermes sighs and leans back, glaring at his aunt.

Sure enough, two servers have appeared, pushing carts filled with food and plates more suited to two-dozen people rather than four.

The Queen of the Underworld motions us over. "I had no idea what you like, darling, so I made sure to order a little bit of everything."

Hades rolls his eyes while sneaking a few strawberries off one of the trays.

"My aunt loves to play hostess," Hermes says as he helps me up. My legs are still wobbly, but his hold on me is firm.

When I look up at him, all I can think is, *he won't let me fall.*

"Careful!" Persephone darts over, slinging an arm around my waist to help me balance. "It appears you're going to have to do a bit of rehab over the next few weeks in order to get reacquainted with walking. Oh, I could just strangle Athena for this."

"Line forms to the left," Hermes says quietly. "But you'll have to stand behind me."

The impulse to lean over and kiss him for such steady loyalty is nearly irresistible, which leaves me even more embarrassed and confused. He is my friend. Why are such thoughts bedeviling me right now?

"Let me do some calling around tonight." Persephone bumps her shoulder against mine. "I want to make sure we get the best."

Once I'm seated (and blushing far too much over needing help to walk over to the table), Hades hands his wife a glass of wine. "Athena has gotten away with far too much over the ages.

It's disheartening how my brother coddles her idiotic whims. I wish you'd let the Assembly know about this sooner, Hermes. How are we ever going to get everyone under control if actions such as these are left unresolved? We cannot have our members running rampant, cursing people simply because they feel like it. Our positions in the heavens are too precarious nowadays to have such missteps."

Persephone thanks her husband for her glass. "Too many poor souls have suffered abuse at the hands of our kind." Her elegant fingers curve around the stem. "Some have perished before we can right their wrongs; others have gone too far into madness and truly became the monsters they were forced to evolve into. And that is something we cannot have happening, especially in today's modern world. Hermes, you know our stance on this. I must side with your uncle—I am sorely disappointed Medusa's case was not addressed earlier."

Those blue-green eyes of Hermes' slide knowingly toward me before refocusing on his aunt and uncle. "Trust me when I say there is no one sorrier than I that it took so long to come to light."

I cannot let them fault him for this, not when he'd held his tongue out of respect for my wishes. I clear my throat nervously. "It wasn't his fault. Hermes wanted to talk to the Assembly for quite a long time now. I was the one who begged him not to."

Persephone sets her glass down, her brow furrowing. "Why?"

I toy with the napkin on my lap, debating how I ought to phrase my answer without outwardly insulting the deities in front of me. As generous as they've been, I do not trust them yet. But my response is not necessary, as Hermes is the one to answer. "Why wouldn't she be leery? Look at what our kind has done to her."

Hades grunts as he butters a roll, anger flashing in his dark eyes. I tense in my seat; is he mad that I've spoken without permission? This is the Lord of the Underworld, after all. For all I know, he could find much offense with me and banish me to a punishment worse than Athena's in some hidden corner of his realm.

Hermes continues, "It was a miracle she even allowed me in her temple, and then, once I was there, to continue coming back."

I haven't been able to blush in millennia, but here I am, doing it again in less than five minutes.

Hades studies me as he quietly munches on his roll. His gaze is even more intense than his wife's or nephew's, so I keep my attention focused on the food on my plate. Only, my stomach in far too many knots, so actual eating is out of the question.

Persephone picks up her fork. "Did he bully you into letting him?"

My eyes fly up, every muscle in my body on high alert. Do they think I have been abusing one of the Assembly? I go to protest, but Hermes laughs delightedly.

"Of course I did."

"It's a wonder you didn't turn him to stone immediately." Amusement sprinkles Persephone's words, but all I can hear is yet another reminder of how people are dead because of me. Or how I could have harmed the most important person in my life at any time.

The control I've been clinging to evaporates. Tears spring forth in its place, along with the impulse to run and hide and have a good cry in private. Knowing my luck, though, these skinny, weak legs would give out within two steps, so my only recourse is to blink rapidly and pray I do not cause more offense. And now my heart's beating hard in my chest, feeling just as trapped here in this moment as I have been for ages.

I'm a killer. I've murdered people. Sixty-three people lost their lives because of me, never to draw another breath. I can only pray they're in the Elysian Fields right now.

I'm a monster. I'm—

I'm the river, pounding furiously at the walls of the dam. Breathing slowly does no good. I cannot get a proper breath. And now I'm clutching at my napkin, the skin across my knuckles white and strained, and a horrible sound escapes me, one born from shame and despair.

This tremulous happiness of having the curse removed—I do

not deserve it. Not after what I've done.

In the next moment, I'm in Hermes' arms, pulled from my chair to his lap for the second hug in our existences together, and he's saying, as one hand bunches in my hair and the other goes to my back, "She was just joking. Don't—you are not what you're thinking. It's okay. It's going to be okay. You are not at fault. None of this is your fault."

The waters in me find the right cracks in the concrete, because the dam explodes. I bawl, clinging to his shirt with my new, smooth hands, soaking the fabric with my hot tears. I can hear Persephone in the background, bewildered and apologizing, and Hades chastising her for careless words, and I ought to be horrified that I've somehow made a goddess feel as terrible as she's claiming, but right now, all I can do is cry.

A good cry, as I've learned over the years, is a cathartic experience. I don't do it often, as it can be a fruitless endeavor—it changes nothing, but sometimes, there's this sweet spot I can find where I simply feel better afterward, even if just for an hour. This time, though, breaking down not once, but twice in front of three of Olympus' own, I find no catharsis.

Hermes has stopped saying anything—they've all stopped speaking—but his heartbeat is steady under my ear as I grapple to get myself back under control. I have no idea how long I've been hysterical, and that scares me. "I'm sorry," I eventually choke out, hating how my voice is as unstable as my emotions. "I didn't mean to break down in your presences. Please, forgive me."

I feel the frustrated sigh Hermes lets go at the same time Persephone says, her hand joining his on my back for the briefest of moments, "It is me who is sorry. I should not have joked so carelessly about something such as this."

I don't know what to do. She seems so genuine, but a goddess, apologizing to—well, I'm not sure what I am anymore. Still an immortal? Or just a mere mortal? But this sort of behavior doesn't coincide with what I know about the Assembly. On one hand, it's obvious Hermes is close to Hades and Persephone, and I trust him and don't believe he'd willingly bring me to gods whose first impulse is to toy with me. But on the other, I can't yet let go of the wariness I've cultivated toward their kind for ages.

"Is there anything I can get for you?" Persephone asks, and amazingly, worry saturates her words. "Would you prefer we wait until tomorrow to talk about the next steps?"

Every muscle in my body tenses again. Hades mutters something to his wife about this being an excellent time to stop talking.

"She means your options," Hermes murmurs, his face lowering down so he can speak in my ear. And then, lifting his head, he says, "Can we have a few minutes by ourselves?"

"Of course. Just—let us know if there's anything ..." Persephone trails off, sounding even more unsure of herself.

"Wife, you've done enough. Leave the poor girl alone," Hades says, voice low and rough even as he takes her hand in his like it's made of porcelain. "Medusa's life has once more been turned upside down by our kind, so I think she warrants a little time adjusting. Hermes, come see me before you leave. There is still much for us to discuss."

The sound of chairs scraping against tile and footsteps sound; soon, the only noises around are the wind through the trees, the fountain splashing softly, and the steady beat of Hermes' heart.

He taps the back of my head softly. "What's going on in here?"

I bite my lip, well aware of the awkward position we're in, of me sitting on his lap and of his thoroughly wet t-shirt. Is he annoyed I'm still here? I've apparently been clinging to him, which isn't proper decorum in the least. I shift in his lap, leaning toward my chair, but he surprises me by refusing to let me go.

So I rest my head back against his shoulder and let out a shuddery breath. I cannot deny how comfortable I feel, sitting here. I would much rather be with him than alone in my chair. Is it because, for so long, it's always been just him and me—and now, here we are again, just the two of us?

64

"Talk to me, Dusa."

I close my eyes and think, once more, of how this god has convinced me with his gentle words and actions to throw caution to the wind. "Can I trust them?"

Whatever he thought I'd say, it wasn't this, because I can hear him suck in his surprise. But he's steady as ever when he answers. "I wouldn't have brought you here had I not believed you could trust them with your life." His hand continues to lightly stroke my hair. "There is nothing—no one—you have to fear in this house. My uncle and aunt are the best kinds of people."

Ha. People. He says this like we're talking about Mikkos and his ex-wife or any other pair of mortals, like Hades and Persephone are normal and incapable of destroying lives with just a thought.

They are the definition of extraordinary. There is nothing normal about them at all. They're gods. And as much as I like to pretend otherwise, so is this person I'm sitting with.

I pull back a little and he lets me, so I can wipe my face. A rueful laugh breaks free at the same time I revel in just how smooth the skin on my cheeks is. These wild non sequiturs remind me of my need to get myself under control. "They must think I am insane."

Because I'm beginning to think maybe I am, too.

"Not insane." I hold my breath when he wipes away tears I've missed. "Although, if you were, no one could blame you. You're simply being emotional, and you have every right to be just as you are."

Sunset has come and gone, and now our table is bathed in soft lights from candles and lanterns nearby. Irrationally, I wonder what it is like back home on Gorgóna—is the weather fine, like it is here? Is it even nighttime? What of my statues—is Niki searching my room, wondering where I am? Are they okay, without me being there to watch over them?

"I must be crazy," I tell him, "because I just thought of Gorgóna as home, and subsequently felt homesick." I pick at the embroidering at the waist of Persephone's fine dress. "I am offi-

65

cially homeless, you know."

He brushes a curl away from my eyes. "No. You are not. This was one of the things we wanted to talk to you tonight about. Hades and Persephone have extended an offer for you to call their villa home for as long as you like."

They did? And yet ... is Hermes not comfortable extending the same offer to me for his home? Squelching down ridiculous yet distinct sensations of disappointment and hurt, I ask, "Why would they do that?"

He's thoughtful for a long moment, like he's trying to choose his words carefully. Finally, "It was best felt you be welcomed in a place that would serve as both safe haven and a home during this transitional period in your life. Hades is extremely powerful; he and Persephone are influential amongst the rest of the Assembly. They will ensure no further harm will befall you."

Harm? I think back to what Persephone said about Athena earlier. Surely she wants nothing more to do with me, right? And there there's now Hermes just made it sound like he will not be around anymore, which alarms me. I attempt to sound nonchalant when I ask, "And ... you?"

His fingers tug through my strands before he tucks curls behind an ear, smiling a secret smile that I've yet to interpret successfully over the years. "What about me?"

Oh, yet another moment I wish I could just hop up and walk off. There's a nice fountain nearby that I'd love to pretend to examine right now, because once more, heat rises to my cheeks. Is he truly going to make me say how much I desire to have him around out loud? Which is a silly concern, since this is my friend, and he's teased me just so for longer than some countries have existed. Knowing I have no escape, though, I relent and ask outright, "Where will you be?"

"Your hair is beautiful," he murmurs, pulling down on a curl. "I still wish I could have met your Girls, though. I bet they were equally lovely. They liked me, you know."

A sensation I've never felt blooms throughout me, where I'm comfortable and uncomfortable all at the same time. But before

I can decipher it, he adds, "I'll be here, too; other than when I'm working, of course. If you're worrying I did not want you at my home—"

Oh, blast it all. Now I'm positive I'm bright red.

"—then you can stop thinking that right now. I would love nothing more than to welcome you there, but strategically, this is the best place for you to get back on your feet."

I groan, "Har-har," as a naughty grin threatens to overtake his face.

I end up eating after all—just a little, but enough to satisfy the both of us. A servant brings Mátia out during the dessert course, along with his bowl of food, and Hermes lulls me into complacency by engaging me in our typical conversations as we take turns fighting for the kitten's attention.

It's exactly what I need: normalcy in the extraordinary.

When the hour grows late, Hermes picks me up in his arms, like I (along with Mátia) weigh nothing so he can walk me back to my suite. And even though sleep is threatening to pull me under as I lean my head against his shoulder, I am coherent enough to thank Zeus that his son is my friend.

Chapter Nine

I nearly fly out of bed when a woman comes into my room, carrying a large tray laden with pastries and what appears to be a pot of tea. How did she get past my lock? Has she noticed me yet? Panicked, I reach for my glasses ... only to remember there is no longer a need.

My hands go up to my hair. There are no snakes. My Girls are gone. I am not in my temple. I am in Olympus, sleeping in a bed large enough to fit twenty, in a villa owned by the Lord of the Underworld.

"My lady, I am your new handmaiden. My name is Kore," the woman says, turning to face me. My eyes instinctively close, but once my heart slows down, I open them back up and study her. I'm startled to recognize her as a nymph, although I should not be, as this is Olympus and all. If my behavior is bizarre to her, she doesn't let on. "Did you sleep well?"

I draw the covers up to my chest as I lean back against the pillows; annoyed at the movement, Mátia squeaks sleepily and bats at my hand. He draws blood—not a lot, but enough for me so quietly reprimand him before answering the nymph. "I did.

Thank you."

She carries the tray over to my bed, chattering on about the weather forecast for the day. I can't help but marvel that there is somebody here—someone other than Mikkos and Hermes—talking to me. She's not scared, she's not in danger ... she's just *talking* to me.

I kind of want to cry again, this time from happiness.

She stays until I'm done eating so she can help me get dressed and do my hair. I feel helpless, like a child coddled by her nurse, which only turns my resolve steely to do such things for myself as soon as possible. Once I'm ready for the day, she brings in what appears to be an extremely fancy wheelchair (much more golden than those I've seen in movies) so she can take me downstairs to where I'm awaited in Hades' office.

Even as she helps me into the chair, I tell her quietly, "I can walk," despite my doubts over the validity of such a statement.

"My lady, my boyfriend is a centaur. I can only imagine what he'd be like if he went from four legs to two." Her soft yet gentle girlish giggling tinkles through the room but it quickly squelched, like she is afraid at getting caught for being so merry. "He'd probably be host to a few broken limbs and maybe a black eye or two from all the falling he did from refusing help." She squats down in front of me, her long brown, wavy hair floating around her willowy body as she adjusts my feet on the footrests, like they are completely nonfunctional.

Again with the *my lady?* "My name is—"

"You are the Lady Medusa," she says, tucking a blanket across my lap.

Whoa. Even pre-curse, I did not carry such an honorific title. "I just meant ... I'm no 'my lady.' Please, feel free to call me by my name."

"You are now a treasured guest in this home." She stands back up and smooths the wrinkles out of her billowy, light green dress. "And as such, you are to be given every respect that the Lord and Lady of the house do so wish."

Before I can counter that, she's pushing me out the door.

"Don't worry about your kitten. I've already set up someone to come and take care of him when you or I are not around." I thank her, and she continues, her voice dropping significantly lower, "May I ask you something, my lady?"

Stars above, please do not let her ask about the people I've killed. I am hesitant with my answer. "Of course."

She calls out a greeting to a satyr coming out of a spare bedroom, linens in his arms before hushing her words once more. "There is a rumor spreading throughout Olympus right now that you and Lord Hermes are ... friends. Is this truth?"

I'm so surprised by this question that I actually laugh. As I have all of two true friends in this world, it shouldn't be very hard for anyone to guess as to who they are. But then, as I consider her question, my laughter trails away. Did anyone know about Hermes' visits over the years? Has he ever acknowledged my presence in his life to anyone before? Unwelcome insecurity descends upon me, fast and furious.

"I beg your forgiveness, my lady." There is worry in Kore's soft voice. "It is clearly none of my business."

Oh! Is she insulted I've taken too long to answer? I quickly say, "No—it's fine. It's—"

But then the object of her question appears at the end of the long hallway. "There you are!" he calls out, jogging down to meet us. Kore stops pushing me so she can drop into a low curtsy, murmuring a reverent greeting to him.

He offers her a curt greeting in return, but his attention is on me. He's got that dazzling smile of his out in full display, making me want to test out my theory that woman cannot resist its allure. I discreetly glance up at Kore, but she's now standing quietly next to the chair, her eyes on the ground. She seems ... nervous. Is this how people act around him? "I swear, this place is like a labyrinth," he tells me, and I refocus back on his face. His eyes are a stable cross between blue and green today. "I tried the other direction first; I think it took me twenty minutes just to find my way back here. I need a map."

I find myself blushing and giggling at the same time. This is definitely going to be a problem if I keep reacting this way around him. Why am I? Was it just my semi-reptilian skin didn't allow such warming before? "How many rooms are in here, anyway?"

He looks back over his shoulder, like the answer is posted on the wall for all to see. When he faces me again, he shrugs in a really boyish, charming way. "I have no idea."

"One hundred and six, m'lady," Kore says quietly from her spot next to me.

And here I'd thought the temple I'd lived in was grand.

Hermes finally looks over at Kore, his eyes narrowing in a way I've never seen them do so before. Did he think she spoke out of turn? She's been nothing but kind to me today. "Hermes, have you met—"

But he cuts me off, addressing Kore in a tone I've never heard, either. "It is my understanding that, after much careful consideration, my aunt highly recommended you for this position."

She curtsies once more, staying silent.

He takes a step closer to where she's standing. "That said, I believe a sister of yours works in another household."

Her eyes do not leave the floor. "Yes, Lord Hermes. My elder sister is in Lady Athena's employ."

Unease slams into me at the sound of her name. What is he insinuating?

"When my aunt told me she selected you to work for the Lady Medusa, I was greatly displeased." No longer smiling, his eyes grow icy blue. "Yet, she was fervent with her belief that you were the best fit for the job, so I conceded to her knowledge in such matters. But now that I have the opportunity to do so, I will reiterate what I told Lady Persephone, although I am sure she wisely has mentioned it to you. If I learn you mention to your sister, or her employer, or any combination there in between, a single word concerning the lady here, you will wish you had never set foot in this house, let alone Olympus."

She pales considerably. "Yes, Lord Hermes. My mistress did inform me of this condition of yours."

My fingers curl tighter around the arms of the chair. I grasp for my voice. "Hermes, what—"

But Kore is not done. "Please believe me when I tell you that my sister and I have not spoken in more than two years, Lord Hermes."

He studies her, and I must give her credit—she does not flinch underneath that piercing gaze of his. "And yet, I do not find that to be a trustworthy enough reason to rationalize your position."

"I will endeavor to prove Lady Persephone's belief in me," is how she responds. And then, with her eyes finally coming up to meet his, "And the Lady Medusa's."

What is going on right now? "Hermes—"

Just like that, his easy smile reemerges. "Hades and Persephone are waiting for us downstairs. Would you mind if I took you instead of Kore? I'm sure she can find herself useful elsewhere."

This is what finally causes Kore to flinch. And when I glance up at her, I can see just how hard she's trying to cover what appears to be surprise. She curtsies again, this time to the both of us, and then turns around and disappears down yet another long hallway.

"What was that all about?" I ask as he grabs the handles on the back of the chair.

He feigns ignorance. "What was what?"

"That—that threatening you did to poor Kore!" I look up at him. A tight knot sickens my stomach. "Promise me you'll never curse her, Hermes. I couldn't stand if anybody was ever cursed because of me."

He stops pushing and is silent for a long moment. And then he comes around to the front, squatting down so he can lean his elbows against the chair's arms, a surprising amount of hurt reflecting back at me in his deep blue eyes. "I don't curse people, Dusa."

Even though I know him well, I'm still skeptical. Friend or no, he is still a god. "Ever?"

He sighs, rocking back on his heels before his head lowers. My fingers itch to touch the beautiful golden hair spilling down so close to my lap. "I cannot tell you I have never cursed a person before," he murmurs after long seconds of quiet breaths. "But I haven't done so in a very long time, and I swear to you it will never happen again."

He looks up at me, and I can see the sincerity and regret in his gaze.

My heart stutters, and a whole host of bewildering sensations rush through me so quickly that they nearly steal the air in my lungs. "You haven't?"

He shakes his head slowly but surely, eyes never leaving mine.

I'm a fool for demanding an answer from a god, but I do it anyway. Too much hope crowds my mouth not to. "Why?"

He reaches up and twirls a piece of my hair, loose and free today with just a hint of wave, around his fingers. "You know why."

The knot now gone, I can't even describe the tingling sensation blooming in my stomach right now. It feels like ... butterflies, maybe. Like tiny wings beating against the tender muscles, anxious to fly free.

He lets go of my hair and positions himself behind the chair again, leaving me unsettled by the emotions raging about in my chest. It isn't until we've turned a corner in the hallway that he finally speaks again. "How did you sleep?"

"Like the dead," I tell him truthfully. I am glad for the change of subject, because my heart is beating too fast. "Also, for such a tiny thing, Mátia is a horrible bed hog. Even in a bed as big as the one I slept in last night."

He laughs at this just as we stop at what can only be an elevator. I've read about them plenty of times. I've seen movies and shows with them, but this is the first time I've ever been in one, considering there were no elevators on the isle and they certainly weren't around in Ancient Greece. So, I can't help myself—I clap delightedly.

And rather than thinking me weird or annoying, Hermes just smiles when I demand to be the one to push the buttons.

Hades' office is probably as big as my temple was: sprawling in size, with windows reaching at least two floors high, it reminds of me photographs I've seen of libraries and museums. Thousands of books line the walls, alongside artwork that spans time periods and cultures. And the statues in here are not painful to look at; they are beautiful, carved of marble until they are smooth and glowing.

I want to have Hermes push me around—better yet hold my arm so I can walk—and examine all these newly discovered treasures in detail, but as Persephone is pouring coffee at a table surrounded by a series of plush couches in the middle of the room, I figure I'll have to wait until later.

"Good morning!" she calls out to me, her words ringing in the vast room. She's wearing an emerald colored modern dress today, appearing if she'd come straight off a catwalk in Paris. "I know you've already had breakfast, but would you like some coffee?"

I decide to take Hermes at his word and trust that I can act like myself here in front of these deities without total fear of persecution. So I wave my friend away as I manage to get out of the chair all by myself so I can scoot onto the couch nearby. My knees tremble, but I love knowing that I did it on my own. "That'd be lovely, thank you."

Hermes sits down next to me, preparing his coffee just the way I know he likes it—half a sugar cube and a splash of cream. Before Persephone hands me the cup she's just poured, he says, "Drown it in cream, Aunt. Dusa likes it more tan than black. And then add as much sugar as you can until it is only a shade of what coffee once was."

Damn him. He's making me blush again. "I can do it myself," I say, but she just grins.

"A girl after my own heart. If I have to drink coffee, this is the way to go."

Hades steps out from one of the alcoves, several folders stuffed with loose papers in his hands alongside the iPad I saw him working on yesterday. "I cannot believe I married somebody who doesn't worship coffee the way I do. What was I thinking?"

Persephone laughs heartily at this. "As I had to twist your arm into marrying me, I'm sure you were only thinking of how to get me to stop pestering you."

I can feel my eyes widen over this. Is this true?

Next to me, Hermes stretches his long legs out. "I had a chat with Kore this morning."

I sip my coffee quietly. He'd shut down our conversation in the hallway, but maybe now he'd be more forthcoming about why he'd gone crazy up there on her.

Persephone sighs. "You didn't."

Hermes merely looks at her over his cup. Hades chuckles as he sits down next to his wife on the couch across from us, tossing the folders and tablet haphazardly on the table.

"Why would you do that? I told you I'd taken care of it."

Hermes continues to merely look at Persephone, his eyebrows raised meaningfully.

She lets out another exasperated sigh. "Medusa, promise me he didn't send the poor girl running in the opposite direction, sobbing." Persephone winks at me as she uncaps a bottle of water. "Because I'm positive she was the president of the Hermes is a Hottie fan club, and that would have destroyed her illusions about him."

Fan club? Hermes has a fan club?

Hades coughs, trying to hold back his laughter, which only makes Hermes glare at him. The Lord of the Underworld points to his coffee, saying, "Damn stuff went down the wrong pipe."

"I did not make her cry, Aunt."

But she looks at me for confirmation. "He—there were no tears." It's ridiculous, but I feel even more confused about what's going on. I turn to my friend. "You have a fan club? Also—what is a 'hottie'? Is this slang I've somehow missed?"

Both Persephone and Hades chortle loudly. "No," Hermes

says, and for the first time, I notice him blush, too, which is an incredibly appealing look on him. "They're just—there's no fan club."

Persephone mock-whispers, "Yes. There is." Then, more loudly, "And a 'hottie' is a handsome somebody girls like to swoon over."

Well, I guess I have my confirmation that the ladies do, indeed, appreciate Hermes.

He glares at her next. "As I was saying, I had a chat with her. I made my position clear."

The laughter fades from Persephone. "All right. Fine. But that's the last time you get to harass the girl." To me, she asks, "Were there any problems with Kore this morning?"

I'm quick with my response. "None at all. She was very agreeable." Persephone continues to wait expectantly, so I add lamely, "Very helpful." I set my cup down on the polished table in between us. "I don't ... I don't want to sound ungrateful, but I also don't want to inconvenience you. But there really isn't a need for a servant. I mean ... I've lived without one for a long time, so ..."

"I know, darling," Persephone says, refilling her husband's coffee cup. "But you have just gone through a tremendous ordeal, and we thought it best if you had somebody to help, at least for the time being. Besides, surely you wouldn't want to deprive Kore of a job? I've recently learned she's planning on going back to school. Tuition can be a mighty burden."

Being a monstrous shut-in, I've been out of the loop socially for the majority of my life, and my only real cues on tone and facial expressions come from movies and television shows, but I'm pretty sure she's left no room for argument.

Hades only confirms this by saying, "You might as well just accept it. Peri is a tenacious little terrier when she has a mind to be." He accepts the cup from his wife; his drink, unlike everyone else's in the room, is as dark brown as his hair.

I can't help but stare at him as he sips his coffee. Today, the Lord of the Underworld is wearing crisply tailored black trousers and a light blue button down, sleeves rolled up on his forearms.

He looks sophisticated and powerful next to his stylish wife, and yet, I can't help but be fascinated by just how easily he seems to play the role of doting yet amused husband.

"How delightful that I'm now a little doggie," she says serenely. And then, over her bottle of water, "Woof."

Both men chuckle; while I want to join in, and despite what I've been told, I simply can't risk her taking offense.

"In any case, my husband is right, I'm afraid." Persephone recaps her bottle. "I'm a tenacious gal. Right now, I want to focus all of that meddling on you, if you don't mind."

My throat suddenly feels dry. What have I gotten myself into? "Um ..."

She holds out a hand, ticking off fingers as she speaks. "You need an entirely new wardrobe. Well—I suppose from what my nephew tells me, there are still some former pieces you may want, but as those are still back in Greece, you'll obviously need quite a bit of new items. Then there's the matter of rehabilitation; you're coming along wonderfully, darling, but it can't hurt to have a specialist working with you on getting yourself back into shape. I've set up an appointment this afternoon. You'll let us know if you feel Telesphorus is a good fit for you or not."

Hermes leans forward. "Telesphorus? He's an arse."

"He's also excellent at what he does," Persephone counters in that same business-like tone she's already used on us this morning. "You wanted the best, I got the best."

He leans back against the cushions, saying nothing further as her attention shifts back to me.

"When you feel ready, you will let us know what you want done with your items back in Greece. From what I understand, you have a few options." She picks up a notepad sitting on the table, along with a pen. "You can leave your belongings there; obviously, the isle is protected, so the chance of thievery is rare. Or, you can have them brought here and we will store them in the basement. This would allow you to bring items you like up to your rooms to help it feel more homey."

"Their basement, which eventually leads to the Underworld,

has three levels," Hermes whispers to me, grinning. "If you think the house is a labyrinth, wait to you see what the basement is like."

Persephone stares at me for a long moment, and it isn't until Hermes nudges me with his elbow that I realize she's waiting for an answer. I wonder if she can find me an etiquette coach, too, because apparently, I'm horrible at reading social cues. "Would it be too much trouble to have my things brought here?"

"No problem whatsoever. I can have movers there this afternoon." She scratches something down on the pad. "We need to get you a new phone—"

"I have a phone," I quickly say.

She looks up from writing. "Yes, but you do not have one that Hephaestus has fitted especially for Olympians. Don't worry, he can transfer all your data over for you. I'll have him get you a new laptop, too."

I sort of don't know what to say to this whirlwind of a goddess.

"I don't know how much Hermes had told you about Olympus before, but we are a large city that has plenty of wonderful sights and places to explore and discover. Our population hovers at anytime around fifteen thousand, and we have some amazing restaurants and shops to fall in love with. I believe you'll like it here very much. That said," she taps her pen against the paper, looking first at Hades and then Hermes before her pale eyes refocus on me, "I ... *we* ... think it best you make sure you always have an escort with you while out and about."

Hades scratches at the back of his neck. Hermes is as still as a statue. And Persephone ... she's looking at me with what appears to be concern.

I swallow. "Escort?"

Persephone looks at her husband again. He sighs and says in a surprisingly kind tone, "Medusa, based on your history, an escort is the most prudent course of action when ensuring your well-being, at least for the time being. If and when you choose to leave the villa, Kore and one of our personal guards will accompany you at all times."

So. I have gone from being a solitary creature to one who will never be alone—and that is not a thought I am confortable with. "May I ask why?"

Hades is blunt. "My brother has apparently been obsessed with you for some time, and my niece is nothing if not vindictive."

Prickles spread across the back of my neck. *Poseidon?* "But ..." I swallow, glancing over at Hermes. His face is expressionless, yet I can see fists curled under his arms as they cross his chest. "Surely I have nothing to fear from either of them. Po—" I cannot say his name, though. "He ... it's been thousands of years. I am nothing to him."

Persephone looks down at her list. Hermes stands up suddenly and heads over to one of the wide windows. "Yes, well," Hades murmurs, "it may seem like that to you, perhaps, but ..."

I can feel my eyes widen significantly. What is he insinuating?

"Not now," Hermes snaps, his back still to us. "She has enough to focus on without having to worry about that sick fuck."

As I've rarely ever heard my friend curse, I'm shocked into silence. Hades' eyebrows shoot up and then back down into a 'v.' Then, to me, he says, "In any case, most of us have escorts ourselves. Persephone's handmaiden always accompanies her out. Standard procedure and all."

The truth is, I'm not comfortable with what they're suggesting, not when independence, even if brought about under the falsest illusions, is so firmly engrained in my character. Yet, Hermes appears more stressed than I've ever seen him before. Persephone's face is creased with worry. And Hades ... The Lord of the Underworld appears as if my agreement to these terms will come one way or another, whether I like it or not. So I bite back the burgeoning frustration steadily growing in my throat and chest and give them a nod.

The conversation turns to more mundane things, but as they talk, my attention wanders over to the windows. Glass separates us from a beautiful vista, of trees and grass, of plants wild and cultured, and of fountains and art. Somewhere beyond that is a city—and yet, somehow, despite the proximity I've finally gained, I feel like Poseidon and Athena still have me trapped in the middle of the sea.

Chapter Ten

As Hermes left an hour back to go on an urgent errand for his father, Kore is the one to bring me to a gym located in the west wing of the villa. Unlike the ones I'd seen on my computer, this one isn't crowded and filled with sweaty people hitting on one another; pristine, sparkling machines and gorgeous mosaicked walls greet me instead.

Meeting us at the entrance, an extremely tall, well-built man says something in a language I don't understand to Kore. She answers in kind, motioning toward me. He's dressed in all black— black t-shirt (fitted so tightly across his chest that I wonder if he can breathe), black cargo pants, and black, highly polished boots that reach halfway up to his knees. Despite us being indoors, he's also wearing black sunglasses. A small corkscrew wire curves from his ear down into his shirt, and from the expression on his face, I must admit, I'm a bit intimidated, especially as I'm at a disadvantage sitting in a wheelchair.

But then he inclines his head toward me and says, "I am Talos."

Uh ... okay?

"Talos is one of Lord Hades' finest Automatons," Kore says, as if this clarifies matters.

I hate feeling ignorant; normally, I'd just whip out my computer or phone and search for whatever has got my mind itching, but as neither are with me, I'm forced to ask exactly what an Automaton is.

"The Automatons are the elite soldiers of the gods," Kore says. Her words are delivered patiently, as if it's not a burden to have to explain even the most mundane things to one as ignorant as me.

So this is the guy Hades said had to, and I use this word loosely, *escort* me around Olympus if and when I choose to leave the villa. He looks less like an escort and more like a mercenary from some war movie. I let out a tiny sigh—can't seem too ungrateful, after all, not when the gods have blessed me so much lately—and say to them, "I take it we'll be spending much time together."

The left corner of Talos' mouth cracks upwards, but he says nothing in return.

"Ah! This must be the fearsome Gorgon that's got Olympus abuzz!" booms a voice from across the gym. I have to peer around Talos, as he makes no effort to move from his position in front of me, to find a small, dark, thin man wearing a ratty baseball cap heading our way. He stops in front of me, arms crossed and yet a finger tapping his chin as if he's in deep thought. "Not much of a monster, are you? You're a bit too pretty for it. Open up your mouth, dearie. Let's see if you've got some ugly fangs inside."

Talos turns and leaves the room without another word. I watch his departure while Kore says flatly, "Charming as always, Tele."

"Am I right on? Too many fangs? Or ... perhaps the cat got your tongue?" he asks me. "Oh, wait. Did Athena take that, too?"

My head whips back around toward where this Tele is standing. Is he serious? Because, help or no, I'm in no mood to be tormented about my monstrous past.

Kore smacks his arm, which causes him to burst into surprisingly boyish giggles. She then hisses, "It would be prudent for you to show proper respect, Tele. The lady here is under not one, but three mighty gods' protections. They would not look kindly upon such disrespect."

This is ridiculous. A servant fighting my battles? As he pointed out, I'm the infamous Gorgon. So I look up at him (which doesn't take much effort from where I'm sitting, as he's one of the shortest men I've ever seen), and say, "The assessment I was given earlier is apparently quite apt. You *are* an ass."

He stops giggling long enough for his eyes to grow nearly twice their normal size. And then he cracks up so hard he actually cries. Drops to the ground, clutches his stomach, and rolls around making the most hideous yet entertaining sounds of hilarity I've ever heard.

Kore sighs and haphazardly kicks at him, which only riles him back up. Hermes was closer to his description of this man-boy than he possibly realized, as he sounds grossly close to an actual ass with his braying. "My lady, this is Telesphoros. Despite his abhorrent behavior, he really is an excellent physical therapist."

He springs to his feet, his laughter immediately stopping. "Damn right I am." Then he smacks my knee before kneading it. His hands are disproportional to his body: fingers long and spindly atop the narrowest palm I've ever seen. "So. You're one of the lucky ones, eh?"

I shove his weird hand off. "Meaning?"

He flips his baseball cap so the bill faces backward. "Not a lot of your kind manages to get their curse reversed before they either are put down like the animals they become by do-gooders or go insane and kill themselves in some kind of mad fury."

As I tried to off myself countless times, his statement takes me by surprise. Others managed to do what I could not? "You've worked with those like me before?"

His head cocks to the side as he walks in a circle around me. "Not many. Like I said, they're usually taken care of before they can make it back to Olympus." He taps the back of my head;

Kore is the one to swat him away. "Is this how you were before the curse?"

A girl, running through the field in a long dress ...

I'm honest with my answer. "I don't remember. It's been a long time."

"You don't remember what you looked like?" I resent the pity that comes with Kore's words. Pity is the last thing I need right now. I've had millennia of pity. What I need right now is strength.

"Two thousand years will do that to an old broad." Telesphoros' grin turns mischievous. "Well, I guess it doesn't matter now, anyway. My assignment is the same no matter if you've got the same legs you were born with or some strange ones Athena thought might be a swell parting joke. I'm to get you walking like you've been doing it instead of slithering this whole time. Tell me, are snakes slimy? I bet you didn't need lubricants, if you know what I mean." He winks over and over at me, like his eye got stuck on repeat.

No, really. Is this guy for real?

His special brand of honking-braying proceeds, "Too soon?"

Kore jerks him away. "I am telling you, Tele, if word gets out you are disrespecting the lady, it will not be good for you, excellent physical therapist or not."

"You gonna tell, pretty girl?" he asks me, grinning maniacally.

Revulsion slams into me. I hiss, "Don't you dare call me that."

That wipes the idiotic grin off his face. Part of me wants to punch him, feel fist against bones and not care if any of them break or bleed. Fight back this time. Not lie down quietly, not be the victim. Who the hell does he think he is, anyway? *How dare he call me that.*

"You mean pret—" this man says to me, but I jerk myself out of the chair, not caring that my knees are trembling just as surely as my curled fists.

I shove a finger into his chest, and he stumbles back in surprise. "Don't you say it again."

"My lady?" Kore asks quietly. She grabs my arm, but I shake her off. "Perhaps we should go back to your suite?"

But the small man in front of me—an asshole of a healer, not the Lord of the Seas—grows a smug smile. "You're angry. This is good."

"Lady Medusa," Kore tries again, "you are tired. Let us retire to your rooms; we can come back again tomorrow."

"No, no—this is good." Now his nods are on repeat. "Anger is good. I can work with anger. She doesn't need your coddling, Nymph-girl. She needs somebody to help her kick some ass." His lips curl so high that I swear, the corner of one side of his mouth closes in on an ear. "And I can do that."

"Prove it," I say.

So he does.

Years of dragging heavy statues around an island were child's play compared to the hell Telesphoros put me through today. I ache in places I didn't even know I could. Wobbly even before the deranged PT got ahold of me, my legs couldn't support me standing up right now if I wanted them to.

I am liquid held together by skin.

"Your presence has been requested for dinner tonight." Kore bends my knee and kneads my calf. A rather embarrassing moan of relief escapes me. I'm laying face down on some kind of special table Telesphoros sent up to my room. Apparently, Kore is a skilled masseuse; well, at least in my mind she is, but as this is my first massage ever, I'll admit to not having much to compare it to. Considering this feels heavenly in contrast to the torment Tele put me through, I'm going to have to stand by this assessment of her.

"However," she continues, nimble fingers digging into my muscles, "I can send down word down that you are too tired from today's session."

I lift an arm and give her a thumb's up. There is no way I'm in the mood to go and be social right now. Not when being social is almost as tiring as exercising new legs.

I can only pray this will not cause offense.

She works in silence for a long time, working both legs and then my back. I swear, her fingers have magic in them. Finally, she says, "About earlier today, my lady ..."

"Eurgh?" is my answer, because even talking right now is exhausting.

"The conversation we had with Lord Hermes in the hallway. I wanted ..." Only her words pause momentarily, thankfully, as her fingers continue to kneed my shoulders. "Please let me reassure you that I would never betray your confidence."

Well, there goes our golden silence.

She sounds so sad and tremulous, so ... I don't know. Maybe hopeful and yet scared all at the same time? But the thing is, I haven't ever had a girlfriend before. My only friends for the last two thousand years have been men—one of them old, the other a deity, so I'm pretty positive I haven't had the best examples of what typical friendships are like. I've no idea how to react to her—is this the moment we hug and I tell her it'll be okay? I've seen that happen in movies, read about it in books. Or should I make her pinky swear to ensure her words stay true? Girls do that with one another, right?

A knock comes at the door, mercifully saving me from doing anything at all. She pulls my nightgown over me before answering it. Soft words float around me, but I choose not to listen carefully. I hover around sleep until a hand presses against my shoulder blades. But it's not Kore's delicate hand; it's large and warm and immediately familiar.

A sleepy smile can't be held back, even if opening my eyes feels like the hardest thing I've ever had to do before.

"I just got back," Hermes tells me. Kore murmurs something in the background; I think she's gotten him a chair for him to sit down on. "And I know you're tired, but I wanted to make sure today went well for you."

That he came here after a long day of work himself warms

me considerably. My words are marbles in my mouth, but he's my friend. He'll understand. "I think I'm worse off than before."

He laughs quietly. He also knows I'm mostly joking. "That bad?"

"Tele is a sadist." Then, realizing he might interpret that incorrectly, I add, "I'm kidding. He put me through a workout, though."

I can feel his fingers twist in my hair; it feels just as heavenly as Kore's massage. "Thought you would like to know that on my way back from my meeting today, I stopped and saw Mikkos."

Now I pry my eyes open. He's sitting less than a foot away, his eyes more green than blue, as they stare down at me. As beautiful as they are when they're crystal blue, I think I prefer them this shade. Not that I'd tell him or anything, because I'm sure gods have better things to do than to listen to people wax poetic about their blindingly good looks. "How is he?"

"He's fine—he and some mates were in a bar, toasting to old times." He leans closer and his familiar, lovely scent curls around me. "Even had a charming lady friend with him, hanging on to every word."

Oh, this warms my heart.

Hermes pulls his cell phone out with his free hand and scrolls through his pictures until he finds one of Mikkos and some woman clearly decades younger than him.

"That old dog," I marvel. I'm utterly pleased to see my friend so happy. He looks content—like he isn't sick, like life is fine and that he has many more days of hanging out in bars and drinking with younger women in front of him.

"Are your duties with Lady Medusa finished for the night?" Hermes calls out. I'm surprised to find Kore standing like a silent sentry in the background; I had no idea she was still here.

She inclines her head. "I have yet to get her ready for bed, Lord Hermes."

He disentangles his fingers from my hair and stands up so he can face her. "You are dismissed."

But Kore does not leave. "I do not intend disrespect, but I am to remain with the lady at all times."

What? I blink and try to focus on her in the distance. She's ... what. Even supposed to *sleep* in here with me? Because I am not okay with that. Not at all.

"Um," I begin, but Hermes is already talking.

"You can inform your mistress that if she has any quarrel about you leaving tonight, she can take it up with me. You may come back in the morning."

Kore's eyes widen, but she nods once and then leaves without another word.

"Are you hungry?"

I stare up at him in amazement. He's really asking me if I'm hungry after that?

"Don't look at me like that. It was Persephone's idea. She can go overboard on these things."

I struggle to sit up; he attempts to help me, but I wave him away. My muscles ache, but I manage to do it. "Am I a prisoner here?"

He does not hesitate. "Absolutely not."

I rub my eyes. It still feels so surreal not needing my glasses when I talk to him. "What are you not telling me?"

His lips purse together before he turns away to pour a glass of water. "There are many things I'm probably not telling you." He hands me the glass. "But I could probably say the same of you, too, considering I've never met a more secretive person before."

"And yet, you know me better than anyone else."

"Thanks to the stars above for that. Is that a no for dinner?"

I let out an exasperated laugh. "No food, thank you. Will they be upset with me for not coming downstairs?"

"Of course not." He pours himself a glass of water, too, but does not drink it. "Do you like it here?"

I glance around me—the overly opulent suite I've been given does not feel like home yet, despite my kitten and my best friend filling it. "It's quite nice."

"Quite nice," he repeats.

I attempt to stand up but my legs immediately give way. He's across the room in a flash, lifting me up into his strong arms once more like I weigh nothing. Not that I'll say it out loud or anything, but being here in his arms is beyond wonderful. "It takes time," he tells me as he carries me over to my bed.

I can't help but wonder if he's referring to the concept of home or walking.

I'm laid gently down, the covers tucked up around me. It's a gesture so unbearably sweet and foreign to me that my eyes prickle at the same time my stomach fills with those incessant wild butterflies that have begun to plague me in his presence lately. I've read about butterflies in stomachs, of course—but I never knew they could be so strong and uncontrollable. And why they could possibly infect me when I am with my best friend.

But this is not something I can talk to him about. Instead, I wait until he's done to ask, "Can I tell you something?"

He surprises me by joining me on the bed; only while I am snug under the covers, Hermes lies on top of them, his hands folding across his chest. "Always."

Why am I so nervous and delighted all at the same time that he's lying here beside me? I force my gaze to the ceiling above us. There are lovely frescos there, depicting everyday life in ancient Greece, little things that I missed out on and only got to learn about thanks to books and stories. "It's different than I thought it would be."

He waits patiently.

"And harder," I admit.

His answer is quiet. "Change always is."

"Whether it's wanted or not, how do you find best to face it?"

His head tilts toward mine; the pillow under us shifts. We're so close right now that I feel a bit delirious. "The only way I can. I keep moving forward."

I nod, folding my own hands across my chest so they mimic his. "Although, as a god, surely change must only come about when you want it."

An exhaled ghost of a laugh proceeds, "You know me better than that. Change happens to us whether we like it not. Sometimes it's for the good, sometimes for the worse, and sometimes, you have no control over it, despite just how desperate you may be to do so. Yet, it is in all our natures to try to bring about the change we wish for."

I roll my head so we're now facing one another. I do know him, which is what confuses me all the more about the surges of lightheadedness that rock me to my core lately simply by looking at him. This is my friend. My best friend. He is a god, and I am an ex-monster. It is not like we are anything else, or ever can be.

Where are these thoughts and feelings coming from? Are they something that was always there, but muted by my monstrous physiology? Or is this something entirely new? Because part of me wonders right now what it would be like to touch his dear face. To purposefully kiss his cheek like he did mine, back on the island.

To press my mouth against his, to discover if kisses can be as sweet as I hope and have dreamed about, especially since the only ones I've ever experienced were markers of pain.

I blink at the onslaught of heat that rushes my cheeks. He and I ... for years we have known each other. Talked to each other. It must be the exhaustion that's confusing me. Because otherwise, I am the most foolish girl to ever live.

I shove an unwieldy mass of hair back off my face. "Are there things in your life you have no control over?"

"Of course," he tells me softly. His green eyes are so intense as they meet mine.

The little butterflies that emerged from their cocoons for the first time in my chest yesterday now swarm frantically, forcing me to avert my attention once more to the scenes above us. I am reminded of a picture I once saw, of the annual Monarch butterfly migration to Mexico, and of how there would be so many of those little creatures brimming the air that magical orange-gold was the new color of sky. I always yearned to someday lie beneath those wings, and now they are here, beating in my chest so strongly I wonder if a hurricane could brew.

I pray that he cannot hear my heartbeat matching their wings.

"Second chances are just that, Dusa. They're chances. There are no guarantees in outcomes, even for the gods. My uncle ..." He clears his throat. "Or my sister—I am sure that they could never have guessed that you would, one day, be laying in a bed in Hades' house as a treasured guest, nor could they have ever seen that you and I would become ... friends. And yet here you are—here *we* are—and you are now in possession of that second chance you never thought would come. Of course it is different than you thought it'd be; imagine how omnipotent you'd be if you could have successfully predicted the true outcome of all of this."

Friends. Yes ... we're friends. Exactly. And that reminder is enough to quell the uprising in my chest, even if done in an irrational sense of disappointment.

Despite my fatigue, we end up talking for hours more, just like we did back on Gorgóna. There's a comfort there, in having familiarity in the midst of upheaval. And when I fall asleep, he is still next to me, his eyes drifting shut, too. And I am glad for it.

Chapter Eleven

"You're not even *trying*. I've seen better efforts from a dead centaur."

I scowl at Tele from the treadmill he has me jogging on. It's been forty-three minutes since I first stepped foot on this torture device. Despite my ponytail, sweat plasters my hair down against my face and soaks my shirt. I feel as disgusting as I do tired.

"Five days ago," I gasp, "I didn't have legs."

"That's a pitiful excuse if I've ever heard one." He perches on the handrails of the treadmill next to me like he hasn't any further cares in the world than needling me. Which maybe he doesn't, because I'm apparently his only client at the moment and he's basically living and breathing Operation: Medusa's Legs.

I push myself past the pain for another seventeen minutes before he lets me shut the demonic machine off. And to think people thought I was a monster. This thing has probably tortured more people over the years than I ever did back on Gorgóna. But if there's one thing I learned from being around Telesphoros, it's to never show weakness. He feeds off it like the vampires I've read about in books.

Despite Kore's numerous warnings to do otherwise, the physical therapist has taunted me, ridiculed me, pushed me to numerous points where I'd been perilously close to breaking down in tears (which, thankfully, I haven't yet), and took great delight in my pain. And yet, here I am, five days after being given legs back, and I just ran an hour. Granted, I'm struggling to catch my breath and I collapse onto a bench within a minute of stepping off of the treadmill, but I have to give it to him. His methods are effective.

"You resemble a drowned rat," he muses, hoping over to where I'm sitting. I've got my head down as I search the room for proper air to breathe.

Kore clucks in disappointment nearby. Unless Hermes sends her away (which he tends to do whenever he's around), she's my shadow. And, as much as I believe I might like her, I'm tired of the hovering. Like right now—there is no need for her to say anything. Was Tele out of line? Yes. Does he know he's out of line? Absolutely. Will her disappointment change his behavior? Absolutely not. So far, the only thing that does is whenever a god comes to visit. Persephone tends to stop by at least once during my daily five-hour sessions, although normally earlier in the day. She's a total creature of habit, I've learned, who has a daily routine she's loathe to deviate from. So, from ten until ten-fifteen each morning, Tele changes his personality to impress his employer.

But Persephone isn't here right now, and Kore is nothing more than an annoying fly to him. "Gee, thanks," I tell him once I'm positive it won't sound like I'm still gasping.

He drops down next to me on the bench. "Sweating profusely like you're doing isn't very attractive; although, I suppose it's a sign you got a decent workout."

"Flattery gets you everywhere."

"You reek, too."

Kore throws her hands into the air; her disgust with him makes me laugh. Tele laughs, too—that awful bray of his that fills the gym until Hades walks in the door. And then his laughter stops entirely.

This is the first time Hades has visited since I've been working out with Tele. While I do see the Lord of the Underworld daily, it's usually in the evening at dinnertime. He's been nothing but polite with me, just as welcoming as his wife, but the fact is, he's intimidating as all hell.

Tele stands up and proceeds to immediately bow; Kore curtsies low. Both keep their eyes on the ground.

As for me, I'm in that awkward position where I'm not sure if I ought to curtsy or not. So far, nobody has expected me to. Persephone has strongly encouraged me to treat them as family, and that as such, I do not need to hang on typical reverences normally bestowed upon them. And yet, this here is one of the three most powerful and important gods in Olympus. So I stand up, ready to curtsy despite my sore legs.

Before I can, though, Hades comes over to where I am and sits down on the bench, patting the space next to him. Far be it for me to disagree. I sink back down, folding my hands on my lap.

He scratches at his five-o'clock shadow before giving me that sinful smile of his. "I had a few minutes free and wanted to check on how things are going in here."

I glance quickly over at Tele, who, for the first time since our meeting, radiates uneasiness. Is he afraid I'll tell Hades just how much he teases me on a daily basis? I decide to set an excellent example and go easy on him. "Good, thank you. I just got finished with a run."

"Excellent." Hades leans closer and I'm no longer pulling air into my lungs—his fingers brush up against my cheek for the briefest moment before he leans back. "Smudge of some sort," he tells me, holding out his thumb.

Nervous laughter releases the apprehension I'd just held in. "I apologize for looking such a fright."

"Nonsense. You are lovely as ever."

Such lies, but he seems so sincere I can't help but blush in gratitude.

"Now that you're running marathons,"—he pats my knee— "Peri and I were thinking that we could all go out for dinner tonight if that's all right with you."

Leave the villa? And he's asking *me* if it's an okay thing? I've spent years in isolation; the last week has brought me more people to interact with, but thankfully in moderation. But to be out and about within a larger population? Just thinking about it fills me with equal parts dread and elation. "In Olympus?"

He chuckles. "That was the thought. We figured it would be best to stay close to home in case you were fatigued from all the hard work Telesphoros is no doubt putting you through."

"He's a task-master, that's for sure," I say slyly. I unfairly delight in watching the man in question pale despite his dark skin.

"I'm sure you are eager to explore the world, too, but perhaps its best to take it one step at a time." Hades' grin turns naughty, as if he knows he's just thrown a bad pun at me. And I can't help but giggle, because it's such a charming smile and one I'd never thought could come from a god with such a dark reputation.

"Will Hermes be with us tonight?" I'm immediately embarrassed for asking. How must that sound? Does Hades think I will only spend time with him and Persephone if Hermes is present?

"Alas," he says, his normally dark eyes a softer caramel, "he will not. Zeus has him out for a meeting that ought to take him through late night. That said, we've invited Aphrodite and Hephaestus to join us." He taps me on the nose. "You will like them."

Disappointment settles down against my shoulders, which mortifies me further. I've known Hermes for years ... have gone days—weeks, even—without seeing him, and yet here I am, crushed because he won't be coming to dinner

I force myself to smile and sound properly excited. "I'm sure I will."

Hades ruffles my sweaty hair, tells me to be ready within the hour, and then heads back to his office to wrap up matters for the day. The moment the door closes behind him, Tele collapses to the ground in a frazzled heap.

I ask him, "Cat got *your* tongue?"

He props himself up on his elbows as Kore hands me a towel. "Interesting that you are dining with Olympus' finest tonight, don't you think?"

95

I rub at my hair with the towel. "Meaning?"

His eerily pale eyes narrow. "Meaning, you are a former monster. They are gods."

"Tele!" Kore hisses as she twists off a water bottle cap for me. I keep telling her she doesn't need to do such mundane things; I'm not helpless, after all. But she just ignores me and does them anyway. I mean, honestly. She opens my water bottles for me. Nonsense, right? Because how lazy do you have to be to have someone habitually open items such as water bottles for you? Nothing is wrong with my hands—monster or not, I would've been able to do such a mundane task. It's only my legs that are in need of help, and after running an hour today, I'm thinking they don't even need much more.

"What?" he throws back. "You can't tell me you aren't wondering the same things. Olympus is abuzz with how this one here,"—he jerks a finger toward me—"has certain gods under her thumb."

The water bottle pauses halfway to my lips as I stare down at him.

He stands up and brushes off his shorts. Then, uncharacteristically serious, he asks, "Tell me, Medusa, why do the gods seem to favor you so much?"

Perplexed, I finish my drink and set the bottle down. Just what is he insinuating? "Are you forgetting that I've spent ages as a monster in exile? I'm pretty sure that's a far cry from favor."

He flips his baseball cap backward. "And now you live as cherished guest at Lord Hades villa and dine with the some of the mightiest of our kind on a nightly basis."

It hits too close to home, to my long-held fears of the fickle nature of the gods. But I refuse to let him see my insecurities. "They are being kind."

He snorts. "Kind? All that was expected, perhaps, was the reversal of the curse. The rare examples who have come before you got that and a one-way ticket back to Greece with a, 'Don't call us, we won't call you,' kick in the butt out the door." Kore hisses his name at him again, but he waves her off. "Kore, you know as well as I the rumors about this girl here—"

I jump to my feet. "What rumors?"

"Shut it if you know what is good for you," Kore warns, stepping in between us. Her lithe frame actually blocks him from my view.

From behind her, I hear, "Is it true?"

"Is what true?" I ask at the same time Kore says, "It is time to get you ready for tonight, my lady." She quickly gathers up my belongings; I attempt to take some from her, but she is a tenacious girl, yielding nothing.

"It is, isn't it?" Tele says when we get to the door.

I pause, looking back at him, but Kore places her hand on my lower back and urges me forward. "You don't want to be late, my lady. We must hurry."

"I'll be damned," Tele calls out. "It is."

What is he talking about?

His wicked smile cuts his face in half. "It was good working with you, Medusa. Be careful, won't you? I wouldn't want to have to help you relearn how to walk again."

Kore forcibly closes the door behind us. In her fluster, I'm able to snatch a bag away from her. "What rumors was Tele referencing?"

"My lady—"

I hold out a hand. "Kore, please stop with this *my lady* bit. I am no lady. Before I was cursed, I was a handmaiden. More years than that, I was a monster. Now, I am just a girl. Please call me by my name."

She looks so stricken by this I can't help but sigh.

"I am sincere in my request. It is what I would prefer. What are these rumors?"

Uncertainty shines in her eyes, but she gives me a small nod. "As you wish ... Medusa." And then, a hint of a smile reappearing, she says, "But I do insist on carrying your bags for you."

I sigh again and pass the item over. She's avoiding my questions, too. I suppose Hermes is right, though; change will come when change will come. Even still, I'm going to work on her easing up on the whole servant bit as much as possible and trusting me a bit more.

After we are in my room and I've bathed and changed into a pretty dress she's picked out for me, I decide to go for it one more time and ask Kore, "What was Tele talking about?"

The hairbrush in her hand pauses in its downward stroke, but she says nothing.

"He said there were rumors about me in Olympus. Have you heard any of them?"

The brush completes its stroke down and then she resumes her gentle styling. "As I spend most of my time here at the villa, I have no time for petty gossip."

"But surely you must have heard *something*. What about from your boyfriend?" Despite being forced to work with me so much, I happen to know she sees him everyday, plus talks to him on the phone as much as possible.

I watch her face in the mirror as her nose screws up and her brow wrinkles, like she's torn from whether or not to say anything. So I sweeten my request by adding, "I swear to you that you have nothing to fear when it comes to me, especially repercussions for speaking the truth."

She bites her thin bottom lip and meets my eyes in the mirror. Why is she so scared?

Oh, this is too frustrating. Surely by now she's realized that she's in no danger of anything from me. "Please, tell me these rumors. It's not like I haven't been talked about before. After all, I've had such lovely, heartwarming things said about me for years. My favorite, of course, was that of my glamorous beheading."

This breaks a bit of the tension, just like I hoped. "Well, my lady—"

"Medusa," I remind her.

Her smile is embarrassed, yet sad at the same time. "Since you insist on hearing it, I will tell you. There are several rumors going around right now, but the most prevalent is that Lord Hades and Lord Hermes have stolen you away from Lord Poseidon."

Images hit me fast and hard, ones I have shielded myself

from over the ages. His hands, on me. His lips, on mine. His body, forcibly entering mine. If anybody has stolen anything, it was that bastard when he took my innocence and then my life. I clench my eyes shut and grab the arms of the chair.

"My la—Medusa, oh, I am so sorry, I did not want to tell you, oh, please do not be angry at me, I promise I won't—"

"Stop," I gasp. These are only pictures from the past, I repeat to myself. Everything he did, it was in the past. Thousands of years ago. I am nothing to him now. Nothing but a distant memory. He cannot hurt me now. I am safe. "Just ... do not apologize. Please."

But she is clearly terrified, tiny breaths sucking in and out from behind me that verge dangerously close to hyperventilation. So I open my eyes and, forcing myself to say as calmly as I can, "What else is being said?"

Her eyes are saucer wide as she rapidly shakes her head, lips trapped between her teeth.

"It is all right." I am impressed with how even I sound, though it feels as if I am across the room, watching another person speak through whoever this girl's body I somehow entered and now inhabit. "Nothing to fear, remember?"

Her voice is barely discernable. "There are some who believe you to be a powerful witch, and that you have bewitched Lord Hermes."

I believe I blink a full four times before laughter bubbles out. And it feels good, pushing its way past crippling anxiety. "A witch? Like—with magic? Hocus pocus?"

A nervous titter escapes her.

Better this rumor than the one before, though. "So, Kore, what say you? Do you think me a witch? Have you discovered my broom and book of spells yet?" I waggle my eyebrows and do my best at cackling; her tittering gives way to genuine giggles.

"Most certainly not. Although," she admits softly when the giggles die down, "I mean no disrespect, but ... I have never seen Lord Hermes so devoted to anyone before, save his family."

Tiny goose bumps spread involuntarily up and down my

arms. Does she really believe this, or is this merely a kindness she is offering? "He and I have been friends for a long time."

She picks the brush back up and once more pulls it through my hair. Her silence makes me uneasy.

"He was my friend when I had no friends. He's a good person, with a good heart." My hands twist in my lap. "See, I'm most likely a charity case. He's quite the knight in shining armor sort of god. Always off trying to save people. Surely you know that about him, right? He ... I think that's why I'm here. He wanted to save me from being a monster. He ... I think he felt sorry for me after listening to me bemoan my fate. It must have been so tiring, listening to it all, you know? Maybe he wanted to stop the vast number of pity fests I threw for myself on a regular basis."

I'm babbling. Full-on babbling, and she's still not saying anything.

Has Hermes heard these rumors? What must he think of them? Does it humiliate him to be linked to me so? Like he would ever be interested in, no, devoted to somebody like me. It's such an absurd thought that my palms begin to sweat. All those stories of gods and mortals mixing, well ... they are nothing but legends.

Right?

"I'm not a witch. How ridiculous is that? Wouldn't these people feel foolish once they met me or saw me. There are no enchantments, no spells. Just ... friendship. Years of friendship. That's why ..." Stars above, my mouth is bone dry. "There's no ... devotion. How silly is that! He's just kind. He's ... friends do this for one another. If there's devotion, it's because of that."

Her answer is a small, albeit knowing, smile.

Chapter Twelve

A long, sleek black limousine pulls up to the front of the villa, driven by none other than Talos, who I've only seen lurking around the edges of my existence over the last week. Other than the one sentence he uttered in Tele's gym, telling me his name, I've yet to hear anything further. And I don't hear anything now when he opens the door for us and helps me into the car.

It's completely irrational, but adrenaline spikes in my bloodstream as I slide onto the rich leather seat. Persephone climbs in after me, hooking her arm through mine as she describes the restaurant we're about to go to. Hades grabs my attention for a small moment, rolling his eyes and smiling wryly, as if he finds his wife and her chatter adorably exasperating.

But this here, this is my first time in a car. My first time in any vehicle other than a chariot, and as that was so long ago I can't even remember what it looked or felt like to be in one, this first is both exhilarating and terrifying at the same time.

I clutch at the seat below me when the limo descends down the winding drive, past olive and juniper trees lining the road and onto the main street. Part of me wants to press my palms and nose against the glass and blatantly stare. There are people out there walking dogs, driving, riding bikes, living their lives, and there are houses and stores and sights so wondrous to see that it's hard to believe it's all real. This is not a movie, though, nor flat pictures in books—no, these scenes are tangible as they flash by me. But to act so uncouth would be utterly rude to my hosts, so I try my best to focus on Persephone and nod and murmur at the appropriate times, even though everything in me yearns to turn toward the window.

"Oh, leave the poor girl alone," Hades says minutes later, breaking through his wife's detailed description of the ambrosia at the restaurant, and of how she felt last time she drank it which sounds suspiciously like drunk. "Can't you see she's not interested?"

My cheeks flame. Is my rudeness so obvious? Hades smirks, winks at me even. But I'm horrified to be caught so uninterested. "Oh, please believe me, I am most enjoying—"

But Persephone merely laughs, her own cheeks red from her husband's good-natured chastising. So instead, she points out the sights for me, telling me which stores she likes to frequent, which directions the other gods live, and of businesses I ought to check out when I decide it's time to explore Olympus. "I'd love to take you myself, darling," she says, squeezing my arm, "but I will completely understand if you feel you need to escape us and get out on your own."

I go to protest, but Hades chuckles. "I'm sure Hermes may have his own ideas about taking her out exploring, Peri."

There I go, blushing again.

"Well, that is up to you, of course." Stars above, her smile could sway the worst grouch in the world back towards joy. "Personally, I would find him a boring tour guide of Olympus, as would my husband here." She blows him a kiss, and he rolls his eyes again despite his indulgent grin. "Do not think you have to humor any of us when you go out exploring. You are free to do so whenever you wish, with whomever you wish. But my offer stands."

She seems so sincere. Persephone and Hades, they've been nothing but generous with me this week. So these words of hers, with her arm linked in mine, inspires an overwhelming rush of contentment and gratitude to flow through me, tempering the adrenaline. "I must thank you two for everything you've done for me. You've certainly had no reason to do so, not with all of my faults and actions in the past, but know it is much appreciated. I will always treasure your kindness."

Neither god says anything for a long moment. But then Hades says, voice rough with an emotion I can't pinpoint, "The pleasure is ours."

Persephone kisses my cheek. "We love having you here."

The rest of the drive, they kindly yet purposely chat together about issues going on in the Underworld, leaving me to do exactly what I want to do: watch the things that have only ever been two dimensional to me bloom into 3-D.

The moment we step into the restaurant, claustrophobia creeps into my bones. It's crowded in here; despite the cool air piping through vents above us, there's still an oppressive heat which leaves my palms sweating. It doesn't help that everyone stops and stares when they notice us. I try to tell myself it's because Hades and Persephone are celebrities in this town, but there's no denying Tele and Kore's earlier words are replaying in my mind.

Plus, it's my name murmuring in soft whispers weighted down by the contrasting airflows in the room. They know who I am. They know what I've done.

No one would dare call me outright for it, not in the presence of these two gods, but I do not think it my imagination that scorn and fear mingles in these murmured gossipings. Part of me wishes I were back at the villa, where, even as I wonder if people are paid to be kind, a safety net stretches out below me at all times. Here, though, surrounded by burning stares and freezing words, the width of the rope holding the net together turns thin and gossamer.

Making eye contact with anyone outside of my immediate party is out of the question. Any time I do so by accident, my head swims. It sounds ridiculous, but there are far too many souls in here. I force my eyes on safe things: smoothing wrinkles out of the soft pink silk I'm wearing; Persephone's mouth, perfectly sculpted as if it were on a marble bust, as she describes just how much she adores Hephaestus; the tiny yet charming constellation of freckles across the bridge of her nose; and Hades' occasional rubbing of his newly grown, dark goatee, like he's contemplating shaving it off because an itch might plague him in this heat. Even as we're led into a grand room filled with chandeliers and white cloth covered tables, where forks and knives clatter against china and laughter mixes with wine and glass, I choose to focus on the clean line of crisp, black jacket the maître d' in front of me wears, and of how his back is straight and elegant as if he grew up with a book on his head and punishment for pages ever touching the ground.

It isn't until we reach our table, front and center of a wall of windows overlooking bright city lights illuminating navy and black sights, that I allow my eyes to meet another pair so vibrantly blue that it would be impossible *not* to ogle them outright.

"Finally!" the owner exclaims, rising up out of her seat so gracefully she just might be floating. Which, with her ethereal beauty, I would not put past her. "We thought you three would never get here."

The last time I saw Aphrodite, she was sitting next to Hermes in the Assembly Room. Apparently, one can never get used to her stunning visage; she steals my breath away just as surely in this moment as she did in that. Blonde hair so fair in nearly glows streams down around a heart-shaped face no other in existence could rival. But I think it's her smile that is the most beautiful thing about her—perhaps a bit too wide for her delicate face, it somehow manages to illuminate her appearance until it dazes you.

"Yes, well, this place is a zoo." Persephone says, stepping forward into Aphrodite's outstretched arms for a quick hug and a pair of air kisses. "I feared we would either be trampled in the lobby or die of starvation from the lengthy wait."

Wind chime laughter floats around the Goddess of Love as she pulls away from her friend. Hades says wryly, "We were out there for all of five minutes, Peri. A person can hardly starve in five minutes."

"He lies," Persephone says. Her lips purse together, as if she's holding her mirth in. "It was at least ten minutes. One can surely pass out from hunger in ten minutes."

"We will have to ensure that the waiter comes back immediately, lest anybody passes out and causes a scene tonight. Only the stars above know how that would look in the rag Angelia puts out," another voice says, and it's then I notice a short, plain man, slightly stooped and standing next to Aphrodite. He's got shaggy brown hair the exact color of dirt, a beard and bushy eyebrows to match, and eyes the color of molten steel.

Aphrodite giggles again and presses a hand lovingly against his ruddy cheek before bending down to kiss him. "Angelia adores you. The day she allows her reporters to say a bad thing about you is the day Olympus falls."

"I am not the one starving nor in danger of swooning," the man says. And then his eyes, equally piercing as the goddess' standing next to him, laser in on me. "Please forgive us our lack of propriety. I know I can speak for the both of us that we are extraordinarily pleased to have you join us for dinner tonight."

My skin heats up ever further, only this time, I cannot blame the crowds around me. Aphrodite disentangles herself from the man and, without warning, steps around Persephone and envelopes me into a hug that smells like a thousand rosebushes in full bloom during a warm Greek summer day. Startled, my arms flail about me, unsure whether I ought to fold them around her slender body or stay respectfully by my side.

She does not seem to notice as she presses real kisses against both of my cheeks before withdrawing back into her space. "You are absolutely adorable. Isn't she, honey? Is she not the most exquisite girl you have ever seen? Oh, I am dying in envy over your hair. Divine. Simply divine. Honey, what do you think?" She turns to the man next to her, who must be nearly a foot shorter than her statuesque frame even when she doesn't wear heels. "Could I get away with this shade? I don't know if I could pull it off like she can, but damn if I don't want to run out and dye my hair right this very minute."

"You will do nothing of the sort. Stop freaking the poor girl out, Dite," he says. I like his grin—it's heavily lopsided, bordering on goofy. Then he steps forward and holds out his hand. "She's been so looking forward to meeting you that apparently she's lost her manners and forgotten to introduce us. My name is Hephaestus; this is my wife Aphrodite."

I stare down at the hand proffered, so large for his size and somewhat stained. A god, offering to shake my hand? Have I been wrong about their kind all of these years, despite the examples Hermes showed me time and time again? When my skin meets his, and his sturdy fingers curl around mine for the brief moment our hands claps, my gut twists in shame.

I've thought them all worse than the monster I was accused of being. Heartless, fickle beings who loved to torment mortals on the turn of a dime. Maybe I've judged them all without getting to know them first, just as surely as history as judged me.

This is all so surreal.

"Oh, Medusa, forgive us," Persephone quickly says, her hand protectively going to my lower back. "I should have immediately made introductions. See? I'm close to swooning. Please tell me that is a basket of bread on the table."

Hades rolls his eyes again but winks as he realizes I notice his playful exasperation. He holds out my seat for me; I scramble for something appropriate to say. "I'm honored to dine with you tonight," I tell them as Persephone gently angles me toward the chair next to Aphrodite. She chooses the one on my left; before he goes to his seat, Hades drops a loving kiss on top of his wife's head.

Aphrodite sinks down in her chair just as gracefully as she'd floated out of it. Her hand immediately goes to my arm, clutching me like I've seen countless girlfriends do in chick flicks over the years. "My brother ... I could just kill him. Kill him! He's lucky he's not here right now or I might just leap across this table and strangle him. I've begged him for ages to meet you, you know. *Ages*. But he'd give me this line of bull with his whole," she drops her voice to a much lower approximation of what I assume she thinks Hermes' sounds like, " *'She needs space, Dite. You come on way too strong; you'll scare the crap out of her.'* " Her voice returns to normal. "Can you believe that? Because you and I ... I just know it. We'll get along like sisters. I feel it in my bones. Honey!" She turns to Hephaestus, seated on her right. "Didn't I tell you? From the first moment I saw her in the Assembly hall, I knew. No wonder Hermes is—"

The table rattles as she jerks back, wincing before flushing bright red and bursting into giggles again. As she leans down and rubs her leg, her husband gives her a pointed yet exasperated look I can't quite decipher. A choking sound comes from Persephone, along with an unlady-like snort. Hades busies himself with the wine menu the maître d' handed over before leaving us alone.

Did I miss something other than a goddess attempting to break the record set for fastest speaker alive?

She mercifully lets my arm go and adds, more slowly, "Yes, um, well ... that is a lovely dress. Just lovely."

Puzzled, and admittedly more than a bit overwhelmed by her boisterous personality, I thank her. Like he knows I need some time to adjust to all this newness, Hades switches the subject by asking if it would behoove everyone to have a bottle of wine brought to the table or if individual drinks would be preferred. Several amusing minutes of good-natured arguing follow, during which I am content to merely watch the interactions between these gods and goddesses. Just as I was when I first observed Hades and Persephone together, I'm surprised by the relationship between Aphrodite and Hephaestus. Either she's an excellent actress or the Goddess of Love is genuinely head-over-heels in love with her quiet yet wry husband. They touch each other almost as much as my hosts do, little touches such as holding hands and kissing knuckles, constant ones that keep them connected.

Not that we ever do such things together, but these actions leave me irrationally missing Hermes something fierce.

Once the wine is selected—Persephone wins out, claiming I need to experience ambrosia or what was the point of us coming to this particular place anyway—the conversation turns toward work matters, which relieves me. I'm not pushed into talking about myself or put on the spot at any moment; then again, I am not ignored, either. The muscles bunching in my shoulders gradually relax (I have a sneaky suspicion I have the ambrosia to partially thank for that), and for the first time since walking into the restaurant, I don't yearn to be holed up in my room back at the villa.

Is this what it's like, the proverbial going out to hang with one's friends that television shows glorify? Because if it is, I think I might very well learn to like it, despite desperately wishing Hermes were here. As comfortable as I have become with Persephone and Hades, and as charming and welcoming as Aphrodite (who has demanded I call her Dite, because that's what her good friends do and we are clearly already good friends, don't I know it?) and Hephaestus are, I miss him. Wonder what he's doing, where he is—is it nighttime there? Is he wining and dining with whomever his father has sent him to see? An image of him sitting at a table much like this, in a similar restaurant fills my mind: him, dressed in a sophisticated black suit with a charcoal gray shirt, unbuttoned without a tie, talking to some beautiful woman. She giggles in a really annoying way that people probably find appealing and finds every excuse to lightly run her perfectly manicured nails across his arm.

It makes me sick to my stomach, which oddly prompts me to drink my second glass of ambrosia so freshly refilled in three long swallows.

I've never really thought about what he does when he goes out on errands for his father. I know from listening to Persephone and Hades talk that he often works in Zeus' stead, wrangling deals and negotiating terms with other pantheons in the heavens.

They've often remarked about how good he is during business meetings, how he's more capable than most to close difficult deals and placate even Zeus' toughest opponents. It'd all been a very nebulous concept to me—one that, despite my affections for him, had never peaked my interest simply because I hadn't thought it my concern. But now ... now I want to know.

"Are you alright, Medusa?" Dite asks me. Her hand is on my shoulder again, jarring me out of my musings. "You're shaking."

I startle and the glass slips from my fingers; thankfully, it's newly empty, or my dress would be ruined as it lands squarely on my lap. Even still, tiny leftover sprinkles dot the thin silk.

"Oh!" She grabs the glass as the table grows quiet. "I'm like the legendary bull in the china shop. Here, come with me to the restroom; I will help you get those stains right out." She digs in the beaded clutch lying on the table next to her plate before pulling out a stain remover pen. "Voilà!"

"I promise you there's no need," I tell her. I mean, it's just a few little specks, and they're already microscopic. But within minutes, I'm in an opulent area off to the side of a gleaming restroom, leaning back into an overstuffed chair as the Goddess of Love gets to work on my now completely dry dress. There are a half dozen other women milling about, fluffing their hair or applying lipstick, whose sly ogling unnerves me to my core. It's an eerie sensation, having eyes trace over you over and over again, as if their owners are trying to riddle out weakness and secrets.

Just like that, I'm wishing I were back at the villa again.

"There." Dite caps the pen and stands up. Small wet circles form a pattern around my upper thighs. "Let's just give it a few minutes to dry before we go back out there." She pulls over a nearby chair; when she sits down, our knees touch, she is so close. "How are you doing tonight? This must all be a lot to take in."

Somebody coughs nearby; it's followed up with another derisive whisper of my name. Aphrodite whips her head around, eyes narrowing into slits as she spots a trio of girls across the room. A low hiss comes from between her lips, one so alien from a goddess who has shown me nothing but a bubbly, enchanting personality that I'm spurred to lean forward and touch her arm, even though my chest constricts in alarm.

"It's okay." I try to mimic cheeriness. "That's to be expected, isn't it?"

She turns back to me, eyes wide in question. The trio quickly leaves the restroom.

It may be suicide, but I say, "I've heard that there aren't a lot of ex-monsters around. Of course they'll be curious."

Her expression smooths out until all I see is the woman I'd met out in the dining room. "Ex-monsters! Are you referring to yourself? Because that's just ridic—"

More risk of suicide, because I cut her off. "I am an ex-monster." I offer a smile, even though my insides quiver uncontrollably. What if I truly offend her right now? I might be right back on Gorgóna before the night is over. "The thing is, I happen to know that for the few lucky enough as I to be changed back are no longer in Olympus. And yet, I'm not only still here, but I'm living at the Lord of the Underworld's home. I'm having dinner tonight with not one, but four powerful and influential gods. And I don't know *why*."

It's something I've wanted to ask Hermes over the last week, but haven't mustered up the courage to do so—not because I was afraid of him, but more because I was afraid to know the real answer. Somehow tonight I've found it, though, and I don't know if it's because I drank much ambrosia, the claustrophobia has messed with my brain, or I'm frankly spooked by her about-face with that weird hissing (truly ironic, coming from a woman who used to hear hissing on a regular basis, when the snakes on her head would get—pun completely intended—snappish with one another) toward those girls, but here I am, using that bit of courage to finally clear the air.

I've taken her by surprise, though, because her perfectly sculpted eyebrows rise high.

"I'm not stupid. I know this isn't normal. Your kind doesn't mix with my kind—"

"What!"

My hands are visibly shaking, but they've got nothing on the full-blown tremors rocking every cell inside my body. I wish I'd drunk more of the ambrosia. Aphrodite has been nothing but kind tonight, and I'm like a rabid dog right now, fully attacking her in a public restroom. There's no turning back, though. I can't stand the limbo that I've fallen into, even if in just five short days. For the last two thousand years, I at least knew what to expect. Life was stable. Predictable. Right now? It's utter chaos. It's like I'm on the edge of a glacier at sea level, finally taken my first steps on land after being lost at sea for ages; yet each time my weight bears down upon my feet as I move, a low groan is unleashed that hints at potential disaster.

The fact is, I'm waiting for the area I'm standing on to break off, so I'm once more adrift at sea. This is how my luck is. Everyone has been kind, that much is true. She's been nothing but kind. But I guess no matter what I thought earlier tonight, old habits die hard, because I can't take it anymore. "Just tell me. Is this some kind of game to you all? Am I some kind of game?"

She's out of her chair, her hair wild and swinging about her shoulders. *"No."*

I stand up, too. She's taller than me, but not by much. "Am I a pet then?"

Total shock flashes across her face.

"There is no reason I can think of that explains why I am being made the only exception."

This has her grabbing my arm. "Stop! Just ... stop this right now. You want a reason?" She's no longer the effervescent goddess from before, and I'm kind of glad for it. Because maybe now that ledge will finally break off already, and I'll no longer have to wait for the inevitable. "I'll give you the very best reason: my brother. Remember him? *My brother* is your reason."

My breath sucks in.

Soft as they are, her words are filled with anger. "Are you telling me that you think you're a game to him? A pet?"

"No," I tell her. Because he is, as he always has been, the grand exception to everything.

Her anger fades somewhat as her fingers uncurl from my arm. Somebody comes into the room, but with one look at Aphrodite, the elderly satyr turns on her heels and leaves without a word. She takes a deep breath, waving her hands around her face like she's drying her nails. "I've totally botched this. Look, I realize you ... distrust us. My psycho-bitch of a sister did something incredibly awful to you." Her voice drops to a whisper. "My uncle ... what he did was unforgiveable." What appears to be genuine sadness fills her eyes. "As the Goddess of Love, you must believe me when I tell you that there is nothing I can say or do that will ever excuse those actions. I would never want to. It grieves me terribly to know that my family has abused innocents more times than I care to count. Please believe there are those of us in the Assembly who are trying to change things. Who don't approve of such actions, who refuse to participate in them." Her mouth, so wide and joyful with smiles at the start of the evening, is now a grim flat line. "Yes, you are the first person changed back who we've happened to take an interest in and have made efforts to get to know. You cannot be surprised that this is due to my brother. I'll admit to it; but I'll also admit that I trust Hermes implicitly. While the family often ..." She pauses, as if she's choosing her words carefully. "Disagrees with one another, he and I have nearly always been on the same side. He is my favorite brother, Medusa. And to be completely honest, the only sibling *I* trust. So when he came and told me, told those of us he is close with, that an injustice had been done by our family and it needed to be rectified, I believed him. *We* believed him. He told us that you two had grown close—and when my brother tells me he trusts somebody, I take that seriously. Because he does not trust easily. None of us do, not in this shark-filled family."

Well, don't I feel like a total judgmental jerk once more.

"I am here tonight, because if my brother cares about you and wants you in his life, I will support him in this. I was sincere when I said I looked forward to getting to know you. I still do. I hope you would like to get to know me, too. That is, of course, your choice. It would please me greatly if we became friends. Not because you are an,"—her nose scrunches up—"*ex-monster*, or because you are a pet, or whatever else you fear you are to us." She leans forward, tentatively reaching out for my still trembling hands. "You had every reason to go mad years ago. And yet ... you didn't. You still have love in your heart. Why wouldn't I want to be friends with someone like that?"

I'm perilously close to breaking down in tears. All these years, I've been so distraught over the rumors about me, over how anyone could judge me without knowing me, and I am absolutely guilty of just the same.

The door opens again, bringing Persephone into the powder room. "Everything okay in here? You two have been gone a long time."

When she looks at me and nods her head in the tiniest way, I realize Aphrodite is telling me that, no matter what I say right now, she will back me up.

Somehow or other, the ice is holding fast. And right now, in this moment, it's also gone silent.

So I turn to Persephone and give her a tremulous smile. It's small, but at least it's not fake. "Yeah. I just ... I had an anxiety attack. It's ... I guess the crowds got to me. I'm sorry that I've delayed our dinner."

She's immediately by my side, concern practically dripping off of her. "Anxiety attack?" Her eyes zero in Aphrodite. "What happened?"

I am so ashamed. My vision blurs as tears fill my eyes. I am hopeless at this. If she'd smote me during my attack, I wouldn't have blamed Aphrodite. Goddess or no, I basically just accused her of lying to me, which isn't friendly in the least.

No wonder I've only ever managed to make two friends.

"Nothing unexpected, Aunt." She squeezes my hands and then stands up. "Medusa and I just had a heart-to-heart, and I think we understand each other the better for it."

I stand up, too, wiping at my eyes. "I'm sorry. I ... I'm not good at this."

Persephone then steps forward and wraps her arms around

me. I let my face fall against her shoulder as quiet sobs that I refuse to let break free shudder throughout me. It's painful, but I just can't lose control. Not here, not now.

"No one expects you to be, darling," she murmurs, her hand gently stroking my hair. And as lovely a feeling as it is, as soothing as it is, this action from her feels completely different than when Hermes does it.

Why is that?

Aphrodite wraps her arms around me from the other side, so that I'm sandwiched in between these two women's hugs. It's a surprisingly comforting for someone suffering from extreme claustrophobia just a half hour before. We stay like that, hugging one another, until the shudders quell and the anxiety passes.

We don't go back to the table; instead, the two goddesses lead me outside to where the car is already waiting. Talos, who'd been standing like a sentinel next to the rear door, comes forward so he can murmur something in Persephone's ear; at the same time, Aphrodite says to me, "Would you be up for some company tomorrow? I could come over and we could just talk. Or, if that's too much, watch a movie. Or take a walk in the groves. Or, play a board game. Lady's choice." Her smile reappears at the same time Hades and Hephaestus come outside.

The truth is, right now, all I want to do is crawl into bed. But I also think I like the idea of making a girlfriend. If she's sincere, I'd be a fool to pass up this opportunity. Hermes adores Aphrodite; I've always heard wonderful things about her. If she wants us to get to know one another, maybe it's time I become open to the possibility of letting somebody else in. Just as I'm about to tell her yes, Hades says in a stern tone that sends shivers up and down my spine, "Ladies, in the car. Now."

Aphrodite's head rears back, almost as if he slapped her. It's clear she's not used to being told what to do.

"Sweetheart, I beg you to do as he says," Hephaestus tells

his wife. Talos has the door opened, and I am the first person he chooses to pull into the limo.

"What is going on?" Aphrodite is saying, but Talos must have grabbed her right after me, because before the last word comes out of her mouth, she's in the limo, too. Persephone quickly follows suit, and the door is slammed shut without an answer given.

"What is happening?" Aphrodite tries again, this time to Persephone. "What did your Automaton tell you?"

Persephone's smile is brittle and altogether fake; it scares me. I've never seen her so unnerved. "Nothing to worry about. It's late, and I'm tired—and I am sure Dusa needs her rest. She ran over an hour for Telesphoros today, you know. It's a miracle she didn't fall asleep during dinner tonight. I think I would have."

Talos gets in and turns the car on. As we pull away from the curb, Aphrodite glances through the back window. "What about—" Her words trail away before her head snaps forward.

Her smile is just as fake as her aunt's.

Okay. What is going on here?

I crane my neck around to see what she saw, even though both goddesses warn me not to. And as we drive away, I see Hades and Hephaestus on the curb in front of the restaurant, seemingly in the midst of an angry confrontation with none other than Poseidon, with Athena by his side.

I go numb. His hands, on me.

His mouth, on mine.

His body, in mine.

Before I know it, I throw up all over Persephone in the limo.

Chapter Thirteen

Aphrodite comes over like clockwork in the late mornings during the next few days so we can have lunch together. Slowly but surely, I allow myself to open up to her. As one would expect from the Goddess of Love, she's rather hard to resist. She's also as tenacious as her brother; when we're together, she gently pushes herself into my life with kindhearted words and what she calls *girl time,* and yet leaves me alone when she knows I need it. We watch chick flicks together (she cries easily, but I suppose that is unsurprising for someone who always yearns for the happily ever after), go for walks in the groves, and meet with Persephone for tea. And I can see why Hermes has long loved her, because she *is* lovable. Hardly a negative word ever comes out of her mouth; she constantly searches for the best in everyone around her. I like this about her, like how she's so sweet and yet devoted to those she adores best.

What I don't appreciate is how no one will talk to me about what happened at the restaurant with Poseidon and Athena. And I figure it must have not been good, because the Automatons on staff nearly multiplied over night. Whereas I hardly ever saw them before as they lurked in the distance, now they are in full view for all to see. Anytime I ask about their presence, I'm informed that, "This is nothing out of the ordinary," and "We always have this many on staff." Persephone especially clams up, usually diverting the conversation to ferreting out new foods she thinks I'll enjoy or surprising me with trinkets she's had shipped in from around the globe. So, for as much as I've been letting Aphrodite in, I think I've been letting both Persephone and Hades in, too.

Although this fills my heart, my days are at their happiest when my hours are spent with Hermes. Usually at work during the daytime, he devotes his evenings and nights to me when he's in Olympus. He takes me into town for gelato and cupcakes, to dinner at small cafés with precious few crowds, and plays board games with me. Nearly every night, he banishes Kore and we talk into the wee hours of darkness. If I'm lucky, when he falls asleep in my bed next to me, I will find myself in his arms.

Upon waking in the morning after such evenings, I devote long minutes to merely watching him sleep, allowing myself the luxury of embracing the butterflies chasing each other in my chest. My best friend is beautiful. I am so, so incredibly fortunate he never allowed me to push him away.

I do not know what I would do without him.

"Where are Hades and Persephone?" I ask, glancing around the empty living room. They are nowhere to be seen tonight; neither are any of the Automatons.

The corner of Hermes' mouth quirks. "Out. Possibly in the Underworld. One never knows with those two."

Relief unfurls in the muscles in my shoulders. Still, I can't help but ask, "Without saying goodbye?"

He's definitely amused. "Shall I fetch them for you?"

"No!" My answer is too quick, which I fear broadcasts just how ecstatic I am at the thought of being along with Hermes right now. And that realization causes me to blush for the millionth time around him in the last month, so I clarify, "Of course not. I was just curious."

"Curiosity killed the cat, you know." To my delight, his hand finds mine and our fingers intertwine. It is a delicious sensation: his hand, warm and worn in mine in just such a way that feels like it's an extension of my body.

It must be criminal to adore touching someone so much.

"Did it, though?" I ask, and he laughs a burst of exasperated air.

"Possibly, but then again, who am I to judge, when I am often struck by curiosity that I cannot help but sate?" He gives me that dazzling grin of his and pulls me through the house. "Case in point: you."

"Me?" I squeak unattractively. There are lights ahead through the French doors leading to the patio, and I am curious enough to wonder what they are, but more so to wonder what he might mean.

"Yes, you." He glances back at me. "I've never told you that I was overcome with curiosity when I heard Athena cursed some girl from one of her temples. It wasn't like it was the first time she'd gone vindictively bonkers, but she was really put out over you. I mean ... one of her *followers*? Even that was low for her." His fingers squeeze mine gently and we stop about twenty feet from the doors. "When I first showed up on your island ..."

I am helpless at looking anywhere but in his eyes. Tonight, they're green. Vivid, beautiful, clear green. "Yes?"

"I'd been warned that you were a monster and that I best keep my distance. That you would slay me at the slightest provocation, and naturally, I believed it, as I could not blame anyone's hatred toward my family after what my sister and uncle had done to you. But once Death handed me that first soul and departed, I heard you crying. My curiosity inflamed tenfold. What kind of so-called monster weeps like her heart had shattered and never would form whole again?"

Like clockwork, my cheeks burn. His fingers brush my reddened skin ever so gently before I turn my face to rest in his hand.

The butterflies in my chest swarm frantically. "My sister misjudged you. I knew that the very second I heard your anguish. I'm afraid I was lost to you from that moment on. I had to discover all that made you *you*, even if I would suffer the same fate as the proverbial cat. And I never cared about the risks, as long as my curiosity about you was sated first."

"Truly?" The word barely escapes my lips.

His eyes are so intense. "Truly."

Oh, it's so hard to breathe right now. And although my legs are strong now, it's hard to stand, too. "You could have died. I could have accidentally killed you at any point."

"Another truth."

I'm so warm. More than just my cheeks—parts of me that I didn't think could turn warm are doing so at an alarming rate. "And yet you kept coming back. Even when there weren't souls to collect."

His lips quirk once more. "More truth."

Do not swoon, Medusa. It would be downright humiliating to pass out in front of him. "You're still here."

"And happier to be so than you probably ever will know." His hand drops from my face. "Come. I have a surprise for you."

Beyond the French doors there is a wonderland that leaves me in awe. Twinkle lights and lanterns hover in the trees and potted plants and rest in a nearby lagoon situated below my suite's terrace, which glows aqua even here at night. There are flowers everywhere: elegant, fragrant blooms that remind me of the fields near my first home so very long ago. I don't even know what to say, I'm so dazzled by just how stunning Hades and Persephone's side patio has become.

My heart is in my throat. "The occasion?"

"Do we need an official occasion?" At the confused look on my face, he lets loose that exasperated chuckle once more. "All right. The occasion is you."

Although this causes an entire field of flowers blooms in my chest, giving the butterflies something to tangle in, I can't help but tease, "I am not an occasion."

"Ah, and there we disagree. You are always reason enough for me to want to celebrate." He pulls out a chair for me at a small bistro table covered in a luxuriously embroidered white tablecloth. There are candles and beautiful yet simple crystal glasses laid out. "But, since you seek further clarification,"—he motions to the amused look on my face, no doubt—"I am celebrating the fact that Hades and Persephone finally left the bloody house, and that my sister chose for once to spend some time with her husband instead of you."

I can't help but giggle, and it feels so good to laugh and know that it's okay to do so. That it's not a temporary, fleeting moment of happiness stuck like a splinter in misery's flesh. I can laugh now without guilt and fear that tomorrow it may all be taken away from me with yet another death.

"They adore you, you know." He pulls a bottle of champagne out of a bucket of ice next to the table. "All of them. If I hadn't made them swear to not take you away from me, I think my uncle and aunt would happily adopt you and cart you off to the Underworld to groom as their heir. Let's not even go into how Dite keeps saying you ought to move in with her."

The cork pops towards me, but Hermes catches it easily. I am stunned by his words—not so much about Hades and Persephone, or even those about Dite (since she tells me this on a regular basis anyway), but the admission that he fears losing me.

I think I like knowing this very much.

I lean forward, chin resting in my propped up hand, attempting to act nonchalant when I am all wild happiness and nervousness. "Surely there would have been conditions such as Persephone's. Six months aboveground, six below."

"Not good enough," he murmurs, and my stomach does a somersault that would put any Olympian to shame.

"We've not seen each other for as many as three months at a time before," I remind him. My voice is shaky, which leaves me feeling awkward. Because nowadays, even two days feel too long to go without seeing him.

He pours champagne in my glass and hands it to me. "Not

by my choice, if you remember correctly." And he's right. Any time that we ever had months separating our visits was due to my request and my insecurity over whether or not I could keep him safe from a beast such as me.

"You could have overridden me, being a deity and all." My voice is even shakier. So are my hands, which can barely hold my glass.

He finishes pouring his own glass and sets it down. "Had I, you would have lumped me in with my less savory relatives and refused to have anything further to do with me. Perhaps even try to add me to your group of explorers at the south end of the temple."

Another somersault. "What if I'd thought you belonged with the poets?"

An easy grin slides towards me. It's incredibly unfair how stunning he is when he smiles like that. "I would have been awful company for those fellows. My prose is appalling."

I can't help the laughter that bursts out of me. "You are a god."

"Even gods can be terrible when it comes to the arts. I am no poet. I would be far better suited to spending my time regaling others like me with tales of adventure and daring." Before I can counter this, he lifts his glass. "A toast, then. To the men and smattering of ladies whose inquisitive natures matched my own, yet are not fortunate to sit here with us tonight: we remember you and value your lives."

I clink my glass against his, tears finding their way to the corners of my eyes. "To my friends," I say softly. Which is a pitiful way to put it, but the hold in my soul they still claim is a powerful one.

I will never forget any of you, I vow in my heart.

We both sip our drinks slowly, his eyes holding mine the whole time. All I can think is, stars above, I am so incredibly blessed to have this man in my life. When he sets his flute back down on the table, he says, "I have a gift of sorts for you. One I think you'll approve of. And then, news you must hear."

As there is no box on the table, I can't help but look to him in question.

He reaches across the small table and takes my hand in his. "Your isle's silent population is no longer there. I have transported them to a place where they will never be disturbed—an unobtrusive, peaceful locale in the Elysian Fields. You do not have to worry about them; I have found a guardian who will take the utmost care of your charges."

My throat tightens, my eyes sting even more than they already were. Was it possible that Hermes could read my mind? Or had it been obvious how I'd fretted over those I left behind? "Niki, too?"

"Even him," Hermes promises. "Every last person accounted for. They are all safe." His thumb strokes my hand. Goose bumps break out across my skin in the sultry heat of the night. "And now, the news I must share, although it pains me to do so. I know we'd planned on heading to Athens to see Mikkos next week, but he has also passed on to the Elysian Fields."

I knew this day would come, had expected it for years now, but it is still a dagger to my chest. The lump in my throat grows larger than a bolder and I can no longer see clearly. "When?"

"Just this morning, in his sleep. Knowing what he meant to you, I made sure I was the one to ferry his soul to the Underworld. He felt no pain, *glykia mou*. He was an old man whose life had come to a natural end."

As shocked as I am that Hermes just called me his sweetheart, I nod and blindly grope for my drink. Hermes gently shoves it towards me and I drink the rest of my champagne in one, two, three large gulps.

Mikkos, dead.

A horrible thought comes to me: *at least it wasn't by my hand.* And then I regret it at the same time I rejoice, because death is still death, and Mikkos is still gone.

Warmth presses against my shoulders; I stand up and fall into Hermes' arms. I cry then: cry for every one of the sixty-three lives I snuffed prematurely, and I cry for the one that lasted long and richly, but still gone too soon for a greedy girl like me. I cry for my youthful naiveté, for trusting a god who I believed to be a man, one who hurt me in ways I still feel to this day. I cry for a goddess who betrayed me after years of loyal service when I needed her compassion the most. And I cry for this god holding me, and for the goodness he's forced me to continue to believe in when it would have been so easy to give in and wallow in misery for the rest of time.

During this release, Hermes holds me in a way that lets me know he won't let go. He won't let me down. He holds me and I cry and the weird thing, when my tears slow, I feel the most certain sense of safety.

A sense of belonging.

A sense of rightness.

He murmurs sweet words of comfort, ones that do not rush me to wrap up nor belittle me for my outburst. And I know, just know, in this moment that I love him. That I am in love with him.

That I have been for a long time and have been too blind to see it before now.

Chapter Fourteen

It is a strange sensation, realizing you're in love with your best friend; stranger still to understand it isn't a recent development, but one born long ago and carefully cultivated. The more I reflect upon this as I lay in his arms on a large chaise next to the pool, the more I am assured of my feelings. I love Hermes. I've loved him for many years. I've just been too scared to do anything about it, be it from using my monstrous visage and deeds as excuses or fear for letting my heart be handled by anyone, man or god, again after what I've been through.

"Thinking of Mikkos?"

I am feeling bold with my new realizations and a glass of champagne under my belt and another in my hand. "Actually, I was thinking of you."

"Favorably, I pray," he murmurs, and it's funny, because he sounds so serious. Like he's worried that I might think anything other than favorable thoughts about him.

"I was thinking ... you are nothing like *him*."

Hermes' body stiffens for the smallest of seconds before he exhales in relief. He knows I do not mean Mikkos. "Praise Zeus for that." His head drops closer to mine, so when he speaks, I can smell the champagne on his breath. "I will never hurt you, Dusa, nor allow anyone else to ever do so again. If you cannot believe in anything else about me, please believe in that."

"I do," I say, because it's the truth.

He takes a sip of his drink and then stares up into the heavily star-laden sky. My eyes only follow his for a split second before falling back to his face. I love his face. It is perfect, that much is true—but it is also that of somebody whose beauty on the outside is matched, if not exceeded, by that on the inside. I've thought myself lucky for some time now, knowing this to be true. So many people don't *know* Hermes, not the person he really is. There are myths and legends, statues and paintings, countless stories, but none of those people who did any of those, who have heard or seen them, *know* him. Not like I do.

He is loyalty and kindness, generosity and tenacity all rolled in one.

I love him. Stars above, *I am in love with him.*

I want to tell him, shout it out for everyone to hear, but how does one go from being best friends one day to declaring their love the other? I know he cares about me—I know this fact as well as I know my name, but ... *love*? Could I ever hope he could fall in love with me, too? I am not a goddess. There have been dalliances between the gods and mortals—even non-divine immortals in the past—but never lasting, meaningful relationships. And yet, I guess there has been one, because even if we are nothing ever more than just friends, Hermes has been consistent in his affection for me for ages. Is that enough, though, now that I know I am in love with him?

I want to kiss him. Feel his mouth against mine. I want my hands in his hair and his in mine. I want my body pressed against his, his against mine. I want all of those things Poseidon ripped away from me on that awful night so long ago. He stole my innocence. I can't offer that to Hermes, can't offer it to anyone. He stole my first kiss, even if it wasn't reciprocated or loving. As painful as those memories are, I wish so desperately to replace them with new ones made with somebody I love.

Kisses, in books and movies, are supposed to be heavenly. I want that experience. And I want it with Hermes.

I want to stop living in fear.

I drink more of the golden liquid courage in my glass and ask for the first time in our relationship, "Why aren't you married?"

He stiffens once more. "What?"

I can't look up at him, though. So I focus on the lights in the lagoon and keep my words light. "Most of your siblings are married. I am curious as to why you aren't."

He clears his throat. "They most certainly aren't. Dite, yes. She's an exception. The rest, though ... not married."

"Hades and Persephone—"

"Not my siblings." He's amused. "But they are lucky exceptions, too."

I try again. "Your father—"

"Also not my sibling. And ... unhappily married most of the time, I think. So he's an exception of the exceptions."

I have another sip of champagne. "All right. I stand corrected, but my question is still unanswered. Why have you never married? You ..." I quickly finish the rest of the glass. "You seem to be the sort that women would want to marry. What do they call that nowadays? A good catch. You're an excellent catch."

I can feel his surprise ripple through the lean muscles pressing up against me. And yet, he says nothing.

"You can tell me." I swallow down the bursts of fear-laced anxiety threatening to surge up my throat. "I'm your best friend."

He's still silent.

A nearly hysterical laugh breaks free from my chest. I have to know the answer to this or I fear I might go as insane as so many people have thought me in the past. "I'll go first. Obviously, the reason I've yet to marry is because I was a recluse of a monster living on an enchanted isle. Most men draw the line at scaly women whose hair can bite them during arguments and eyes which can turn them into stone—in a bad way." Oh, stars above, did I really just say that out loud? I need more champagne, but that would require me getting up and going and getting it. And *that* would mean I might have to make eye contact, which would make all of this even more humiliating. I'm botching this; he's got to be utterly confused over why I'm suddenly asking all these things I've left alone before. More hysterical laughter escapes me. Like a lunatic, I waggle the ringless fingers on my right hand in front of us. "Thus, my singleton status. Your turn. You're not married or ... dating, I think?" I nearly groan at myself. Smooth moves, here, Dusa. That doesn't sound like blatant prying at all. "You've never mentioned dating. Fess up, friend. What's your reason?"

His hand comes up to meet mine, still dangling uselessly in the air between us. And then he laughs, too—that exasperated breath of a laugh of his that I've come to love over the years. "You really don't know, do you?"

My heart joins the anxiety rising in my throat. What does that mean? "Well, we've never talked about it, so ..."

I feel the deep breath he takes, long and steady and calming. "Are you sure you want to know?"

Yes. But then ... not if it means my heart is going to break when he tells me he is in love with somebody who is not me. The chances are good—excellent, really. Just because he never admitted it before doesn't mean it hasn't happened. But even still, even under the threat of agony and despite how my heart has decided to leap out of my throat so it can run a marathon, I'm left dizzy as I lay still against him in the wide chaise in his aunt and uncle's backyard, in desperate need of an answer. It's funny, just flat-out ridiculous that I've had years and years to ask such a question, yet never did. And now I think if I don't get one, I don't know what I'll do.

He's my best friend, somebody who has seen me at my very darkest and weakest, and it's only now that I am terrified of losing him.

I love him.

I love him.

I force myself to sound bemused. "I asked, didn't I?"

His fingers knot in mine in our still raised hands. And then my breath leaves my chest to fly up toward the constellations when he pulls our enjoined hands down so he can kiss the back o mine. "The reason I'm not married is that you are my best friend."

The back of my hand is on fire—aching, lovely, torturous fire. It spreads out until every last bit of me is consumed, which is so unfair, because here he is, telling me he is in love with somebody who apparently won't marry him because he was foolish enough to become friends with me.

I have the worst luck. Absolute worst luck of anyone ever born.

My hand is still so close to his mouth, so when he exhales that exasperated, quiet sigh of his again, a shiver rips through my body at the mere brush of his breath against my skin. "Dusa ... how is it that this is so painfully obvious to everyone except you?"

How do people breathe in situations like this? I wouldn't be able to catch my breath or slow my heart right now even if I tried. How do hearts break and race at the same time? I want to ask what he means by, about the girl who is cruel enough to withhold her love because of our friendship, but my words are disappeared just as easily as the air in my lungs.

He presses another kiss on the back of my hand, enflaming me once again. "You want to know why I haven't married yet? Because I have yet to ask the girl who owns my heart entirely, let alone actually *tell* her what she means to me. I've been too selfish to do so, because I've been fearful that once I do, things will change between us for the worse if she does not feel the same way, and I know I can't lose her. So I've held on to what we have, even though I want to be with her more than anything else in the entire universe. See, I am completely, irrevocably, in love with the best person I know. And I have been for a very long time."

I hate her, HATE whoever this nameless girl is. How could she be so cruel? Hermes loves her. *Hermes*. He is the best person *I* know. I would trade places with her in a heartbeat. She has no idea how lucky she is. I'd like to see how she'd feel when she has no love, locked away on an island for years. Maybe she'd wise up then.

But for now, no matter who she is, if my friend is unhappy, then I will do anything in my power to change that situation for him. Even if it destroys my own heart. I say, shamed at how my voice cracks just as easily as the brittle muscle in my chest, "Maybe if I talk to her for you ... explain how things are between us ... she'd not object ...?"

He shifts in the chaise, rolling over to his side so he's now facing me. I blink the tears back, praying he can't see them, but it's a moot point when he gently tugs my chin until I turn to face him, too, my body following suit.

His eyes are so green tonight as they pin me to where I lay. He's so beautiful. So wonderful. The best kind of friend.

I love him.

Our faces are so close to one another right now, and all I can do is selfishly think how easy it would be for me to lean forward and kiss him like I've dreamed about for the last couple of weeks. One kiss, and then I'd let him go.

One kiss, to replace the one stolen from me.

This would be my first kiss. What happened with Poseidon didn't count, because a kiss should be born from love, and want, and need. A kiss should be beautiful, something a girl can hold onto for the rest of her life, to pull out in her memory whenever she wants butterflies to come back. A kiss shouldn't be roughly ripped away from her and turned into a thing of nightmares.

I want that kiss, and I want it from my best friend.

So I do it. I take the risk. I lean forward in the scant few inches between us until our foreheads touch and our champagne-tinged breaths mingle in the miniscule slice of space left between our lips. I don't want to steal this from him, not like mine was stolen from me. I give him this moment to pull back, but ...

He doesn't. Our hands, still clasped, are wedged in between our bodies. I can feel the beating of his heart right now against the back of my hand.

It's racing just as fast as mine. That's ... good?

My lips brush ever so lightly against his. It's lovely, just absolutely the most lovely sensation, because tingles flare up and down my body and my head swims and I burn and float and all that happened was the delicate slide of skin against skin.

There.

My first real kiss.

I pull back, ever so slightly, but a low moan escapes him. And then his hand is in my hair, bringing my face back, and our mouths come together again. This is no brush, though, no soft slide: this is his mouth, on mine and mine on his, and oh stars above and everything wonderful in the world, this ... impossibly *this* is more beautiful than what happened before. But I have no time to process it, because his lips are moving against mine and it is everything, *everything* I could have ever dreamed it would be.

I'm melting right into him. My body melts right into a useless puddle of nerves and heat and it's just soaking right into him, it has to be. Because I can't feel anything other than his mouth on mine, his breath against my skin, and I don't think I want to feel anything right now if it wasn't one of these things.

I love him.

His tongue touches the seam of my mouth and I gasp, and then it's in my mouth, twining with my tongue and all of that melting that just happened happens all over again. Something in me switches on, some need that tells me I must do the same with him, and when I do—when I ease my tongue into his mouth—he makes that same, low groan that just might be my new favorite sound in the world.

For the first time in two thousand plus years, time stands still. I pray it stays that way, because this moment here?

Divine.

He shifts in the chaise, his mouth never leaving mine, until he's above me. My heart thunders in my chest as I reach up both hands and dig them in his hair, just like I'd imagined earlier. I'm drunk, and I can't blame any of it on the champagne. It's all him, and of how he makes me feel.

When we come up for air, we're both breathing heavily, and as I gaze up in his eyes, so bright green in the moonlight, I can't even begin to piece together all of the sensations wracking my body right now.

"Dusa ..." he murmurs, my name word barely voiced against the songs from crickets and frogs surrounding us.

Don't do it, I think. *Don't tell me what just happened between us was a mistake, because if you do, I don't think I can survive that. I'm not ready for this dream to be done.*

His head shifts just a tiny bit so he can press a lingering kiss against the corner of my mouth. "In case it wasn't patently clear, that was me finally telling you how much I love you."

My hands, currently on his shoulders, still. Surely, he did not just say what I think he did? Because—

"I am in love with you," he whispers against my mouth. "Desperately. Hopelessly. In. Love. With. *You.*"

Something long-lost yet effervescent bubbles up in me, threatening to tear me apart in its efforts to burst free: joy. Blissful, radiant, incandescent joy. "That's a good thing," I whisper in return, a hand coming to cup his dear face. "Because I'm in the same situation."

I can feel his mouth curve against mine. "You're also hopelessly in love with you?"

I can't help it. The elation filling every single one of my cells won't let me do anything else—I laugh. And then I kiss him again: deeply, so he has no doubt of what I mean.

I can't stop touching him. He can't stop touching me. Even now, as I lay back in his arms once more, staring up at the stars, one of his hands runs lightly up and down my waist; the other twines through my hair. I'm tracing patterns on his chest, marveling how there is no awkwardness, no fear as I lay here with him—just love, all-consuming, effervescent gorgeous love.

"So," he murmurs, his mouth lingering against the top of my head as he leaves a kiss there, "when did you finally decide to give me a chance?"

I play with one of the buttons on his shirt. "What do you mean?"

Another lingering kiss finds its way to my forehead. "I've been waiting a very long time for you to wise up and realize your feelings toward me."

My fingers pause in their effort to undo his button. *"What?"*

I feel his chuckle before I hear it. "Was that unclear, too? Wow. I'm apparently horrible at this. But that's okay—as long as I finally have you in my arms, I'm more than content."

I shift and lean myself up on an elbow so I can look him in the face. He looks content. Amused. Happier than I've ever seen him before.

But surely, there is no way his feelings for me could be older than just a few weeks old. Friendship, yes. I have no doubt about the validity of our friendship. But love? There is no way he was ever in love with me, because I was a monster who killed people.

"What's the matter, *kardia mou?*" he asks me softly, a hand smoothing stray strands of my hair away from my face.

He calls me his heart, but he is mine and has been for so long. "I love you," I tell him. I let every last ounce of that very real, very valid feeling coat every syllable I speak. I've never said those three words out loud before. And now, now I want to say them all the time, as often as I can, as long as his ears are the ones to hear them.

He groans quietly, his lips finding my neck, and I arch toward them. "I cannot tell you how long I've dreamed of this ... being here, with you," he tells me, his words soft and sweet and hot all at the same time. "I've imagined it thousands of times, in a thousand different ways, but ... you taste better than anything I could have ever imagined in even my best dreams. And believe me, there have been plenty of those kind when it comes to you."

I struggle to focus as one of his hands runs the length from my waist to my breast. The arm propping me up turns to jelly, making it difficult to stay upright. He catches me easily, his mouth once more claiming mine. I shiver when his fingers dance across my skin to circle my breast, cupping it in a way no other man has done before.

I fall apart all over again.

"Do you know what I used to dream about?" he murmurs in my ear as his hand drifts to my other breast.

I manage to whisper, "What?" even as he steals my breath away when he lightly pinches my nipple. I jerk, but not from pain. No, there's only delirious, delicious pleasure here. This must be what odes were written about, infinite movies attempt to depict, books desperate to describe—the perfect, exquisite sensation of lust and love all rolled into one.

"What you sound like when you're kissed." His mouth brushes mine. "What your body would feel like under mine." His index finger traces a light circle around my hardening nipple. "What you would taste like." His teeth lightly graze my neck. "What it feels like to hear you tell me you love me, too. I cannot tell you how delighted I am to finally have those answers. How it makes me feel like I've been given the best gifts in the entire universe."

My eyes go blurry; too much happiness threatens to spill out. After all that I've done, after all I've gone through, how did I ever deserve this? Him? "Then listen closely. I love you, Hermes. I. Love. *You*."

He groans. And then I gasp when his lips travel to meet where his hand is, my back arching so he can easily capture my breast, still hidden behind my dress, in his mouth. Oh, sweet stars in the skies, surely Zeus has just struck me with one of his lightning bolts because I have been electrocuted. Nerve endings I didn't even know were there before flare to life, turning achy and hot.

I need something—desperately need it, but I don't know what it is.

Suddenly, he pulls away from me and calls out something in that language of Olympus I don't understand, his hoarse voice ringing out across the courtyard. Faint rustling follows.

I struggle to form coherent words. "What did you just say?"

An embarrassed smile slides across his tempting lips. "I basically told the Automatons patrolling the villa that if they came within a two thousand feet of us tonight without me or you giving explicit permission first, I'd personally ensure that they would lose their jobs."

It takes a few seconds for his words to sink in before I jerk into a sitting position over him. "Have we been *watched*?"

He leans up on his elbows, eyes drifting to my chest. This, of course, makes my embarrassment grow tenfold. "Dusa. Love." He eyes finally meet mine. How do they manage to pierce me so? "No. They—while I certainly never guessed that this would happen tonight, I always make sure that when you and I are together, it's just us. They are on the property, yes. They are within a safe distance if needed." He lets out that wonderful exasperated breath of a laugh. "The only people here ... it's just us. I would never expose you to anything that I would ever think would harm you—not even if my lust threatens to get the better of me."

I want to look around the patio, ensure for myself that his words are true, but he's captured my attention so fully. "We're alone?"

He nods, biting his lower lip, like he's worried that I'll somehow take back what I've said, how I feel. What we've done.

For some reason, that undoes me. This god—this powerful, popular, wonderful god has fallen in love with *me*. All that bad luck I thought I'd cultivated over the years evaporates out of my pores. Because I am the absolute luckiest girl to ever live in this moment.

He gave me my first real kiss. He's given me his love, his friendship, and his devotion. But I am suddenly greedy, because I want more than that. I want to entirely erase what's come before. It's been two thousand years, yes, but I want that memory completely overwritten in my life with one from this man here.

So slowly, oh so slowly, I reach down and grab the hem of my dress. He's still up on his elbows, watching me as if he would rather cease existing than look at anything else. It empowers me, makes me feel like in this moment, I am calling the shots.

Me. I am choosing to do this. Me. *My choice.*

"Medusa," he half-whispers, half-moans, using my whole name for the first time in forever. Something hard presses against my bottom, and I revel in it—proof of his desire for me. Rather than terrifying me like it did so long ago on another man, I now ache at the thought of it being in me.

I pull the dress over my head, tossing it on the ground nearby.

His breath rushes in loudly, and I can't help but blush. He stares at me for what feels like forever, eyes moving up and down my bare body, trembling in the warm breeze. Then he looks up at me, eyes wide and yet glazed, mouth slightly parted with no words coming out. He tries to say something but all that manages to come out is that delicious moan that heats me every further.

A thrill shoots through me. Have I rendered him speechless?

I reach up and free my hair, haphazardly arranged in a loose bun. It spills across my shoulders, earning me yet another audible inhale from Hermes. I delight in how his hand trembles when he reaches up to touch a strand of hair grazing the tips of one of my breasts. His fingers brush against the peak and something in me tightens and strains.

His voice is husky. "Are you sure?"

The fact that he's asking, that he's waiting for permission makes me all the more sure. I nod, my hair swaying around my shoulders.

His fingers still in their tracings. "I need to hear it," he whispers. "Please."

Part of me is terrified to say it. Because, as sure as I am, it also means there's no turning back. Tiny insecurities surface: what if, despite how much I love him, it's just as painful as the last time? But I also know it could be beautiful—everything else tonight has been.

As I have done for years, I place my trust in his hands; only this time, I do not just trust him with my heart, but my body, too. My words are just as soft and shaky as his. "I want to make love to you."

He leans back and blows out an unstable breath. "If ... if you need to stop, just ... I'll understand ... just—you'll need to tell me—"

I reach down and slowly unbutton his shirt, effectively robbing the rest of his much-appreciated assurances. I only get half-way done before his hand curves around the back of my head, pulling me down for a reality-shattering kiss.

Because that's what's happening. Reality, as I've known it for thousands of years, is no longer the same.

Our mouths crash together as our hands frantically explore each other's bodies. His shirt finally comes off, and I marvel at his beautiful, smooth skin. This is why people glorified him in art—he is magnificent. But I don't get to study him too much, because his mouth finds my breast again and now, with no fabric between us, the heat between my legs flares so strongly that I find myself whimpering from need and want. As his tongue and teeth turn me inside out, one of his hands traces a path down from my other breast to the top of my panties. Except, as needy as I am, I find myself stiffening the moment his fingers dip below the thin elastic.

He stops, his hot, hard breaths puffing against delicate skin. I know why he paused, and I love him for it. Yet, frustration builds in me, too—I cannot, *will not* let my past dictate this moment. "Please," I whisper brokenly.

His eyes, so emerald in this light, meet mine. There's lust there, yes. But so much love and concern it rocks me to my core.

I swallow hard and say, "I need you."

He groans again, leaning up to capture my mouth as his hand once more dips into my panties. The air in my lungs stills as he skims his fingers lower still until they slip in between my legs. And then, sweet heavens above, he touches a part of me I never knew existed.

If I'd thought I'd come undone before, I was wrong.

Everything blurs and heightens as he kisses me—my mouth, my breasts, my neck—and all I am is feeling: feeling him, feeling his fingers, feeling this hot *need* in me build and I ache, just ache in a demand for something I can't quite reach. And then, his fingers ease inside me and my mind just scatters, just up and explodes out of my head and floats away in the breeze. My body follows suit and shatters, too, until his name is ripped out of me and I go limp against his hand.

Before I can process the miracle that just happened, he kisses me—hard—and then shifts so he can slide his pants off. Just seconds before, I thought myself to be a puddle of bliss, but the sight of Hermes naked—sculpted, golden muscles that would make an artist weep—sends my heartbeat back into overdrive.

"I adore you," he whispers hoarsely. "There's only ever been you for me."

It's my turn to grab his head and pull it toward me. Our tongues are at war with one another as we kiss, and it's hotter than ever before. I thought I'd found relief for whatever need ignited in me minutes before, but I was wrong, because it's back and stronger than ever. "Please," I tell him again, not knowing what it is exactly I'm asking, but knowing all the same that he's the only one who can help me.

A long, deep kiss follows before he pulls back—just far enough for his forehead to rest against mine. His hot breath hits my mouth; his racing heart beats against mine. And then slowly, gently, the tip of his need presses into me. I gasp; not in pain, not like the first time so very long ago, but because spikes of ecstasy threaten to tear me apart again.

His moan only serves to intensify the ache consuming me. "Are you okay?"

"I'm ..." I gasp again as he pushes further into me. "Yes. Just ... stars, this is ..." I cling to his shoulders, my hips instinctively rocking into his. "Hermes ... please ..."

He pauses, his breath coming out in hard, short bursts. Is he afraid of hurting me? Because nothing could be further from the truth right now. So I thrust my hips once more toward his, driving him in deep and sure. I eat up another one of his delicious moans. "Dusa ... you ... I have never ..." He doesn't finish, though. Slow thrusts which make speech impossible eventually give way to frantic ones as we memorize one another. And when I fall apart a second time, it's only moments before he suddenly goes still in me, my name falling from his lips.

And I am content, truly content, for the first time in ages.

Chapter Fifteen

"Have you had a chance to look at the list yet?"

Hades doesn't look up from his iPad, on which he's been reading the morning's news and reports from the Underworld. "No."

Persephone sighs and sets her fork down and stares at him, hard.

Her husband reaches for his coffee. "I gave it to Talos."

She picks her fork up only to drop it again, making sure it clatters loudly. He finally looks up and says, "Light of my life, the two of us have gone over the plans for Friday at least a dozen times each. It is in the hands of the Automatons now. Have a little faith that things will go well. When have any of your parties ever gone badly?"

"I can think of a few," she mutters darkly.

He sets his cup back down. "Let me rephrase—when have any of your parties in the last millennium gone wrong?"

This prompts her brows to crease. The next thing we know, she's standing up and heading out the door, shouting for Talos.

Hades angles one of his droll smiles toward me with a small

shrug of his shoulders, as if to say, "What can you do? She is who she is, but I wouldn't ever have it any other way."

I hide my laughter behind my own cup of coffee. Persephone has been planning Hades' birthday party, set for three nights from now, for months. I find it humorous that she does so, as he's repeatedly mentioned how he doesn't feel the need for one, especially now that he's reached "middle age." Of course, this makes me wonder just what "middle age" for the Assembly entails, but I'm not going to be the one to ask him.

That said, Persephone is on edge about the attendance list and security, and while nobody will confirm why, I have an unsettling suspicion that it has to do with me. I'm always told it's because these are typical issues for members of the Assembly—there are those who will always try to crash the parties in efforts to curry favor from the gods. But as I know I'm under constant surveillance, I can't help but worry once more that something is going on that I don't know about yet.

What I do know is that the last week has been heavenly. Since Hermes and I finally admitted our feelings for one another, my feet have finally found firmer ground. We had a conversation the morning after making love for the first time that really shook me to my cor, yet strangely strengthened my happiness.

"Last night," I asked him as we ate breakfast in my room, "you said something strange."

He looked up over the toast he was buttering and flashed me that dazzling smile of his that gets me every single time. "Was me telling you how much I adore and love you the wrong thing to do? Because I can't take it back, love. Now that it's finally out there, there it will stay."

I blushed furiously. "Not that. I liked that very much. I meant ... you said you've been in love with me for a long time."

He reached over for the pot of strawberry jam on the table. "That's bad?"

I was nervous all of a sudden, which was unsettling. Having known him most of my life, I shouldn't feel this way. But since the moment we decided to alter our relationship, those pesky butterflies in my chest won't leave me be. "Hermes," I said to him quietly, "I was a monster just a few weeks ago."

His eyes, still a vivid green that morning, met mine as he slathered the jam on his toast. "And?"

"And ..." I twisted a piece of my hair in my fingers. "I mean ... there is no way you could have been in love with me longer than the past few weeks."

He looked at me like I was insane.

"I was a monster," I reminded him. "I ..." I had had to swallow, and then whispered, "Killed people. Had ... snakes on my head. My skin was ... not right. Scaly. I didn't even look like a *person*. There is no way you could have ever loved that. I get why you would now—now that I'm not hideous—"

"Stop." He put the toast back on his plate and got up, coming round the small table so he could kneel down in front of me. "I hope you don't think me so shallow that the moment the curse reversed, I decided I suddenly had feelings for you. Dusa ..." He took my hands in his and kissed them. "I'm afraid I fell in love with you shortly after we met. I told you last night, you fascinated me from the very beginning. The more I got to know you, the more I found myself falling. You were, and are, unlike anyone else I've ever met before. You have a goodness in you others would have long let die away in such circumstances." He pressed a hand against my heart. "This is what I fell in love with. Not your body—which, I won't lie, I enjoy very much,"—I blushed again—"or your beautiful hair—because you know I most certainly was fascinated with your snakes, too—or those eyes of yours I find myself so easily lost in on a regular basis. Dusa, I love *you*. Who *you* are. I hadn't tried anything before now simply because I never thought you would go for it. It was hard enough ensuring you'd keep me around as a friend. I wasn't willing to risk declaring anything else until you were ready."

I cried many more tears of happiness, and he kissed them away and made love to me again. And now here I am, hopelessly in love with my best friend and delighted to be so. We didn't make a grand proclamation of our new relationship, although I know Hermes talked to Hades about it at one point shortly afterward, but it didn't matter. Everyone seemed to already know. In fact, Aphrodite took me to the side when she came to visit so she could tell me how relieved she was that I "finally came to my senses" and put her poor brother "out of his misery."

"You knew?" I asked her as I looked across the room at where Hermes was talking with Hephaestus.

Wind chimes filled the room. "Of course I did. I am the Goddess of Love."

And now here she is, bounding into the room while Hades and I finish brunch, carrying what must be a half dozen shopping and garment bags, and already talking a mile a minute. "I popped down to Paris yesterday and found this amazing boutique," she says, breezing past Hades with a kiss on the top of his forehead, "and I saw a dress I had to have for the party. Obviously, I bought it. Better yet, Dusa, I found a dress for you! I know we'd talked about going shopping here in Olympus, but when I saw this one, I knew that nothing local would do you as much justice as this. It's like it was made exactly for you."

"Paris!" I sigh when she sits down next to me. "I've always wanted to go to Paris. It's been one of my favorite cities to read about."

She quickly presses kisses against both of my cheeks. "Well, there's no reason now at all that you can't go. Tell Hermes to take you there—stars above, we know there's precious little he would ever say no to you for."

One of Hades' eyebrows lifts as he smirks, making me blush uncontrollably again. I really need to learn how to get a handle on this, because it's humiliating to resemble a tomato most of the time.

"Where is my brother?" Dite asks, looking around the room, like he's hiding behind the drapes or the like.

It's Hades who answers. "Work, niece. Some of us have it." He gives her a pointed look, which only makes her giggle all the more.

"I've taken the day off. I just wanted to come by and give

Dusa this dress I found. Want to see?" She unzips one of the garment bags and extracts an emerald green silk dress that shimmers. At first, I think it's gorgeous. But then ...

Then I realize it has a slight print to the fabric. And that print is a python pattern.

I jerk back in my chair, refusing to take what she holds out to me. Is this a joke? She must see the look on my face, because she quickly says, "Wait. Listen to my reasoning for this. Dusa, you have nothing to be ashamed of. *Nothing*. The truth is, yes, you were ... altered for many years. But I think the worst thing you could do is pretend like it never happened. It did. Sometimes, terrible, awful things happen to people, things you can't predict or wish for differently that happen just the same. But you can't let them consume you. You can't wish it away. All you can do is pray you've learned from it, that it's made you stronger, and that you will move on. I bought this dress because it's beautiful, but also because it's *you*. I felt like if you wore it, embraced who you are and what you've been and done ... it will help you move on."

I'm not a huge fan of her logic here—I mean, I'd spent the better part of my life part-reptilian—but I can see her point. I glance down the table at Hades, who is watching us carefully. I no longer fear that I'm some sort of pet of theirs, or a charity case. And I sincerely believe that Dite would never give me a dress like this for the sole purpose of humiliation. It's not her style, nor any of the gods that I've begun to let into my heart.

But still. I don't know if I'm ready to embrace such a dress.

She unzips another bag. "Here's the one I'm going to wear." She pulls out a blue dress that matches her eyes perfectly. And this dress, like the one she'd bought for me, also has a python print. "But I'll leave it up to you with what you want to wear. If you still want to go into town and pick out a dress, then I'm down with that. But this one would be lovely on you."

I take the green dress from her and stare at it.

"How about this," she says. "We'll go to town anyway—you need shoes no matter what dress you're going to wear—"

"There must be thirty pairs of shoes in my closet already," I tell her wryly.

"A girl can never have too many shoes." She waves at Hades. "Am I right, or am I right, Uncle?"

"Stars forbid me from ever denying any woman shoes," is his answer. He's amused, though.

This seems to satisfy her. "We can lunch—"

"I am just now finishing brunch." I smirk.

"*After* shopping. If not lunch, then tea. C'mon. You've barely left the villa in days. We'll take Kore and that thug of my uncle's, and I bet you anything we can sweet talk Heph to come and join us. He's been working on something for Hera, but I know he'll be glad to get out of the workshop for a bit." She grabs my arm, nearly bouncing in her seat. "Shoe shopping is a wonderful treat, Dusa. Let's go spend my brother's money, huh?"

"You might as well go," Hades says from his end of the table. "She's annoying when she doesn't get her way."

"Love you, too, Uncle!" She blows a kiss at him, and he chuckles.

"Fine." I let out a shaky laugh. "We can go."

She squeals, bags go flying, and within twenty minutes, we're in downtown Olympus, pulling up in front of a stretch of Dite's favorite stores. I do not think she's taken a breath since we left the villa. I don't mind, though. I've needed the time to center myself. I've never actually gone clothing shopping before—plenty of so-called trips on-line over the last few years, but this will be my first time in one. And as much as I'm dreading being around a lot of people, I'm also excited about this new experience. It feels so ... normal, or at least, what I'd like to think normal is. Because while normal for me for so long was to garden and dust off my statues, I've craved what the rest of the world took for granted.

Shopping is one of those things. Shopping with friends even more so. I ignore the fact that I'm followed by a hulking Automaton, which I get is *not* normal, and instead focus on stepping through the door, listening to the bell ring above me, signaling our presence, and taking in the overwhelming smell of fabric and leather mixed with incense. Aphrodite immediately pulls me toward racks of clothes and waves at a willowy salesgirl chatting on a phone behind a large glass counter. To my relief, the boutique is nearly empty, so I do not have to fight my claustrophobia quite yet. It's enchanting, though, and exactly what I thought it'd be like, which prompts a burst of pleasure. She claims that we're here to buy me a dress if I so wish to, but none of the items she gravitates toward are dresses. Shirts, pants, skirts, tank tops, jeans ... these are all modern pieces that have yet to make it in my already overflowing closet yet. Persephone, for all her generosity, tends to favor designer clothes best suited for black tie events rather than daily life. Shallow as it may seem, I'm completely thrilled to finally get a chance to feel what it's like to wear such clothes after looking at them in magazines for so long.

"Let me set up a dressing room for you, my lady," Kore says softly, taking a stack of jeans from my arms.

I'd almost forgotten she was with us, she's been so quiet. Almost as quiet as Talos, who never speaks and is currently positioned outside the door. Except, now that I've turned to face her, I notice her mouth is in a flat line, her brow furrowed. "Are you okay? And stop calling me that. I thought we agreed you should just use my name." I widen my eyes and smile so she knows I'm not annoyed.

"I am fine." She glances quickly over my shoulder and then back at me. "But ... if I may ...?" She cuts the space between, clutching the jeans to her chest. "My la—I mean, Medusa, I feel as if I must—"

"THESE are adorable," Dite exclaims, shoving several t-shirts my way. I startle and take a step back from Kore. "You need to try them on. I can just see how my brother would love you in them. He's hopeless when it comes to fashion, you know." She chuckles. "Of course you would know. Tell me you agree that his propensity toward dressing like one of those stereotypical frat boys in old t-shirts and flip-flops gets old fast."

Kore takes the shirts away from me and goes over to where the salesgirl is. "Actually," I begin, ready to argue how I have no qualms with how Hermes dresses, but Dite isn't done. "I mean, obviously, you will not follow suit with shirts that are barely held together after decades of wear. I just meant, he'd probably be very pleased at the sight of you in a t-shirt and jeans."

Is Kore arguing with the salesgirl? It sure looks like it—she's leaning in close, eyebrows down in a 'v', as she whispers furiously with the fellow nymph. I've yet to ever see Kore look so angry before. "What do you think—"

But once more, Dite is already off and running on another topic as she flips through a rack of clothes. "I texted Heph a few minutes ago. He'll meet us at one of our favorite dives near his workshop in about an hour. It's a little sandwich shop that you'll love. Hardly ever a crowd."

I take the sequined skirt she hands over. She knows about my unease with crowds?

"Sounds great," I murmur, glancing back to where Kore is. She's now heading over to where the dressing rooms are. The salesgirl retreats to the counter and picks up the phone again.

"You could always text my brother." Dite knocks shoulders with me. "Let him know where to meet us if he's hungry." She waggles her eyebrows.

The action is comically bizarre on her lovely face. Does she have something in her eyes? Oh—*oh*.

She laughs, delighted. "You're too cute with how much you blush. No wonder Hermes is constantly trying to get you to do so. Here. Go try this on already."

Nonetheless, it takes me a good ten more minutes before I make it to the back of the store where the door to the dressing rooms is. Kore is standing there, tense as she wrings her hands together. "My lady—"

I give her a pointed look.

She glances over my shoulder, stepping directly in front of the doorway. "Perhaps it would be more comfortable if you simply purchased all of these items and took them home to try on? Who knows when these rooms were cleaned last?"

Why is she acting so strangely? She's even more nervous now than when Hermes confronted her in the hallway that one morning. "Kore, it's okay. I'm fine with being here."

Yet she doesn't move. "Please," she whispers, nearly in tears. "Let us go home."

I'm just about to ask why she's so insistent, but Dite yells out from where she's knee deep in designer t-shirts, "Make sure you come out and show me how those jeans fit, yeah? Kore? Would you mind helping me pick some things out for her? You know her size well."

Kore's eyes drop to the ground as she skirts around me. I follow the hallway down to where an ornate mirror hanging on a door proclaims my name. Tingles of excitement burst into goose bumps across my skin as I go inside the large room. I immediately head over to where Kore has hung several shirts; there's a yellow one Aphrodite picked out that I really like—

"Hello, little monster."

My hand freezes just as it's about to touch the hanger. I did not just hear that voice. I did not.

And yet, I did, because when I slowly turn around, I find none other than Athena leaning against the freshly closed and now locked door. She's got her hair up in that tight bun again, making her face appear severe and unforgiving.

My stomach jumps into my throat. I have no words—none at all.

"You've been an exceedingly tough little whore to get ahold of," she says, her voice quiet yet cutting against the wooden walls. "I think this is the first time they've let their pet be alone, isn't it?" Her smile is icy, and I hate that I physically flinch at her vehemence. "My sister is always supremely stupid, but I thank her for that. I knew she'd fuck up and drag you to someplace like this. It's time we had a little chat, don't you think?"

My back hits the wall behind me, scattering shirts and hangers onto the ground. The urge to scream conflicts directly with the fear choking my throat into silence.

She takes several steps forward, her sensible canvas flats silent against the plush carpet, until they come flush against my own satin ballet ones. Her face is far too close to mine, forcing me to press even harder into the wall. "You think you were so clever, brainwashing my brother into convincing our father to reverse your punishment," she whispers harshly. "But here's the thing, *monster:* nobody ever said I couldn't do it again."

Terror squeezes my heart so hard I'm positive it's stopped entirely. How did she know I was here? Why is her anger just as strong today as the day she cursed me? It takes effort, but I manage to get out the prayer she never answered: "I worshipped you. What did I do to make you hate me so much?"

"You—," she jabs a finger into my shoulder so hard I don't doubt it will leave a bruise, "—are nothing more than a slut. You desecrated my temple."

Surely she can be reasoned with. "But—"

"Shut up!" she hisses, grabbing my cheeks in one hand and squeezing until black dots dance before my eyes. Once I do as she commands, her thin lips curve into the most evil grin I've ever seen. *This* is the Goddess of Wisdom? Hermes is right—she's *insane.* "I miscalculated where I banished you to last time. I wasn't thinking clearly; it was foolish of me to put you where he would find you. I won't make that mistake again."

Oh, sweet heavens above, please let this be a nightmare.

"Dusa?" Aphrodite's voice floats down the hallway and into the dressing room. "How's it going in there?"

Athena shoves her hand against my mouth, pushing so hard I taste blood. "Not a word," she mouths to me.

"Medusa?" Dite's voice is closer now. "Sweetie, can I see? Was I right about those shirts or what?"

The shock of Athena's appearance and threats finally wears off, leaving behind a strong sense of self-preservation. I kick against the goddess pinning me against the wall, shoving as hard as I can. Even though I know there's a good chance she'll strike me down in seconds, I still need to try.

I can't go down without a fight. Not this time.

Athena stumbles back, tripping on one of the hangers on the ground. I scream my friend's name and lunge for the door. Athena grabs my ankle, yanking hard until I go down, too. I scream again, clawing at the carpet as I try to pull myself forward. Aphrodite shouts, too—this time for Talos, and then the door handle in front of me rattles as she tries to come in. "Medusa! What's going on?"

"Little bitch!" Athena's grasp is vise-like as she drags me back toward her. "I warned you!"

"Dusa—is that Athena?" Dite is now pounding on the door; it sounds like she's kicking it, too. "Sister! How the—how— TALOS, GET THE FUCK IN HERE AND BREAK THIS DAMN DOOR DOWN!"

I kick at Athena, pray that my fists make contact, but it does no good. She is not only the Goddess of Wisdom, but she is also the Goddess of Warfare. She manages to twist me under her within a split second, pinning me to the ground. I thrash against her, screaming as Aphrodite pounds on the door, yelling at her sister to stop, but it's all for naught.

She's going to do it again.

She's going to make me a monster again. Oh, gods. Oh, gods, oh, gods.

Oh, Zeus—please let it go fast this time—

The door crashes open; Talos stands there, fists clenched and covered with plaster and splintered wood. Aphrodite darts past him and throws herself at her sister, shouting at her to let go of me, but then Talos is there, too, wrenching Athena off. The Goddess of Wisdom is snarling, threatening Talos, threatening me. Dite hauls her hand back and smacks her sister straight across the face so hard she goes flying out of Talos' grip.

"You dared to do this when she is under my protection," she snarls as Athena hits the wall. My friend looks nothing like the Goddess of Love right now. "Talos, get Medusa out of here. I will take care of my sister."

"We're not done," Athena rages as Talos takes my hand, helping me up. "Not by a long shot. I swear this to you."

I collapse the moment I put pressure on the foot she'd dragged me by. Talos catches me before I hit the ground, hauling me up in his arms.

Aphrodite delivers a perfect roundhouse kick straight from

a martial arts movie, sending Athena sprawling against the wall. "Now, Talos!"

He doesn't need to be told twice. He turns and swiftly exits the dressing room, carrying me like I'm a baby. Kore is there at the doorway, tears streaming down her face. "My lady—my lady, I am so sorry—"

"Follow us, and I'll kill you," Talos tells her in his deeply accented voice. I jerk in his arms, but he does not slow down to hear what Kore's saying. We're out the door and into the limo in less than a minute; and then we're on the road back to the villa. I'm not even placed into the backseat like normal; Talos has me sitting in the front next to him.

I want to thank him for getting me out of there, but I must have lost my voice screaming back in the boutique. And when I look down, I see my hands are shaking. I'm bleeding—Zeus Almighty, I'm bleeding and didn't even know it. Scratches lace my arms and calves; half-moon, bloody circles ring the ankle that brought me down.

She attacked me. Flat-out attacked me in a store.

My hands aren't the only things shaking. My whole body is now. And it keeps shaking until we get back to the villa, surprising me that my tremors don't rip the car apart.

Chapter Sixteen

I awake to muffled shouting coming from somewhere behind closed doors. I blink in the hazy morning light—how long have I been asleep? I remember Talos carrying me inside. Hades and Persephone met us in the foyer, both gods attempting to stay calm when I could tell they were anything but. And then there was Tele coming up to my room to look at my ankle and give me something to help me sleep. That was ... afternoon, right? Aphrodite and I went out around eleven yesterday, so ...

I'd slept a whole day.

Mátia mews as I roll over. I murmur an apology, stroking his head as I focus on the voice outside. Relief floods me, because it's Hermes. He's shouting at ... I can't tell. That voice is quiet, or at least far softer than his angry one.

I ache everywhere. A glance down shows me multiple bandages on my arms, more on my leg. The ankle that had failed me yesterday is wrapped. I lean back against the pillows, clutching the sheets.

Athena had attacked me yesterday. She still hates me. She wants to turn me back into a beast.

All of the tears I'd held back yesterday leak out as I muffle my sobs against my pillow. Mátia nudges my hand with his cool nose, licking the skin with his rough tongue, and it only makes me cry harder. I knew this was all too good to be true.

The door opens, and I frantically try to wipe away the mess on my face. "Dusa? Are you awake?" And then Hermes is with me, pulling me gently into his arms, and I just can't manage to keep the sobs silent anymore. They burst out of me, filling the room. He holds me close, rocking and saying soft things I can't discern through my hysterics, kissing my face over and over again. But it only serves to make me feel worse. Because this, here? This man I love? He will be gone just as soon as Athena fulfills her promise to me.

Because she's sworn to put me somewhere where he'll never find me.

I don't know how long I cry. Long enough until dry heaves wrack my body. He doesn't leave, doesn't move from where he is, and it only hurts all the more. I love him; it's taken me years to finally understand that, and he will soon be lost to me just as surely as the bit of life I've just reclaimed.

It isn't until the dry heaves stop that I finally hear the things he's telling me. He loves me, he says. He's so sorry he wasn't there yesterday when Athena got to me. He feels like he's failed me. He swears it won't happen again. He's so sorry. He loves me. Athena will pay for what she's done. He's disavowed her; she is no longer one he calls sister. He loves me. Do I hear him? He loves me. He'll do whatever it takes to keep me safe, no matter what. Hades will be conferring with Zeus this very afternoon to rein Athena in. He loves me.

I hiccup the last bits of hysteria out and blessedly fall silent. I'm exhausted, and not in a good way.

"Will you tell me what she said?" His thumb grazes across my cheek, wiping stray tears away. "I got some of it from Dite, but ..." I feel his Adam's apple bob as he swallows hard. "Please, love. Tell me what she said to you."

I stare out at the window. I'm hollow again. It's a feeling so familiar to me that it's almost comforting. My words are hollow, too, when I tell him, "She's going to make sure I'm better hidden next time."

"There will be no next time." He presses kisses against the top of my head, tension tightening the muscles in his body. "I swear I will do whatever it takes to keep you safe. You will never—"

"You can't make that promise." It's a gray day outside, hardly any sun streaking down on the grove outside my window.

He cups my face in one of his hands, but I can't look up at him. Not yet. "I can. I vow to you now that you will never be cursed again. Do you hear me, love? *Never*."

I let him think this. I don't want him unnecessarily blaming himself, not when none of this is his problem.

I think back to the night Poseidon raped me. Was there something I did to entice him? Lead him on? I think not, but ... he could have had anybody. Why me? And why there? And why did it enrage Athena so much that, over two thousand years later, she's still convinced I haven't served my punishment?

I don't leave my room again for the rest of the day. Hermes stays with me despite his phone ringing with requests from his father, making me remorseful for keeping him from his duties.

I might as well still be on Gorgóna for all the good my so-called freedom has done for me.

"Don't be silly," I tell Persephone. She's hovering next to the couch I'm lounging on. "Why would you cancel the party? You've been planning it for months."

"It doesn't feel right to celebrate after what's happened." She sits next to me, making sure she keeps clear of my sprained ankle. It's healing quickly, though; I'm already able to put my full weight on it without collapsing. For all his smack talk, Telesphoros is a miracle worker.

Hermes is downstairs conferring with Hades. It's the first

time he's left since I woke up yesterday, and only because Talos is standing inside my room at the door.

I tear my gaze away from the Automaton and ask quietly, "Where is Kore?"

She scratches her upper arm and sighs. "In custody."

I sit up, startled. "What! Why?"

Persephone stands back up and paces the length of the room. "Hermes was right, you know. Kore ultimately could not be trusted. I beg your forgiveness on that end."

"What?" But Kore was always so kind. I just don't understand.

"That was one of her younger sisters' boutiques," Persephone says, floating back toward the couch. "While we knew her older sister works for Athena, we've only just learned so does a younger sister. Apparently, once you came into the store, the sister immediately contacted Athena. Kore stood by and said nothing. She had plenty of opportunity to tell someone about Athena's visit, but she didn't."

Poor Kore was so nervous in the boutique; she'd tried to get me to come home rather than go into the dressing room. "That's not true," I say quietly. And then I tell her about the failed stops and starts of Kore's attempts to warn me.

"And yet," the Queen of the Underworld says to me, "she could have told Talos or Aphrodite as soon as you went into the dressing room. Or the moment you walked into the store and she saw her sister. She did not. Darling, do not worry. Hades is ensuring that Kore will be properly punished for her betrayal."

I push myself up to a sitting position. "No—please. *No*."

She sits on the coffee table in front of me. "Medusa—"

But she doesn't understand. "As a person who has been punished by the gods, it's not something I would ever wish on my worst enemy. Please, do not harm her. I could not bear if she was hurt due to me."

Her pale eyes narrow in confusion.

"I do not blame Kore in the least. She was trapped. I beg you to have her released so she can come back and work here with me." I pray that they will keep her on staff, even when Athena has her way with me. I grab Persephone's hand. "Please."

She sighs and leans forward to kiss my forehead. "If this is your wish, I will respect it. I will talk to Hermes in the morning about it."

Relieved, I slide back down on the couch and fold my hands across my chest. "Also, please don't cancel the party. I couldn't bear it if you did that, either. Just because I'm up here, hobbling around, doesn't mean the rest of you can't have fun."

She sighs again. "If you insist, darling. Maybe you can come down if you feel up to it. Dite made sure your dress is pressed and waiting for you if you want it."

Her touch is too kind, too motherly. It hurts, knowing this goddess will be lost to me, soon, too. I turn away to stare out of the window. "I appreciate the offer, but I think I'll stay in and watch a movie."

She kisses me once more and heads downstairs to prepare for the party.

I end up having the same argument with Hermes an hour later. He doesn't want to go, preferring to stay with me, but I force him to promise to go for at least part of the time. *It's your uncle's birthday*, I tell him. *Your family will be here. Don't let me ruin your night.* He argues with me but caves in the end, just like his aunt did, although he draws the line at two hours of socializing.

"I'm planning on taking a long bath. You'll be bored stiff. Stay a few hours, drink some wine for me. While you're at it, give Dite a hug for me, too," I wheedle. My friend has not seen me since the boutique, but not from lack of trying. Apparently, the person Hermes had been shouting at in the hallway the morning before was none other than his favorite sister. In addition to blaming himself, he unfairly blames her for what happened to me. I tried to insist that it was not her fault, and that she saved me, but it was as if I was talking to the statues back on my island.

He pours himself a glass of bourbon from a decanter on a nearby bar. "Enough about parties and sisters. I've talked to my uncle, and if it's okay with you, we'll just stay here at the villa until we can find a place of our own."

I drop the remote control I'd just picked up, my eyes flying up to see if his mouth is indeed moving, and that he just said what I think he just did.

He recaps the decanter. "The security here is much tighter than my house," he continues, like he hasn't just dropped a bombshell. "Plus, you're already settled in, and I don't want to upset that right now. But he's vowed to help us find a place that meets the criteria I'm looking for as soon as possible, plus assign us a number of his Automatons when we're ready. I've never bothered with employing more than a few in the past, so it'll be nice to gain some of his."

I must look like a fool with my mouth wide open, but it cannot be helped. He's ... planning for our future when I know it to be ending so soon?

My shock must finally be noticeable, because he sets his drink down and comes to kneel down by my side, eyes more blue than green and filled with concern. "What's the matter? Is it your ankle? Do you need something for the pain? I can go—"

I grab his arm as he goes to get up. It takes a good second to piece together my hope. "You—you want to live with me?"

If I weren't so blown away by this, I would laugh at his obvious confusion. "Isn't that what we've been doing, love? Even if we haven't officially put a title on it yet?"

As I go over the last week—no, *weeks*—and realize, yes, outside of work, he's been here every day. Spent the night in my bed each evening, making love to me until I no longer knew my name or his, but ours. Woke up with me every morning, his naked body warm and tempting next to mine. I have not wanted it any other way. But he is a god, and I am not a goddess. He loves me, of this I have no doubt, but to break tradition and live with someone that is not of his kind?

Surprise flashes in his eyes, surprise and an unexpected hint of hurt. "If I have yet again been unclear about my intentions toward you, then I apologize." My hand is in his, and then his forehead lowers to press gently against my flesh. He stays that way for just a moment before brushing his mouth first across my knuckles and then, oh so sweetly, across my lips. "I love you. But if this is something you don't wish for ..."

Oh, for the love of— "Hermes." I pull him closer. "It is. Of course it is. It's just ... I am not a goddess."

"So?"

His sweetness cuts me to the bone. He doesn't understand. He's just always too generous, too much of a knight-in-shining-armor to get it. I try to explain, but I think I botch it, since it comes out as, "Dogs and cats can be friends, but do not live in the same doghouse. Or in other words, gods in the Assembly do not form long term romantic relationships with ex-monsters, even though I want nothing more than just this." I groan in embarrassment, knowing I'm not the most eloquent girl out there.

All of my gibberish leaves him with that exasperated sigh/laugh unique to him. "Where do you come up with this stuff? You could not be more ridiculous right now." Any protest of mine is swallowed and then scattered when he kisses me. My toes curl, my hands snake into his hair, and once more, the mere touch of his tongue against mine propels me high into the heavens. He kisses me slowly, heating me inside out until I'm panting. Kissing leads to touching, touching leads to my dress on the floor, and then his clothes. And finally, he's exactly where I need him to be: deep inside me, moving maddeningly slow as his tongue in my mouth matches these strokes. I hold onto him tightly, hips rising to meet his in perfect synchronicity, until my body swells and explodes in the bliss that only he's been able to bring to me. He follows moments later, and when he's breathing heavily, trailing kisses down my cheek, I revel is the comforting weight of his body against mine. He is still in me, and as always, I am reluctant to let him pull out just yet. I like this connection between us, this feeling that we are, despite all the odds, one.

"There is something you need to understand about the gods,"

he says softly in my ear. "I know you think us flighty and subject to whims of fancy, but the solid truth is, we are the most consistent creatures in the universe. I love you. Do you understand that? *I love you.* That is not going to change, not ever. When we finally fall in love, it's forever love. Even if you decide one day that you do not love me anymore, I will still always feel this way for you. I will let you go if it's what you desire, but Dusa ... please do not worry about whether or not our happiness together depends on what you think the Assembly might think. I can easily deal with them—I've had loads of practice over the years." He kisses me again, hot and slow. "I want to spend my life with you, if you'll let me." His tongue traces my jaw line; passion stirs in my belly once more. "I want to spend forever with you." He gently bites my earlobe; I moan softly. "I don't care if you are mortal, immortal, or a so-called ex-monster. I just want you."

I hate to say it, say anything, especially since his hand is sliding in between our bodies, down to where we are still joined, but I have to. "But, Athena—"

He cuts me off with another kiss, his fingers making contact with my pleasure point, and all of my argument goes flying out the windows. I gasp, arching into him, lost to anything but the newly swelling ecstasy his fingers bring about. His mouth lowers to close around my breast; I moan, bucking as he sucks greedily. I twist strands of his hair around my fingers, reveling in how I can feel his length harden in me. I squeeze tightly around it, needing him to move within me once more. He groans that delectable groan of his, and our bodies once more dance in perfect synchronicity.

Athena and her threats be damned. If he's willing to risk it, so am I.

"I'll be back in an hour, tops."

I laugh, straightening the collar of his green button down shirt. Apparently, when Aphrodite had bought my dress, she'd bought him a matching shirt and suit. He's criminally gorgeous in it, sleek and handsome, like he could be the world's most famous movie star. I pity all of the women downstairs, for the swoons they'll try to ward off when they see him, and for all the men who will realize they'll never be as desirable as he is. "Don't you dare. You promised me at least two."

"I did nothing of the sort."

I pat his cheek and press a quick kiss against his lips. Except, he's in no mood for anything quick, because his mouth reclaims mine for long, scorching minutes that threaten my already tentative balance until a knock sounds on the door. "I don't have to go," he whispers against my mouth. "I can stay right here with you and be perfectly content."

It's completely tempting, but I know how important his presence is there tonight. Anybody who's anybody in Olympus will be there, and he'll be expected since his close relationship with his uncle is well known. I reluctantly lean back and smooth the lapels of his smart black coat. I love that he has no tie on. "Go. Have fun. Believe it or not, I'm actually looking forward to that bath and then snuggling up with Mátia while we watch a movie. You need to hang out with your family."

"You say you want me to go, yet you tell me that?" He half-laughs, half-groans, dropping his forehead in the crook of my neck. "You must realize I'll have a very vivid image of you, naked and delectable in a bathtub, in my head for the rest of the evening now. Everybody will know what I'm thinking, because it will be hard to hide it."

I can feel what he means, pressing up against my belly. My own image of Hermes, naked in a bathtub with me, has me seriously reconsidering my urging for him to go to the party. I drop my hand and cup his hard length, eliciting another one of those delicious moans and a knee-knocking lick on my neck. "Maybe—"

The door swings open to reveal an atypically nervous Aphrodite, flanked by two Automatons. I drop my hand, my cheeks bursting into flame. Hermes sighs and glares at his sister.

"I was just—oh!" She turns pink—a lovely pink, unlike my own tomato red—when it's obvious what she just interrupted.

"Most people at least wait until the door is answered before inviting themselves in, Dite," he growls. "There's normally a reason people shut them, you know."

She blinks and then blushes harder, which would be amusing to see on the Goddess of Love if I weren't so embarrassed at her catching me feeling up her brother. "Nobody answered when I knocked. Just wanted to see if you were still coming downstairs, brother. People are asking for you."

There's a question in his eyes as he looks down at me. "I think I'm going to stay—"

"Yes." I nod, giving her an earnest smile while rubbing her brother's back. "He was just about to head on down."

Aphrodite drifts closer. She epitomizes all the legends about her tonight, with her hair perfectly styled yet sexy, her makeup and jewelry minimal (she has no need of it, obviously), and the dress she'd bought in Paris fitting like a glove. Wait. She's still wearing the python print dress? Invisible hands massage my heart. "I also wanted to see how you're doing, Medusa." She reaches in between us and hugs me tightly; the overpowering scent of roses nearly swallows me whole. I'm instantly transported back to my roses on Górgona, and of how those plants helped me get through life one day at a time. And here I am, smelling them on this goddess after she went and saved me from her own sister.

Life is funny that way.

"I'm so sorry, friend," she murmurs into my hair. "So very sorry I failed you."

Hermes is unhelpfully silent as he continues to glower at his sister, hands stuffed in his pants pockets. I love him, but he cannot think to blame her for this.

I squeeze her back before we let go. "What are you apologizing for? If anything, I ought to be thanking you for saving me."

She smooths a stray hair away from her cheek. "If I hadn't insisted we go to that particular boutique, none of this would have happened."

"How could you have known that one of Athena's girls worked there? Along with your godliness, do you guys also know every single person who works in Olympus and where? Because if not, Dite ... you need to stop feeling bad. The truth is, I was happy to be there. I've never gone shopping for clothes before in an actual store, so it was a treat. I'm genuinely disappointed I didn't get to pick the right pair of jeans."

"We'll go again. As soon as you want." There's that wide smile of hers again, and it's good to see it again. "In Paris even."

"You'll have to wait to take Dusa to Paris until after we go for the first time." Hermes' hand rests on my lower back. "I've been dying to take her for years."

Stars above, I love this man. He remembered all my chatter of Paris?

His sister smiles knowingly at us. "It's a deal then."

Chapter Seventeen

I'm in a scalding bubble bath a half hour later, eyes closed while relaxing to soft music flowing over the bathroom's built-in speakers. I let the heat sink into my muscles and then my bones until I'm a content blob of jelly. I've got so much to be thankful for right now, so very much. I've got my life back, real friends, the love of my best friend, and a loyal kitten. And, as uneasy as I am about Athena carrying out her promises, I'm choosing to look ahead at the life I get to build. For a long time, my life never felt like it was *mine*. Worse yet, I stole lives from others. These last few weeks, I've stopped trying to rectify that. I can't bring any of those brave, yet misguided, souls back. But there must be something I can do in their honor, to balance the karmic scales and ensure that their lives were not snuffed out too soon in vain. Maybe I can ask Hermes to help me get into my bank account, so I can start sending donations to my favorite charities again. Maybe there is charity work here in Olympus I can get involved in.

I wish I could talk to Mikkos about all of this. For all the wonderfulness I've embraced recently, it hurts more than I can articulate that I never got to see my old friend again. He died on vacation in Corinth, never to know the extent I valued his friend-ship, or how he saved my sanity more times than not. And as much as I appreciate my new friends, I also mourn the loss of the only other person, outside of Hermes, who stood by me when I was a pariah.

I wonder if his son buried him, gave him a place of respect and peace. While I know he's now roaming the Elysian Fields, I yearn to visit where his body lies in rest. I bet if I ask Hermes, he'll take me there. We could go there together and—

"Pardon the pun, but if this isn't a wet dream come to life."

My eyes startle open, only to find someone worse than Ath-ena sitting on the edge of the tub, inches away from where I lay.

Poseidon.

He's dressed in all black, eerily resembling one of the Au-tomatons. Except where they are all bunchy muscles, he is lean and sculpted, his hands laced together and dangling in between his knees like he's been here all along.

Like he belongs here.

I jerk upwards, water sloshing out of the tub and over his pants; but then, realizing how I'm naked and vulnerable to his piercing eyes, I immediately slide back down into the dying bub-bles. What is he doing here? How did he get in? There's absolute-ly no way he was invited. Hades claims he hasn't spoken to his brother, outside of Assembly meetings, in at least a decade—the Seas and the Underworld are not close, nor have they ever been. Plus, I happen to know there are two Automatons stationed out-side my door, and at least two-dozen patrolling the grounds to-night.

I grab a nearby washcloth and clutch it at my chest. "What—how—" But it's no good. He's got me over a barrel, and the bas-tard knows it. His smile, so unfairly genuine, grows as his bright blue eyes—so disconcertingly similar to Dite's—caress the length of my body, and then back up again to linger where the skimpy washcloth desperately tries to cover my breasts.

The urge to vomit nearly strangles me.

"Do you know," he says softly, his voice just as familiar to me in this moment as that horrible night so long ago, "that one of my greatest pleasures is reliving the day you became mine?" His fingers dip into the tub, swirling a path through the bubbles until they close in on my knees. I jerk away; more water sloshes out of the tub, but he acts like I'm not cringing at all.

His? *His*?

I scoot back in the tub, away from his fingers, not caring that the pressure of my foot against the porcelain edge as I push myself sends spikes of pain through me. But the pain is good, because I use it to snap, "I am not, and never have been, *yours*."

Genuine concern and hurt reflects back at me in his eyes. "Pretty girl, I've tried to give you time to get used to things. I gave you space. I indulged your whims by not making a scene when you were clearly brainwashed into staying here." He runs a wet hand over his face, sighing quietly as I gape in horror at how he comes across as so blatantly sincere in his beliefs. "But ... it's time to come away from this nonsense. I've missed you." When I cringe in the corner, he reaches out and traces his fingers across my bare, wet flesh.

Bile rises in my throat. My skin crawls. I am in a nightmare, I have to be, because there is no way this bastard is putting his hands on me again. And yet he is—he's here, I can feel him, and all I want to do is scream and throw up and beat him with my fists. I hiss, "Don't touch me." But his touch has shaken me. Shaken my words.

Shaken my confidence.

Because now my voice is tiny, just like it'd been when he'd raped me that rainy night so long ago.

"Sometimes," he says quietly, "I wonder how we got to this place." The corners of his mouth lift just a tiny bit. "Remember how easy it was between us in the beginning? How many hours we spent together, just ..." His fingers skim up past my knee, onto my thigh. My tremors turn into convulsions. "Talking," he continues, acting like he's oblivious to my disgust. "Being ourselves with one another. I've never been able to be just me before, not until you came along. Stars, am I grateful for stumbling across

163

you in my niece's temple."

He's crazy. Just ... *crazy*. He sounds so reasonable. So ... sad. Resigned. Like he's a victim just as much as the one he made me. I scoot further back, shuddering so hard water is sloshing everywhere.

"I'm more sorry than you could ever know about what Athena did to you."

He raped me, brutally tore away my innocence, and he's apologizing for *Athena*?

"Had I known ..." He swallows hard, his fingers travelling toward my upper thigh and it's close, too close and too familiar and too awful to even imagine them going any further. I jerk hard and slap them away.

Poseidon has the audacity to play wounded angel. "Medusa, you must believe—"

"Don't touch me," I gasp again.

He holds his hands up in surrender. "Okay, pretty girl," he says, voice deceptively soothing. I hate him for this, because I'm reminded of all the conversations we used to have with one another, the ones he just referenced, where he hid his true nature behind that of a kinder, gentler man with just such a voice. One that I might have fancied myself falling in love with at some point. And that thought revolts me. "There's all the time in the world to talk about the mistakes we've made once we leave Olympus."

Once we—*what?*

No, no, no, no, NO.

Not caring that his eyes are on me, that I'm naked, or that my ankle feels like it's been through a grinder, I launch myself out of the tub and toward the door. Talos' name is on the tip of my tongue, but strong arms wrap around me, pinning me to a hard chest. One hand comes up to cover my mouth, the other wraps around my waist. "Shh," he soothes into my ear. "It'll be okay, sweet girl. All you have to do is hear me out. Give this time. You'll see. It'll all work out. You'll remember in no time." And then he does something that sends me over the edge.

He kisses the skin right next to my ear, turning my stomach

over.

I kick against him, arms swinging. I'd give anything to be as adept as Aphrodite three days ago, to possess such a kick that sends gods sprawling, or a punch that could fell a tree. But I don't. I'm weak compared to the Lord of the Seas. All of my kicking and attempts at hitting does nothing but make him sigh.

"I'm sorry. I know I'm springing all this on you suddenly, but my brother has refused me access to you. I just ... Stars, pretty girl. I've missed you so much. To have you here in my arms again?" His deceptively soft words precede his tongue tracing the length of my ear. Bile surges once more in my throat, gagging me. How is it when Hermes does such a thing, my insides melt, and when Poseidon does it, my skin crawls in agony? "I've never been able to resist you. Not since the first moment I saw you. And now you're in my arms once more. You feel so good, so very, very good." His tongue dips behind my ear, and it's then I can feel his excitement press hard against my bare bottom.

Revulsion slams into me harder than his waves ever could. I bite his hand until I taste blood and kick as strongly as I can into one of his shins. Under normal circumstances, I think this would've at least made him stumble, but no—Poseidon merely grunts and somehow manages to readjust his hold on me.

And then he says something that steals all the fight out of me. "It's exactly as I feared. They've turned you against me, haven't they?" He's all sadness. "I didn't want to have to do this, but ... if you choose to keep fighting me in this moment, know I'll stop at nothing to destroy my nephew until he's nothing more than a memory to mortals and gods alike."

The bastard stabs me where it hurts the most. Tears flood my eyes, but I do as he asks.

"It's time to go, Medusa. My Automatons are waiting for us." He leans in closer, his breath hot against my neck. I shudder hard, but he doesn't seem to notice or, worse yet, care. Because his hand, the one that's been holding firm around my waist, drifts upward until it reaches just underneath my breasts.

I flat-out drown in terror. Athena's threats are nothing compared to this. *Nothing.*

Somehow, a miracle happens, because he doesn't grope me further. Instead, he whispers another bitterly sincere apology and then instructs me to dress quickly. To my horror, he's already laid out something for me to put on, something that he must have brought himself—matching all black, so we can blend into the night. My hands shake, and I drop the clothes repeatedly as I try to get them on, especially as I can physically feel his eyes caressing me; but in the end, none of this matters. I'm dressed as he wants me to.

The French doors leading out to my balcony are open; the soft white curtains flutter in the breeze. So that's how he got in. And apparently that's how he'll leave with me in tow. I can't believe this is happening. Just an hour ago, I had hope. A future. And now—now this sick bastard is going to take me back to the deep end of the sea so he can continue to drown me.

He takes hold of my arm, a deceptively gentle action, as he steers me toward the open doors, whispering reassurances the entire way. Each step brings a stronger sob. *This is happening. This is real.*

I'd rather die than go with him. I think about his threat and realize he only restricted me in that moment. Hermes could still be safe.

So I do what I have to do. I break out of his grasp, adrenaline spiking my bloodstream. And then I run as fast as I can until I reach the metal railing circling the balcony. "Medusa!" he shouts, stumbling after me. "What do you think you're doing? Medusa!"

I scramble up and then, without a backward look, I fling myself into the air. He screams behind me, my name, agony lacing every syllable, but I'm free as I hurtle toward the darkness below.

Away from him.

And that's what counts.

When I crash into the villa's surprisingly deep lagoon, my breath is smacked straight out of me. I sink straight to the bottom, supernova-filled blackness threatening to overwhelm me. But adrenaline is a powerful thing, because as much as I want to allow that blackness to take me, I also register another body crashing into the water, one much more adept at swimming than me. One that controls water like it's part of his own body. So I kick back up to the surface, gasping as I break free. And then I scream.

Hands grab at my ankles, but I manage to twist free long enough to drag myself to the side. I cry for help again, desperately trying to haul myself up onto the pavement, but this time, Poseidon manages to grab hold of my sprained ankle. He jerks me hard; my pleas are lost in the dark water. I kick desperately, making contact with what feels like his face. *Oh, thank you, Zeus!* My ankle is freed so I can barrel toward the surface.

Except, I go under once more the moment I surface as a strong wave rolls over me. One, then two more bodies crash into the lagoon with us. I claw at the surface, gasping for air, my feet thrashing in an effort to stay away from the fingers that keep grazing them. It's no good, though. No matter how hard I kick, no matter how much I try to push myself upwards, he manages to make repeated contact just long enough to keep me under. My air supply is rapidly dwindling.

I'm going to drown.

As terrified as I am, I'm somewhat comforted, too. Drowning is preferable to a life with Poseidon. It's bitterly ironic that I'd be dying in his element, but if the alternative is to give into him, I'll gladly take the irony. I won't go down without a fight, though; chances are that if I let myself sink, he'll manage to haul me back up. So I continue to struggle, letting more and more of my air bubble out of me.

Within seconds, it's all gone. The thrill of vicious victory suffuses me as I breathe in water. It floods my lungs, weighing me down.

And just as I think death has come to meet me at last, strong arms reach down into the pool and pull me up into fresh air.

Chapter Eighteen

I'm choking. More precisely, I'm vomiting up water and, well, vomit. I think Talos might be breaking some ribs as he hammers his sturdy hands down on my chest. He's also yelling something— the longest sentences I've ever heard him utter—in that language that seems prevalent in Olympus, but foreign to my ears.

In my waterlogged haze, I think: *I ought to rectify that.*

Out of the corners of my bleary, stinging eyes, I watch several Automatons hauling Poseidon out of the pool. He's shouting my name, begging me to reassure him I'm okay, but they've got him firmly by the arms. I jerk backwards at the sight of him, at the sight of desperation and heartbreak in his eyes, but Talos quits his yelling and chest pumping long enough to say, "Have no fear."

Easy for him to say.

He helps me up so I can bend over, expelling the rest of the water in my chest as he beats against my back. Poseidon fights against the Automatons, pleading over and over for me to answer him, and I dry heave into the grass. And then I hear Hades' voice, and then Hermes', thank the sweet stars above. As much as I want to stand up and throw myself into his arms, my legs totally give out on me, until I'm lying in vomit-soaked grass. No matter. He comes to me, anyway, his arms pulling me into his body as I shiver uncontrollably.

"Don't you touch her, Hermes!" Poseidon's words roar through the air, crashing over me until I feel like I'm in the lagoon, drowning again. "I will break every bone in your body if you do! You have no right!" Then, looking at me, "Medusa! Do not go with him, I'm begging you—please, sweet girl, just ... just let me explain!"

As if he hasn't heard a single threat Poseidon just issued, Hermes lifts me up in his arms as he stands; I throw my arms around his neck, grateful he's clutching me so closely. He doesn't say anything, just strides away from the scene as two of the three most powerful gods in all of Olympus shout at and threaten one another. He doesn't take us in, though; we skirt around the side, down a paved brick path buttressed with juniper trees, until we reach the kitchen entrance to the villa. A large driveway opens up to it; several cars, including Talos' limo, sit out in front. Caterers dart in and out, resplendent in their white chef's coats and hats, only to stop and stare when they catch sight of us. Hermes deftly sidesteps the gawkers until we come to a small, black sports car parked behind a catering van near the back. Still not saying anything, he gingerly sets me into the passenger seat, buckling my seatbelt for me and shutting the door before coming round to the driver's side. He flips the shade down; keys fall into his waiting hand. The car roars to life, and before I can blink, he's barreling down a driveway I've never been down before, and turning onto a street I've never seen.

As we head around a corner, he adjusts the heat and then grabs my hand and squeezes. I'm alternating between shaking hard and shivering, my teeth clattering in the quiet car. But his touch is calming, and gives me enough strength to squeeze back.

He does not let me go.

We drive in silence for over an hour before new city lights spread out before us. Are we still in Olympus? Over the weeks, I've never thought to ask how Olympus works, or where it is even located on a map, if it is indeed located on such a thing. From what I saw, it looked like any other modern city—well, except the population, of course, and the hints of Greek culture in the architectural styles of certain buildings. But here we are, moving into what appears to be another city, a very different looking one than Olympus, and I have no idea where we are. I don't bother asking Hermes, though. Every glance over at him shows me that he's trying desperately to keep himself in control.

It hurts to see him like this. It hurts more to know his pain and fury stem from what I've just gone through. He's hurting because *I'm* hurting.

After another half an hour of driving, Hermes turns into a residential area that reminds me in a small way of villages in fairy tales. Single story homes with moss covered, sharply steeped roofs covered are stacked next to each other with only small slivers of grass and riotous roses to separate them. He weaves in and out of the cobblestone streets in a maze, until we finally come to a nondescript-whitewashed brick house with lilies of the valley growing like wild in front of large windows. The door to the garage opens the moment he turns into the driveway and closes the second he turns off the car.

Where are we?

And yet, he still doesn't say anything. He gets out of the car and comes around to my side. I'm gently unbuckled and lifted out. A door located up a staircase over to the left of us opens, and standing there in the bright light is a short, stocky man. He steps to the side when Hermes and I pass, shutting and locking the door behind us.

"Is everything taken care of?" Hermes asks as he carries me through a small kitchen and into a hallway.

The middle-aged man trots around him and then jogs down the hallway until he gets to a closed door. "Yes, *minn hirra*."

I try to pinpoint his heavy accent—possibly Scandinavian in origin? I root through my catalogue of languages collected over the ages. *Minn hirra* ... hmm ... that's Old Norse for *my lord*, I think? I glance around us, but nothing on the walls indicates a particular culture one way or another.

He opens the door for us and stands to the side. Hermes sweeps past him and carefully sets me down on a bed pushed up against one wall and covered with a patchwork bedspread. He turns back toward the man and says, "Thank you, Amund. Please bring us some tea." He glances at me. "And soup?"

I swiftly shake my head. No food. Amund ... Amund. Yes. Definitely Norse.

He tells the man, "Never mind. I'll let you know if there's anything we need."

"Yes, *minn hirra*." Amund shuts the door; Hermes goes over and clicks the lock shut. Then he turns back toward me, the misery and fear in his bright blue eyes vividly piercing as they take me in. I don't need to ask him what he's thinking; it's plain as day on his dear face.

I don't need his apologies. He has nothing to apologize for. What I need, though, is him. I open up my arms, and he comes to me immediately, folding me up into him until I feel safe and the shudders lessen. Until I can breathe again.

"Medusa ... love ..." His words are gentle, tremulous, and yet are only masks for the rage I feel in his muscles. "Did he hurt you?"

"He ..." I swallow hard, my throat and lungs still sore from all the water they suffered from tonight. "Nothing like before. I swear."

Every muscle in his body tenses as he struggles to pull in calming breaths.

My skin still crawls with the lingering traces of Poseidon's influence, and I hate it. I lick my dry lips and glance around the room; another door sits to the side. "I need ..." A shaky hand pushes still damp hair out of my eyes. "I need to get him off me. I want him off me." Hysteria clamors back up my throat, sending me into another round of shaking. I wipe frantically at my arms, at my belly. "I—I need—"

It's all the encouragement he requires. He carries me over to the door, shoving it open with a foot. A quick flip of the switch reveals a small shower, toilet, and pedestal sink. I am relieved there is no tub.

"Do you want me to wait in the other room?" His question is soft as he turns the water on.

I shake my head. No. I don't want to be left alone right now. I'm too afraid that I'll let Poseidon isolate me once more. He did that before, and I'll be damned if I let him do it again.

Hermes is gentle as he helps me out of my damp clothes. I want to burn them; they are nothing more than reminders of Poseidon's insane claims of ownership. *He really believes he loves me.* I'm sick to my stomach once more. So when I step into the shower, I tug at my love until he undresses and follows. It's cramped, but I don't care.

I can't let Poseidon's touch stay on me a minute longer.

This is love. This man here? This is real love, not that sick, warped kind Poseidon thinks he has.

My legs quiver, my stomach twists in ugly knots, but I tell Hermes, "Kiss me."

Hermes' hand pauses midway in his reach for the soap; he stares down at me in concern. Am I acting crazy? Maybe. I don't know how others survive moments like this. I wish I did. I wish I knew what was appropriate. Maybe some of them withdraw into themselves. Maybe some need to be around people right away. Most probably don't jump right into sex after their attacker comes after them. But all I know is that I need the memory of that bastard's hands to be obliterated. He cannot be allowed any control or influence over my body. His love cannot be the one I hold onto.

My plea falls out of me, just as broken as I feel inside. "Hermes, please."

His hands cup my face as his mouth captures mine. His kiss is tender, like he's trying to heal me. I love him for that, but right now, it's not what I need. I need him to do more than help me heal. I need him to help me erase what's just happened. I reach up and lock a hand around his neck, my tongue diving deep into his mouth; the other hand goes down to stroke him until he's hard. It doesn't take long, since my kiss and touch ignite him just as fast as his does me. "Dusa," he whispers into my mouth, but no—no talk. Not now. Now has to be about new memories.

I'm using him; I know I am. But I can't help myself. I'll die if I don't wash this away.

I let go of him long enough to snake his hand down my body, in between my legs. He needs no further encouragement. I collapse back against the cool tile behind us, letting the hot water burn away at the horror of the evening. Soon, I'm gasping into his mouth, writhing against his hand, and letting the passion his lips and touch bring incinerate the lingering vestiges on water-wrinkled fingers against my skin. I dissolve in his arms, crying out his name—so glad it's his name that comes, and that it's born from true love, not hate. But before I come completely down, I wrap my arms around his shoulders and lift myself so I can twist my legs around his waist. "Dusa ..." he tries again, voice hoarse in the steam around us, but right now, I need him in me. He's hard—so hard it must be painful, so it doesn't take much convincing for him to adjust me until I slide right over his need.

My back hits the tile again; one leg slides down while he lifts the other up. I match him stroke for stroke, kiss for kiss, moan for moan until an orgasm swells once more inside me. And now it's my name falling from his mouth as he breaks apart in my arms, and I hold that close.

Poseidon will never, ever have the ability to do this to me.

I will never allow him to touch me again.

When I wake up in the morning, I'm in Hermes' arms. He's wide-awake, though, staring up at the ceiling. Dark smudges of exhaustion ring his eyes. Has he slept at all?

"Where are we?"

He presses a lingering kiss against my head. "Somewhere safe."

A knock sounds on the door. Hermes gets out of bed and pulls on his pants. "It's me, *minn hirra*," a deep voice calls through the door.

Hermes unlocks the door, opening it just far enough for me to see Amund standing there, wearing a stained white t-shirt with a chicken on it and cargo shorts, his greasy hair pulled back into a ponytail. "They're here."

Hermes nods and shuts the door. He leans his forehead against the wood for a long moment before turning back around to me. He says quietly, face and words devoid of any emotions, "Hades and Persephone have come to talk to us."

I draw my knees up to my chest so I can wrap my arms around them.

"I can assure you that they weren't followed."

It hadn't even been a concern. I have to clear my throat; it's scratchy and still raw from last night. "What do they want to talk about?"

His eyes close briefly, as if he's debating whether or not to tell me the truth. But then, he opens them—today, they're crystal blue, and sad, so sad—and says, "It's best we discuss this all together."

Alarm tightens my muscles as I pull my knees in tighter. The threats from last night rear their ugly heads. "Poseidon—he said—"

"Please, for the love of all that's good in the world, do not say that bastard's name." He's anguished as he comes back over to the bed. "Not right now. I need—I need to stay focused, and I can't do that if all I want to do is go rip him limb from limb." His hands are soothing on my arms, my back. "No matter what happens out there, Dusa, you must understand that I love you and that from this moment forward, you are safe. Trust me in this, love."

Another knock sounds just as I press a hand against his stubbled cheek. "Okay," I whisper, because I do trust him, even though the alarm in me intensifies.

Why does it feel like he's apologizing? Or, worse, saying goodbye?

He passes me his shirt from the night before, the one that was to match the dress Aphrodite bought me. I slip it on, fingers trembling as I button it up, glad that it's long enough to hang midway down my thighs. I refuse to put on the clothes from the night before.

We follow Amund down the hallway into a small living room that clearly stopped evolving in the 1970s. Orange shag carpet runs wall to paneled wall, and mustard yellow-brown couches covered in slick plastic litter the floor. Above an ancient television is a dusty mounted oil painting of a Viking longship resplendent with dragonheads. There, to the right, stand Hades and Persephone, still dressed in the same clothes they wore to the party the night before, looking just as exhausted as their nephew.

Persephone rushes me, enfolding me in her arms even as a still shirtless Hermes refuses to let my hand go. "Darling, I cannot begin to apologize enough for what happened last night. If we'd only—" She pulls away, shaking her head. Are her hands trembling? "Thank the stars that you're okay. I don't know what we would have done if you weren't so."

Amund turns and leaves the room. Hermes' grip on my hand turns viselike.

"Wife, you know our time is limited." Hades steps forward, putting an arm around her thin shoulders. To Hermes, he says, "It is as we discussed. "

I look up at Hermes. He's wooden. Expressionless. The only thing that tells me anything is wrong is his grip on my hand, like he's afraid I'll disappear. "What's going on? When did you have a discussion?"

Persephone begins to cry silently, further confusing me. Hades says quietly, "Medusa, my brother—"

"Don't," Hermes snaps. The rage so present in his eyes last night has returned with a vengeance.

"She deserves to know," Hades says, more gently now. "Nephew, I know this is a difficult time, and I would give anything to have this outcome different, but we cannot keep her in the dark about his intentions any further. You know this."

Hermes says nothing, staring right through his uncle like he isn't even there.

I'm instantly wary. "What are you talking about? What do I need to know?"

Hades wipes his brow, even though there is nothing there. "After last night's events, my brother has brought a petition to the Assembly stating that he has every right to you as he'd ..." I've never seen the Lord of the Underworld so troubled before. "He says he claimed you as his prior to the curse. Says now that the curse has been reversed, he has every right to ..." His dark eyes flick toward Hermes, standing still as one of my statues on Gorgóna. "He has this idiotic notion that you're to be his bride or ... lover." He coughs, bringing a clenched fist up to his mouth.

My heart sinks straight out of my chest, through my stomach, and onto the floor. This is ... what? *"What?!"*

"It is ridiculous, of course," Persephone quickly adds. "Everyone knows this. Nobody has listened to his ravings, but we cannot ignore them any further now that he's filed a formal petition. When one of the governing Assembly brings a petition, it must go through thorough debate and then judgment. Burden of proof must be brought forth from both sides. While that happens, we figured it best to get you out of town to where neither Poseidon nor Athena can find you." Her hands twist together.

I can't catch my breath. Sweet stars above, he thinks he'll *marry* me? "He's ..." It takes a moment to process her words. "Has he been saying this before last night?"

Hades coughs again, looking pointedly at Hermes.

"Tell *me*." I jab at my chest. "What has he been saying?"

Hades rubs at the spot between his eyes. "He mentioned it at the initial petition where we decided to reverse Athena's curse. Our brother told him that if he was serious, he'd have to file another petition, but that you were to be granted a grace period. We kept him at bay for the last few months, making sure you never heard about any of his insane ravings while we attempted to find loopholes in his claims."

My mind goes into overdrive. He'd been there at the restaurant that one night, arguing with Hades and Hephaestus after the limo pulled away. Athena had been there, too. Are they conspiring together? And there was that stupid rumor Kore had told me about, the one where gossip in Olympus had accused Hermes and Hades of stealing me from Poseidon. Fury rocks me to my core. "He does not own me. I am not a toy that can be passed from owner to owner." My words spit out of me. *"I am a person, and nobody owns me!"*

"Of course, darling," Persephone says as Hermes wraps an arm around my waist. "We know this. This is why we—"

"Why did nobody tell me?" I'm close to full-fledge shouting, but I don't care. Don't they hear what they're saying?

"Because he's a sick fuck," Hermes growls, "and there was never going to be a point in time in which I would allow him to follow through." I look up at him; he's shaking, he's so angry. "Telling you would have only upset you, and you've suffered enough at his hands."

I reach up and grab at my hair. "Why me? Why is he—" I can't even get it out, I'm so furious.

Hermes lays a hand against one cheek and tilts my face toward his. When he speaks, it's like he has to tear the words out. "Do you remember how I told you that, even if you fall out of love with me, I will always love you? That the gods, as fickle as mortals believe us to be, are actually very constant once our minds are made up? He ... he fell in love with you all those years ago. It doesn't matter to him how you feel, or how much time has passed. To him, you are the person he wants. The one he's *always* wanted. As sick as it sounds, he loves you."

This is *insane*. "Don't I have a say in this?"

"Of course you do," Persephone says, glancing quickly between both her husband and nephew. "But I hope you don't mind, we naturally assumed you were not interested in what he has to offer."

"Damn right I'm not!" Heat flushes up my neck as hopeless rage threatens to tear my chest open. "That ... that bastard—he ... he *raped* me. He ... last night—he ...!" Hysteria chokes the words right out of me. *"I would rather die that ever allow him to touch me again!"*

Hermes' arms circle me; between his shaking and my shuddering so hard, it's a wonder we're even upright. "He won't. I swear he won't. Medusa, I—I failed you yesterday, but I swear, I won't again. This is why it's best you leave Olympus."

Will he stop this nonsense about failing me? It's totally ridic—wait. *What's this about leaving?*

"I'm going to make sure he can't find you, and then I will do everything in my power to ensure the Assembly rules against him. When I am done, you will never have to fear him again."

The room around me spins. Wait. Hold on. This is going too fast. Wait.

"We will be fighting for you," Persephone is saying. "This is the best solution. But darling, time is running short. The Assembly is set to meet in two hours time. You must be long gone by then."

Are my feet even on the ground? I try to be rational; it's the only way I think I'll be able to get through the day. "Okay." I nod my head. Take a deep breath. "Okay. I'll pack a bag and get Mátia and—"

"There is no time to get him." Hades sounds sad as he tells me this. "Be rest assured he will be well taken care of, though. A bag has been brought for you."

They want me to leave behind Mátia? I blink once, twice, three times. "When do I leave?"

Hermes' lips drop to the top of my head and stay there. It's Hades who says, "Within minutes."

"It's for the best," Persephone says softly. "To this I swear."

Okay. Well, this isn't ideal, but ... "Where are we going?" My hands press against Hermes' bare chest.

Much like the night before, every muscle in his body tenses. Unease blooms in my belly.

"He cannot go with you," Hades tells me in a flat voice, and my world officially comes grinding to a halt as I step outside my body.

"None of us can," Persephone whispers.

They're sending me away without my cat, without my best

friend, without anybody I hold dear?

I try to pull away from Hermes, to see his face, but he won't let me. He holds on tighter, his chest now rising and falling rapidly. So I stare out accusingly at Persephone and Hades.

"An associate of mine will be taking you to an undisclosed location within the next ten minutes." The Lord of the Underworld assumes a business-like tone. "None of us in this room know where it will be; it will be best this way. If the Assembly petitions us for knowledge, we will not be able to disclose it, even under pain of punishment. You will be transferred from being under our protection to this person and those they choose to work with you."

I'm completely numb. Even my fury is gone. Here I am, hearing how my life is once more changing, and I can't dredge up a single emotion.

"There will be rules you will be expected to follow while you are in their care. Medusa, you will not be allowed to speak any of our names. Not a single one—not mine, not Peri's, especially not Hermes'. You will not speak your own name; a new one will be assigned to you, one we will not know. Names are like beacons to the gods; if you name us, we will be able to find you wherever you are. My brother will be able to locate you if you use any of these names; it does not need to be only his that is voiced." He pushes back the dark hair spilling onto his forehead. "There will be no communication between any of us and you, nor will there be any communication between us and your protectors, at least in relation to you. There will be no praying to the gods, silent or spoken."

I can't feel my feet. Not even Hermes' arms around me.

"We do not know how long you must stay in hiding. Obviously, the goal is to defeat my brother's petition, thereby paving your way back home, if it is what you so wish for then. However ..." He coughs into his fist, once more flicking his dark eyes toward Hermes. "However, if things do not go our way, if my brother somehow manages to sway the Assembly ... then we, of course, will do everything in our power to make sure that neither he nor Athena will have access to you again."

His meaning sinks in, slowly but surely. I will never see Hermes again. Or my cat. Or anybody I have grown to love. I don't even have Mikkos anymore. I have nobody.

I think I was better off cursed, on an island.

Amund comes into the room. "Five minutes out, *minn hirra*."

Hades thanks him. "Do you have any questions for us?"

I stare blankly, not really seeing them anymore. I try one more time. "Do I have a say in any of this?"

"Of course you do." The Queen of the Underworld is on the verge of tears again. It's funny how hers can come so easy, and mine are nowhere to be found. Why is that? I should be crying. Flat-out sobbing. But I'm not. I can't feel the fear I know I surely must have, the anger, the helplessness, or the desperation that must be constricting my lungs. "You can choose to come back to Olympus. It's just ... darling ..."

They cannot guarantee my safety. They thought they could, yet in the end, Athena and Poseidon found me, anyway. *Why me?* Why am I such a draw for these gods? I guess it doesn't really matter, though. I'm going to be sent to exile again.

"*Minn hirra* Hades?" Amund holds his hand over the base of his phone. "Border patrol says the Greek Seas is thirty minutes out. They tried to detain him, but it appears he's had help from within our Council."

"Fuck. **Ægir**, right?" Hades picks up a nearby vase and smashes it against the wall. I don't even flinch, not like Persephone does. Not like even Amund does. "Give me the damn phone. If they're looking for war, they've got it. Peri, say your goodbyes." He quickly presses a kiss against the top of my forehead and then storms out of the room.

"We love you so very much. Stay safe, stay safe," Persephone whispers, kissing my exposed cheek. She wraps her arms around both me and Hermes, as he's refused to let me go yet, squeezing hard and then hurrying out after her husband.

The heart of the man I love races in his chest below my ear. He expects me to just say goodbye? We've been—he's been my best friend for over two thousand years. And while it hasn't been until just recently that I've seen him every single day, there's never been an extended period of time when we haven't had access to one another.

And now ...

I may never see him again.

I want to rage, accuse him of giving up on me too easily, except I'm hollow. This isn't how it was supposed to be. Love conquers all, doesn't it? Being a good person, trying your best ... those should count. I've tried so hard over the years.

His strong hands once more cup my face, angling it so I look up at him. "I swore to you that I would do whatever it took to make sure you are safe. I will do anything to keep this promise. Even rip out my heart and send it with you. Because that's what I am doing today, Dusa. I am sending you away, and I am sending you with my heart, because I cannot stand the thought of you being punished one more second because of my family."

I'd say my own heart is breaking, only I can't feel that, either. Maybe he's already taken it out of my chest. "You don't want to come with me?"

"Of course I do. You think I like the idea of letting you go, that having no way to find you is easy?" He shoves one of my hands against his heart. "He would be able to find me. The Assembly has always had the ability to find one another; it's been a failsafe of our governing body. I cannot risk him getting to you. For as strong as I am, as influential as I am, I am not one of the Three. I cannot fight him alone, Dusa. None but the Three are alone a match for each other's strengths. I need my uncle, my aunt—I need my sister and her husband. I need us to outweigh any and all power he might amass in this fight." He kisses my forehead. "More importantly, I need you to continue to be strong."

I laugh quietly. Bitterly. "I am the weakest person alive, haven't you noticed? If you are no match for him, then I am nothing."

"In that you are wrong." He presses a kiss against the corner of my mouth. "He thinks you will kowtow to him immediately. He thought that last night. And yet, you fought back. You went against one of the Three's wishes and refused his demands. That's strength, love."

I look into his eyes. Stars above, I love his eyes. How can I live without them in my life? "He threatened to kill you."

This amuses him. "He can try."

How can he be so flippant? Doesn't he understand what his death would do to me? Somebody calls out his name. Oh, stars— our time is growing too short. I lick my dry lips. "Promise me something?"

Another kiss on the other corner of my mouth. "Anything."

"Stay at your uncle's." I swallow. "Take care of my ... *our* cat. Do not let that bastard hurt you. I'll never forgive you if you do."

Another kiss, a light brush across the center of my lips. "I will fight for us, Medusa. I will not give up. Please do not give up on yourself, either. Never forget that I love you. Never forget that you mean everything to me."

Amund comes in, carrying a small bag. "Andlát is here."

Andlát ... Andlát ... I cannot translate the word immediately.

Hermes kisses me: hot, desperate, and deep. I can taste his frustration, taste his love and pain, and somewhere in me, something finally breaks.

Our lips part far too soon for my likes. And then Hermes is walking me to the garage, where the small black sports car no longer resides. In its place is an empty room with oil-stained floors and a man with graying hair and a hawk-like nose.

Amund hands the man the bag, gives a respectful bow, and then leaves, shutting the door behind him.

"It is good to see you, old friend," the man tells Hermes. "Although I wish it was under different circumstances."

Hermes pulls me close. "She is my heart. Do you understand the consequences of failure?"

The man smiles patiently, as if this threat from a powerful god is nothing. "Of course."

Hermes holds out his hand; out of seemingly nowhere, the man pulls out a dagger and slashes my beloved's palm. Just as I'm about to shriek in horror, Hermes' other arm pulls me in tighter. "Do not worry," he whispers to me. "This is as expected."

The man smiles blandly and then cuts his own hand in the same spot. Within seconds, Hermes and the man press their palms together.

"It is done," the man says.

Hermes squeezes his hand shut; the blood and wound disappear. He gently tips my chin upward so our eyes meet. "I trust this man, Dusa. I've known him a long time. He will not fail you."

You're leaving me, is what I want to say.

Our foreheads touch. "I love you. Hold onto that. I did not wait two thousand years for your love only to lose it so easily."

And yet, you're letting me go, is what I want to say.

When we kiss for the final time, emotions roar to life within me. Overwhelming love fills me up and overflows into this dingy garage, filling up the hollow spaces carved out just minutes before.

Then he is gone, back through the door in which Amund first led us through. And the funny thing is, he calls me his heart, says he's sending his with me, but he just took mine out the door with him. I am left behind with the strange, composed man holding a bag and the key to my future.

"I am Death," he says calmly, smiling serenely. "But you may call me Jocko. It's best we hurry. I feel the Greek Sea's wrath, moving like a hurricane to dry shores in our direction. The Greek Messenger's benediction he just laid upon you will only act as a shield for so long through my portal to the afterlife. Our journey there will be brief; just long enough to get us to where I need us to go. Shall we?"

He holds his hand out, the one that now shares my beloved's blood. I stare at it in wonder. Hermes just blessed me?

"Come, child. Let us make haste."

The irony is not lost on me that I finally make Death's acquaintance just when I decide life is worth living.

jackson

Chapter Nineteen

"Wyoming?"

Jocko chuckles as I pan around. There are mountains and open spaces and trees and they look nothing like any I've ever seen in Greece or Olympus. "Why not? We're hundreds of miles away from the coast. I thought you'd appreciate that."

I'm apparently horrible with gratitude. "I do!" I quickly tell him, but he winks to let me know he isn't offended in the least. Which is good, because it would truly be further testament of my wretched luck if I were to get off on the wrong foot with Death so quickly. I add, "It makes a lot of sense." And it does.

"Jackson is a small town." He motions out of his car window. "Pretty touristy at times, but it's got everything you need to alleviate boredom, yet but also maintain anonymity."

I stare out the passenger window at the boutiques and cars. "It seems nice."

"One of my favorite places," Jocko tells me. "It's why I picked it. I love to ski, and the snow is prime here."

I unsuccessfully hold back a snort of disbelief. Death, a skier? Death as, well ... anything other than what I've long believed him to be?

"You should try it," he tells me, and I'm surprised to find he's absolutely serious. "Skiing's good for the soul. Or so I'm told. Can't verify that one for certain, as I'm soulless."

I already know the answer, but I ask anyway. "Does anyone know you've brought me here?"

The crinkles around his eyes soften. "No, child. My lack of soul is exactly why I was chosen to be your guardian. No god can find me unless I wish to be found."

I turn back toward my window and nod. The loneliness I'd been dreading finds me and pulls me under. The rest of the drive is done in silence as I languish in a vicious undertow of misery, until we arrive at a smart looking two-story log cabin. Jocko cuts the engine and pats the steering wheel. "This is yours to do with as you please, as is the house."

Mine. So different from the temple I inhabited for millennia, but in so many ways, it feels like a worse punishment. I am being unfair, I know this, but it can't be helped.

I don't get out of the car right away, even though Jocko does. I watch him head up the paved pathway, but refuse to look at the house much. Why should I? It's nothing more than a prison, my newest set of cells. Hate, loathsome and potent, threatens to suffocate me. Hate for Poseidon. Hate for what he's done to me, what he's taken. Hate for Athena. Hate that I ever could have worshipped her.

It's all too much. I don't know if I can take a step out of this car, because I just ... can't.

A short, plump, elderly woman steps out of the door onto the front porch and confers with Jocko for several minutes before I'm motioned to join them. It takes Jocko calling out my name two, three times before I manage to open the car door. I am a coward in the worst of ways. Getting out of this car means it's all true. I will have officially started a new life robbed of anyone I hold dear, even my cat.

How can I do it? How? Hermes wants me to be strong, but I don't feel strong enough to even get out of the car right now.

Jocko is at the car door, his hand outstretched. "You can do this, child," he tells me, and the weird thing is I want to cry, rail that I can't, but all I end up doing is placing my hand in his. He extracts me gently and leads me up to the woman, now leaning heavily on a cane. His hand still at my back, he says, "Bernadette, your ward."

"Ain't she a pretty thing?" the woman named Bernadette says. She's missing a tooth on the bottom row. "A face to tempt the gods indeed."

I hate my face. I hate that she lays a hand against it like it's precious. Like it's a gift I ought to be proud of. But it's not. My face, both ugly and beautiful, has brought me nothing but misery.

Jocko says nothing in correlation to this statement. Instead, he propels me through the front door into what appears to be a very comfortable sitting room. Once Bernadette shuts the door behind us, he asks, "Is everything prepared?"

"Got the paperwork just a bit ago from our contacts," the older woman tells him before lowering herself into a chair. "Wouldn't be surprised if you passed their car on the way here. Everything is clean. Untraceable."

Jocko steers me towards an overstuffed chair. My back is ramrod straight when I sit, my bottom at the very edge. "Excellent. It bears repeating that there can be no mistakes, Bernie. Your master has made it quite clear that the punishment for any failure to comply with his orders will be dealt with the swiftest and harshest of consequences."

Bernadette's eyes settle on me. They are so clouded that I can't help but wonder if she actually can see anything. "I'm not an idiot, you old fart. I know what's at stake. The question is, does this one?" She shoves her cane in my direction.

I thought it rhetorical, but as nothing else is said and expectant eyes fall on me, I tell them I most certainly do.

Jocko says in that bland, calm voice of his, "What name has been selected?"

Name? I blink and look up at him. I'd forgotten that they're even stripping my name away from me. I don't even get that.

Bernadette lifts herself out of the chair with some difficulty and limps to a nearby table. She picks up a manila folder and hands it to Jocko. "Madeline Gregorson."

One of Jocko's eyebrows goes up.

The older woman cracks the smallest of smiles as he sorts through the papers within. And, as hideous as the thought of going by anything other than my own name is, I can't help but let loose a tiny smile of my own. Madeline. Maddy. Meddy. Medusa. It wasn't too far apart, was it? And Gregorson is almost laughable in its similarities to Gorgon.

"I afforded her twenty-three years, based on your description," Bernadette is saying, "but I could nearly smack your skull, Jocko. The girl looks like she belongs in school. How old are you, child?"

"Two thousand—" I begin, but she waves her cane at me so closely I'm forced to retreat further in the chair.

"Lords, not that one. The age you held before this all went down. How old were you when it all went to pot?"

"The same—the very cusp of twenty-three."

Bernadette harrumphs and taps Jocko on the shoulder with the tip of her cane. "She'll be constantly asked for ID because nobody will believe she's twenty-three. What an inconvenience that'll be."

"I am sure she will be able to handle herself quite capably in any circumstance." He bats the cane away. "She's already shown such aptitude time and time again."

My eyes widen in surprise. He thinks me capable? What a joke. Much to my everlasting chagrin, I am the most helpless train wreck alive.

"Child," he says calmly, as if he can hear the words in my mind, "there are few who have survived what you have and come out the other end intact. And yet, here you are." He smiles; it's not a fantastic smile, nor is it hideous. It's just a plain smile for his plain face.

Bernadette seems to agree with me, though. "Hmph. We'll see." Her milky eyes swing my direction. "None of this Bernadette bit for you, by the way. You're to call me Granny."

She's kidding, right?

Jocko keeps on smiling that nondescript smile of his. "It was decided you needed somebody with you. Somebody who could protect you when I am not around."

And *Bernadette* was chosen? An old, overweight woman who relies on a cane and has bad eyesight? "And this came from Ha—"

"You are not to say any of their names," Jocko snaps, cutting me off. I jerk back at the bite in his voice, so unlike any tone he's used before. But just as quickly as the anger comes, it fades to the one I've become familiar with. "Names are like beacons. Remember that, if you remember nothing else. And this particular request came from Bernie's mistress, who determined her to be a suitable guardian. If I am not mistaken, Bernie, your master has no idea about your placement with Madeline?"

She taps the side of her nose. "A lady's got to have her secrets."

I can't help but stare in mystified horror at Bernadette.

"Looks can be deceiving." Her cackle is so very witch-like. Plus, those eerie eyes pierce me just as easily as the gods' do. Can she actually even see? "Wouldn't you know that best?"

"Bernie," Jocko sighs, "we haven't time for that at the moment. I am needed across the globe shortly, and as we all know, mortality cannot wait. A few things bear repeating, old friend. Anything Madeline wishes for is to be accommodated,"—he glances down at me—"within reason, of course. It is up to her whether or not she chooses to work or goes to school. We've been instructed she be allowed to pursue whatever she likes locally, as long as we can ensure her safety in said endeavor." The manila folder is passed to me. "Details on your bank accounts are within, along with a driver's license, birth certificate, employment history, and notable particulars on your past."

I glance at the folder in my hands. It's not too thick, but big enough to hold an entire life history of somebody who never existed. Something akin to panic blooms in my lungs. "I ... I don't know how to drive."

I know it's a dumb thing to say, especially when Jocko and Bernadette trade looks steeped in exasperation. "You'll learn." Bernadette thumps her cane against the floor.

A clock chimes somewhere deep in the house; Jocko straightens his coat before laying a hand on my shoulder. "I must go now. An earthquake is set to strike in Southeast Asia and my presence is required. Due to my job, I will not be here at all times, but if you need me, I can come to you within seconds. Bernie here will show you how to contact me."

I trail him to the door, where he hands me the keys for the Range Rover outside. "Bernadette thought it best you had something sturdy, especially with the weather around here. Personally, I thought you could do with a bit of flash, but what do I know?"

"Not much," Bernadette says. She ducks under my arm and steps out onto the porch with Jocko. "There's a reason the mistress wants me here, and you and I both know it has nothing to do with my spellbinding personality. It's because I'm the best choice at keeping my granddaughter safe. And safe is not behind the wheel of some convertible hot rod better suited to cinema. Or," she adds, jabbing her cane forward, "somebody who has nothing to fear from Death."

She's apparently taken to the whole grandmother bit quickly.

One of Jocko's thin, gray eyebrows lifts in amusement. "Madeline certainly has nothing to fear from me, old friend."

"Not with me here, she doesn't. Be gone with you, lovely—as you found fit to point out, your presence is required elsewhere." Bernadette's face is soft despite her hard tone.

As for me, I don't say much at all. The panic in my lungs expands to the whole of my chest. Jocko, the last link I have to ... to anything, fades from sight as he walks down the front path.

"Might as well come on in and get acquainted with your new home," Bernadette calls out, already back in the house. "Don't want to leave the door open too long. My bones get chilled more often than not, nowadays."

I close the door behind me. I consider about what I know

about Wyoming. "And yet you are now somewhere where snow piles up."

She cackles. "True enough, that." Her cane juts out at me, but thankfully, I'm a good fifteen feet away. I'll need to remember to always keep at a distance if I want to stay away from that thing. "You want something to drink?" She doesn't wait for me to answer; instead, she shuffles further into the house, leaving me no option other than to follow. "Didn't know what you were into, so I made sure to stock up on a little of everything. Got us some coffee, tea, lemonade, both flat and still water, wine, hard liquor ..." Her head tilts toward me, those bizarre eyes narrowed. "Well? Speak up, child. What's your poison?"

There's a generous wine cabinet here in the kitchen behind Bernadette, alongside a built in hutch populated with various sized glasses and decanters filled with different colored liquids. I can't help but flash back to the last time alcohol passed my lips, of the night Hermes and I lounged next to Hades' fountain, drinking champagne and making love for the first time. How his kisses felt while his body moved inside mine, and how that magical experience was headier than any drink ever could be. Even now, I can taste him on my lips, hours after our last kiss—a kiss broken apart all too soon because of Poseidon.

"Goodness, child! I had no idea asking for a drink preference would be so traumatizing," Bernadette says, and she's right in front of me, concern etched all over her worn face. And I am crying, and it's so strange that I am and not knowing exactly when it started.

She doesn't hug me, though. Instead, she pulls down a bottle of whiskey and gets to work filling a pair of shot glasses. Hers is held high when she says, "To freedom."

I clink mine to hers. Funny how freedom can burn in your throat and taste like prison.

My bedroom could be taken directly from a designer magazine

layout. It's the master suite, which I initially balked at when Bernadette showed off her much smaller room down the hallway, but she brusquely reminded me that this is my house, and technically, she's a guest (although I should never get it in my head to order her out, because there would be literal Hell to pay). Enormous yet sparsely decorated, it has a very Parisian feel to it, in terms of fabrics and furniture. I love it, I truly do, but at the same time, I can't help but feel out of place in it.

Nothing of *mine* is here.

"Did you do this?" I ask Bernadette after she shows off the luxurious bathroom attached to my suite.

She's affronted. "Of course not. I hired designers. I was told you fancy Paris, so I thought I might bring some of it here to you."

My eyebrows lift. "You did this all in one day?"

"You'd be surprised what you can do when you have buckets of money to throw around, missy."

I pick up a small statue off of the dresser, the one thing in the room that looks remotely Greek. It stands out like an argyle sock amongst a sea of whites: a statue of myself, of when I was a monster. I wonder if I can get rid of it. "It's nice. Thanks."

"Well, that's good to hear, because they were warned that it better suit to your tastes or they'd get no money from me," Bernadette says. She taps the cane on the dresser. "Even if it's ridiculously French. Good gods, child. Why French?"

What if I never get to go with Hermes? I keep my voice light, even though I want to curl in a ball as I set the statue back down. "I don't know. I've just always wanted to go to Paris." I stare down at the hideous face, frozen in porcelain. Had my face looked like that? Was this what Hermes saw all those years?

Could he have truly fallen in love with such ugliness?

"You'll still be wanting that wish, as it won't be possible for some time, now." Her cane hovers near the statue. "This is from me, child. Don't go looking like those hoity-toity designers had the wherewithal to place this in your haven."

Haven? Does she really think I could ever view this place as my haven? I whirl around to face her. "You thought I would appreciate such a gift?"

"As a matter of fact, I do." At the incredulous look on my face, she clarifies, "Well, you will, at some point. This I know. We always must remember who we've been, child. It's just how things are."

"Easy for you to say," I spit. "You weren't a monster."

The milky orbs focus in my direction. "Some may disagree."

"Meaning?"

"Meaning I think you need a reminder, that's all."

I pick up the manila folder she'd laid down on the dresser when we'd first come into the room. "Funny, I was pretty sure you all wanted me to become somebody different. I wasn't even aware I had any say in the decision." I flip the folder open and tap on my new driver's license. "Madeline Gregorson wouldn't want that ugly thing in her beautiful, impeccably French themed room."

"I disagree."

I bark out a laugh. "How is that possible? As *Madeline*, I'm apt to know my own mind."

Her cane whips out and strikes my upper arm. I yelp and jump back, clutching my bicep. "You are most certainly not in the right frame of mind right now to know much of anything. You are scared and confused, and I will be patient with you to an extent, but know I will not coddle you simply because you want to feel sorry for the hand dealt to you. You think you are the only one to have life go in ways not imagined?"

Stars above, does my arm ache from where she struck me. "And you have?"

"I wouldn't be here had it not, would I?"

The numbness is finally thawing. "So you've been screwed over by the go—*them*, too?"

"Listen to the mouth you have on you." She sits on my lilac colored bed. "I'd heard you've been good at languages and slang. Personally, I find such talk disgraceful."

I stare at her until I finally bark out a laugh. "Do you know who I am?"

"Are you addled in the brain? Obviously, I know who you are. I found a statue of you, didn't I?"

Anger seeps through the ice. "Do you know what they did to me?"

"I know that you're here with me right now," she snaps, "and not back where it was you were, possibly facing a worse future. So shut your mouth, missy, and be grateful for the gifts you've been given today."

I bite back my frustration. This isn't her fault; I shouldn't be taking out my anger on her. "I'm sorry. The room is lovely; I thank you for it."

Her cane swings out and clips me again. "Not those gifts, you daft girl!" She stands up and shakes her head. And with that, she exits the room far more gracefully than I would have suspected an elderly, plump woman reliant on a cane would be able to.

Chapter Twenty

Dear H,

Bernie brought me this journal this morning, saying she thought it would be therapeutic for me to write in. When I asked her why she would think that, she said that's what she heard girls do, which seems like a lousy reason to me. But who am I to disagree with the cane (more on that later)? So here I am, writing in this damn journal at the kitchen table while she makes me lunch and watches me like a hawk. If you ever get to meet Bernadette, do not be fooled by her eyes. She may appear blinder than my cat, but she's got better vision than anyone else I've ever met.

In all the years I fantasized about travelling, I never imagined Wyoming would be one of those places. I'll grudgingly admit it's beautiful here and the people so far kind. It's not crowded, which makes it easier to breathe when Bernie takes me to town. She's been trying to teach me to drive—I'm hopeless, I'll admit it—and she's got me helping with grocery shopping, trips to the post office, library, and out to lunch with friends of hers. In between her numerous lectures about how spoiled I am (AS IF, but arguing with her is pointless), she seems to think me diving into NORMAL life is exactly what I need right now. And NORMAL means shopping, doing chores around the house (which I tried to point out I always did anyway, but that made no difference here or there), and cooking (another thing I already know how to do). Nevertheless, the point is, Bernie is not letting me hole up in my bedroom 24-7 like I want, so I can drown in how lost I feel lately. She's forcing me with that wicked cane of hers to get out and learn how to, and I quote, LIVE.

The only thing is, I'm not sure what I want to LIVE for. She says this is my chance to decide for myself—says that back at the villa, all I thought about was how I felt sorry for myself. I disagree with her, by the way. That at my old home (pre-villa), all I thought about was how I wished I were something different. But now, without any influences from your kind, she thinks I ought to focus on me.

I got mad at her for saying these things. Who does she think she is, telling me what I've thought and done? But then I got to considering it (while I was at lunch with her network of elderly friends—sorry, even though I am far older than they are, I just felt like I couldn't relate to tooth problems, brittle bones, and adult diapers yet), and maybe she does have a point. For a long time, I hated what I was, what I did, and what I allowed to happen to me. So here I am, fourteen days in, and I've decided that maybe I do need to find out WHO I AM and WHAT I WANT. And it's probably the scariest thing I've ever decided to do.

After Bernie demanded I get my butt off the couch and do something other than eat ice cream while watching sappy movies that left me ugly crying, the first thing I decided to do was sign up for a self-defense class. It was ridiculous; I knew it was ridiculous. Even Hermes told me he was no physical match for Poseidon, but there was no way I was ever going to be left in a position again where somebody could grab me and leave me dangling and flailing. I was going to follow Aphrodite's lead and learn a proper roundhouse kick. At the very least, I could stand my ground with Athena (although, that was questionable, too, considering she is a goddess and I am ... well, whatever an ex-monster is). But the point was, Bernie was right. I'm done with being the gods' toy. It was past time to take control of my own destiny.

Bernie seemed to approve of this choice, despite a well-placed comment over how it shouldn't have taken me two weeks to arrive at a decision a four-year-old could've made in minutes. Fourteen days into our new relationship, I already knew better than to let such words get to me. The day Bernadette heaps praise on a person without a pointed comment first is the day the apocalypse is upon us. Snappy comments aside, all that mattered was that she helped me pick a martial arts studio in town, and faithfully drove me to it for the private. Initially, I considered joining a class, but even ten people seemed overwhelming. One-on-one was much more doable.

"Baby steps," I tried to rationalize to Bernie.

"Hmph," alongside a slight sneer was her answer. Yet, she sat in the back of the dojo, watching my instructor (a woman of about forty named SanDee, who I came to realize doesn't know how to frown or lower her voice below a chipper shout) carefully mold my body for sixty minutes a day. And then Bernie watched me practice at home for hours afterwards and on the days in between. I'd call her my cheerleader, except I know that would earn me a whack on the thigh with her cane.

A week after I begin lessons, she orders me a punching bag, gloves, and mats. I continue to journal, writing letter after letter to Hermes that he may never see. A week after that, she helps me strip one of the spare bedrooms so I can create a mini-gym. Three days after my gym takes shape, and I tell her I need to build up my endurance, she orders me a treadmill. "I'm not going to be running after you, missy," she tells me one afternoon as she knits in the rocking chair installed in the corner of the gym. I'm practicing my kicks and am going on my second hour. I'm achy but determined. I may not be able to control a lot in my life, but I can control my body. She adds, "Best to do it in here where I can watch you."

I let loose another kick, one that knocks the bag back several feet. Satisfied, I turn to face her, wiping my sweaty hair back from my face. "Maybe we can order you one of those scooters. You could scooter after me."

This does not amuse her, but before bed, she does it because I tell her I need to get outside and let the cool morning air sting my lungs. The sheer fact that I'm finally admitting I need to get out of the house and go somewhere other than the dojo and our normal stretch of errands seems to please her. We pay for rush shipping, and two days after we order it, her scooter arrives.

I start slow, jogging an hour the first day. My lungs burn, my sides sting, but Telesphoros would be proud. I breathe in and out, in and out, until all I hear while wearing my noise cancelling headphones are the sounds of my breath and of my heartbeat. My body slides into automatic: feet pounding the pavement, one in front of another, arms swinging, ponytail flying in a comforting rhythm. Each day after, I add five minutes to my time. I run, I kick, I punch, I practice. Every motion, every mile helps clear my head, helps me focus on being in the moment. Helps me maintain some kind of control over my life. Helps me not dwell on how I still haven't heard one word from Hermes. I try my best not to focus on how much I miss him during these times, even though I now write to him daily in my journal. But I can't stop the thoughts when I lay in bed at night, or the dreams I have of him each time I sleep. During the day, though, I'm able to force my body and mind to conform to the reassuring regulations of discipline.

Nearly a month and a half after my first martial arts class, I turn my body into a lean, clean fighting machine.

"How much money do I have?"

Bernie looks up from the stew she's cooking. "Hasn't anybody ever told you it's gauche to talk about money?"

I've just finished an hour of yoga out in the living room; during downward dog position, I had an epiphany. Or rather, I remembered something that used to be important, but seemed to fall by the wayside over the last few months. It's time I brought it back. I gather my sweaty hair and clip it up before I lean against the counter next to her. "Isn't that more applicable to talking about other people's money? I'm asking about my own. How much do I have?"

"Am I your banker?" Her milky eyes narrow. "Why are you asking about your funds? Planning on spending a bunch?"

"Actually," I tell her, sneaking a carrot off the cutting board, "yes. I am."

She swats at my hand. "What do you need now?

To balance my karmic scales. Nearly seventy people died because of me. I can't bring them back—oh, sweet heavens, how wonderful would it be if I could. I even asked Jocko about it recently, but he was firm in his response: nobody escapes death to return to the living, not if it was his or her time to leave. So I have red in my ledger, and I'm ready to literally pay my debts. "I want to make some donations."

She taps the wooden spoon on the edge of the pot and lays it down on the counter. "Hmph. It's about time you got your head out of your ass, missy."

I'm not insulted. Rather, something warm stirs inside me as I soak in her backhanded compliment. "I have a list of favorites that I haven't given to in several months. Think we can go to the bank and make some transfers tomorrow?"

She shuffles over to the cabinet where the plates and bowls are. "I suppose we can."

I turn toward the table to find Jocko sitting at it. I start, but at least I no longer drop the plates like I did the first dozen times he surprised me like this. "You are looking well, Maddy."

Bernie hands me another set of dishes. His sudden appearances and disappearances never bother her.

"Thanks. Any word from our mutual friends?"

It's the same question I ask him every day when I see him. And each time, the answer is the same—an enigmatic smile that tells me absolutely nothing. "It was a busy day. I had little time for meetings."

Of course he didn't. I bite back my frustration and set his

plate in front of him. Nearly two months into my exile in Wyo-ming, and I'm still in limbo. I can control my body, I can control my money, but I cannot control the outcome of a petition in front of the Assembly—if, of course, it hasn't already been decided.

If it has ...

Then this is no longer temporary exile. This is it. This is my life.

"I'm glad you're keeping yourself busy, Maddy. I must admit, I was a bit worried early on when Bernadette informed me you spent much time lamenting your situation, but it appears you've turned a corner." Jocko drapes the napkin on his lap, his flat eyes challenging me to contradict his assessment.

Which I won't. Complaining does me no good. It never has, especially to Death.

Bernie passes me his bowl of stew so I can set it in front of him. "I am worried that you have isolated yourself, though. You ought to be out making friends. Exploring your options."

Friends. All of my friends have been taken from me. My best friend ... I took a chance, a leap of faith, and I allowed myself to fall in love with him. And now he's back in Olympus, and I'm here, and the distance between us is greater than any sea Poseidon could create. "I'm doing great!" I force myself to sound happy. "Granny and I get out of the house everyday, I'll have you know."

"You go grocery shopping," he says dryly. "That is hardly what I mean."

I pour him a glass of wine. "I go to the dojo, too." I snap my fingers. "We also go to lunch with friends several times a week!"

He gives Bernadette a rueful smile. She shrugs. To me, he says, "What about friends your own age?"

I pour Bernie a glass, then one for myself. "Well, if you point me in the vicinity of the multiple millennials, I will be more than happy to introduce myself."

He sighs. "Maddy ..."

It's my turn to give him a look that serves as a challenge.

"I am simply saying that it might be healthy for you to go out and meet like-minded people. Join some clubs. Volunteer. Perhaps seek out some support groups. Go out to dinner, the movies—"

"Like a date?" I hate that I've snapped at him, but *really*. "Are you saying you want me to go find ..." I'm furious. "Some *person* and go on a stereotypical *date*?"

He merely stares at me with that mild look that could either be supportive or disapproving. I glare back. And then I glare at Bernie. She's radically unapologetic, like always.

My fingers clench around the wine glass stem. "Do you know something I don't know?"

Bernie reaches out her hand toward me, but I jerk out of her reach. "Maddy—"

"Do you guys know something? Was there a ruling?"
Silence.

My breath catches in my throat. "There was, wasn't there?"
More silence.

Is the room spinning? "Did ... did he win?"

Bernie says in an uncharacteristically soft voice, "Maddy, we—"

I stand up; wine sloshes out of my glass. "I'm going for a run." I'm at the door when Bernie unhelpfully points out it's dark outside.

I let the door slam behind me. Neither follows for once.

Bernadette is sitting on my bed when I come back an hour and a half later. It's my second run of the day, so my muscles are burning. All I want to do is soak in the shower, but here she is, clearly wanting to have a discussion. I bypass her to head straight to my closet. "Save it."

Her cane thumps against the bed.

It isn't like I haven't thought about what Poseidon's victory would mean a thousand times already. During tonight's run, it was no different. As much as I tried to push the thoughts out and onto the tarmac below me, I couldn't. *I'll never see Hermes again* became the ultimate in earworms.

It became hard to breathe. It's still hard to breathe.

"Child ..."

I yank my pajamas off a hook. "I don't want to talk about this with you right now."

"Then shut your mouth and listen. I should not be saying this to you right now, but ..." She stands up and shuffles over to where I am. "I do not believe Jocko has heard one way or another about any kind of verdict."

Right.

"I don't know how much you know about Jocko and what he does. He is, how can I put this ... a free agent amongst the different ..." She waves her hands around, motioning to the sky. "He owes no allegiance to any group, which is why he was selected to be your guardian. That said, it is my understanding that once he accepted the deal certain,"—she waves her hand upwards again—"*people* made with him, he took those terms seriously. A breech of contract on either side could lead to serious consequences."

My anger fades into curiosity. This is the most I've heard about Jocko and what he does since ... well, ever. "What does that mean?"

"That I cannot tell you. The deal concerning you was struck between Jocko and a certain two ... friends. The terms were not made common knowledge. Now, child—if he is silent, if he does not answer your questions, it is because he is unable to. You should not make assumptions one way or another." She stands up and stretches her back. "You overreacted tonight, missy. Plus, Jocko does not understand a girl's angst. He left completely baffled as to why you were upset. He thought it might be indigestion, although he thought the stew delicious."

I sigh and slump back against my dresser. "I know. I'm sorry. It's just ..."

She waits patiently, her cane tapping on the hardwood floors.

"I'm trying." I laugh quietly. Stars above, I am a mess. I've tried so hard in the last few months to mold myself into something strong, but here I am, emotionally weak. "I lived by myself for thousands of years. I had all of one friend until the last fifty years. Then I made another—just one more, mind you. When I was changed back ..." I shake my head. "I was like a fish out of water. I still am. I'm trying, Granny. But right now, I've not only lost the two best friends I've ever had, but also the love of my life."

One of her hands comes up to gently pat my shoulder.

"It's stupid, right?" Tears blur my vision. "I have more important things to think about than just how much I miss him, right?"

"Love is never stupid."

I swipe at my eyes with the back of my hand. "I'm trying so hard to be in control. I just need ... I need to be in control of something in my life."

"You are, child." Her voice is surprisingly kind. "Do you not see this gift you were given? You could have had all your choices stripped away from you. But you are here instead. You have been given a second chance to do what you will with your life."

What must she think of me right now, falling apart after two month's worth of progress? "I know. I know. I'm being silly. I'm totally aware that I have an opportunity rarely afforded to others. It's ... it's just ..."

She surprises me for a second time tonight by stepping forward and wrapping her arms around me. I lean into her embrace—she smells strongly of floral perfume and, to a lesser extent, stew, but rather than be off-putting, it's reassuring. Maybe this is what a true grandmother might feel like: warm, accepting, and understanding.

My starved heart soaks in every second of being in her arms.

"It's just," she says, rubbing my back, "you know what true love feels like."

And that's the problem. Because I'm greedy—I want control, I want my second chance, and I want my love.

Chapter Twenty-One

There's a flyer on the dining room table—sherbet orange and rectangular, with black lettering. *Support Group*, it says. *Survivors of Rape and Sexual Assault*. An address is given along with dates and times already circled with blue ink; a building dedicated toward community safety located in Jackson proper houses the meeting. I stare at the single sheet of paper for a long time, at the picture below the capitalized words declaring a person's greatest shame: there are women there, and men, and they are looking up at me with flat mouths and expectant eyes.

It shakes me to my core. Did Bernie leave this here while I slept? Jocko?

I go running without Bernie, who, from what I can tell, is still slumbering. I had trouble sleeping last night and need my head cleared. But the more my feet pound the pavement, the less I'm able to ease into the lulling zone that running has afforded me these last couple months. I want silence in my head, but all I can hear is *survivors of rape and sexual assault*. Familiar yet unwanted frustration builds up in me—not only for my own situation, in which I was raped and then nearly kidnapped during a second assault that would have, no doubt, ended in yet another rape—but for the countless others who have also suffered similar fates. Women, men, children, old, young, straight, gay ... violence is not picky when it comes to its victims. And it's distressing, thinking of these other people, faceless yet dear to me. We are part of a group no sane person wants to join, and yet we are members anyway. We come from every walk of life, of every race and religion. There is no way to exit the group once we've joined; all we can do is try not to let it define us. I've tried to put two thousand years between me and what happened, yet it's still here. I lied to myself for ages, desperate to believe the lies, insisting I've moved on, and yet each time I remember that bastard's hands on me, his hand across my mouth as he pushed himself in me, my stomach turns to knots. I told myself it no longer mattered. I told myself, even as I fell in love and learned that sex could be wonderful and not painful, that if I just ignored it long enough, it would go away. Yet, time, the great official healer of ails, wasn't enough.

Hermes was right after all.

I need to be strong enough to finally confront what Poseidon did to me. Truly confront it and own that it happened to me. And then I have to be strong enough to finally move past it.

Bernie drops me off ten minutes early before the first meeting I'm not too cowardly to attend. I've missed two so far: two I swore to myself I'd go to, only to find myself in possession of a thousand and one excuses as to why I needed to do something else, instead. So here I am, in front of a nondescript house in the middle of a residential neighborhood, knots which would make sailors proud twisting in my stomach. I tighten my wrap-around sweater a bit more snugly, take a few deep breaths, and go inside.

About a dozen people are milling about in a room that features a ring of chairs and a table filled with donuts and coffee. Some people are talking quietly with one another; others are standing by themselves, playing on their phones. A few are even laughing, and I marvel at this simple yet powerful emotion in a room such as this.

These women—they were raped. They are here to talk about rape. And yet ... they are laughing.

It's not like I haven't laughed since Poseidon's attack. I've laughed plenty of times. And the weird thing is, I don't begrudge these women their precious laughter in this moment. I *envy* them it.

A slightly overweight, pretty woman comes in and claps her hands. She's got long brown hair and soft brown eyes and twin dimples on her cheeks that wink even when she isn't smiling. "Good morning, friends! Could everyone find a chair?"

I hover in the background until most the chairs are filled before selecting my own. The woman, a counselor named June, starts off by telling us, "When I was seventeen, I was date raped at a party at my best friend's house. The person who did this to me was my boyfriend at the time. We'd been fighting, and he put something in my drink. I woke up the next morning with blood in my underwear and no knowledge of what happened. I'd thought I just passed out. But a video went around school showing what he did to me while his friends taped it." She lifts up her arms, wrists out. Sharp white lines crisscross the inner skin. "Two weeks later, after a lot of teasing and finding the word 'whore' painted on my locker and my car, I tried to commit suicide. Thank God I failed."

There is a smattering of murmuring, alongside heads bobbing in understanding. I can't help but stare at her in wonder. So much pain, and yet ... here she is. Strong. Owning what happened to her. Refusing to let it define her.

One by one, people in the room open up with their stories. Some have been here before, some many times. Some are new like me. Every story is different, but end the same—they were raped: by friends, by boyfriends or girlfriends, by people they trusted. A few even mention strangers assaulting them. My heart cracks and breaks for every single brave person in here, but also swells at the signs of their strength. Some have attempted suicide. Some became outcasts either by choice or forced by a skewed society. Some have tried, like me, to pretend it didn't happen. Every person has a different story, a different path they've walked. But it happened all the same, and now they're here, taking the steps to move on.

I debate the entire time whether or not to share my story. It isn't required—June makes it quite clear we are free to speak when we are comfortable. Part of me wants to run and hide, but when the hour closes in on us, I decide I can't be merely treading water in the deep end any longer.

I begin the long journey of swimming toward shore.

"My name is Maddy." My palms are sweaty, my voice hoarse. My story is known, yes—but never from me. I don't talk about the details, but ... I think I finally need to. They can serve as my life jacket as I make my way home. "I was raped by someone I thought was my friend. After it happened, people ... they thought I was a monster. I became isolated. I stopped trusting others. A few months back, he ... the asshole who did this to me, he tried to do it again. And ... I'm tired of him having this power over my life."

Supportive murmuring breaks out, alongside the same understanding head bobbing I'd seen earlier.

I twist my hair back behind my ears. I take another deep breath, and then I let the air out slowly. The constriction on my lungs has eased a fraction.

"You need to keep some money," Bernie says, peering down at me as I type in an amount to donate to another charity. "Gotta live and all, child."

"From what I can tell," I say, squinting at the screen on my laptop, "I have enough money to run a small country." I click send and lean back. "Unless you expect us to build ourselves a mansion here in Jackson and hire the entire town to work as our staff, I hardly think we'll miss it."

She grumbles and sits down next to me. Bernie has no problem with me giving money to charity. I've even wheedled out of her several causes she found worthy of our funds. But the one I just wrote seven figures to is an important one, because it's the foundation June mentioned to us in the last group meeting. It's the one that helped her when she didn't think she had any other choices, the one that so many other people sought out in cries of desperation, looking for ways to understand what happened to them.

Seven figures seems like a lowball number, but for today, it'll do.

I've been going to the group now for over a month. We meet twice a week. There are plenty of days I say nothing. There have been a few in which I've broken down and cried while listening to others, cried when I unfolded more of my own story. But each day loosens those screws around my lungs.

I run. I kick. I punch. I listen. I write. I give.

I live.

Stars above, I *live*.

Chapter Twenty-Two

You'd think that my first trip out of Jackson since arriving four months ago would be a welcome event, but after joining a regular karate class that meets four days a week, plus picking up a few weekly volunteer shifts at the local animal shelter (stars, I miss Mátia, and this is the closest I can get to him), my days are starting to fill up. I've gotten to know some of the girls from the support group; we've gone out for coffee a few times. While I wouldn't classify them as friends yet, I'm enjoying the time we do spend together. I appreciate the people who work at the shelter—there's one guy, Frank, who always has the ability to make me laugh. SanDee teaches my new brown belt class at the dojo, and she's forcing me to break out of my shell and get to know some of the other students. I even got asked out on a date few times by a very persistent yet nice guy who I spar with. I told him no, naturally.

Bernie says this is progress.

There's been no news from Jocko one way or another about what's going on in Olympus. Outside of him regularly appearing and disappearing in front of me (and being, of course, Death), my life is now free of anything supernatural. No gods, no goddesses, no monsters except people whose hearts and actions deem them so. I have gotten used to the silence, even though a thread of unease still stitches itself throughout each day.

What I still haven't gotten used to is letting Hermes go. I've tried. The heavens above know I've tried. I keep telling myself, now that four months have passed, the chances of me seeing him again are slim to none. I was warned about this, after all. They told me that if the Assembly ruled in Poseidon's favor, they would ensure I was never seen again. Each day I wake up and remind myself of this, attempt to let the reality sink into my bones, but it's hard.

I miss him.

He is—*was*—my lover, yes. But for over two thousand years, he was also my best friend. And, in many ways, he is *still* my best friend. And I would give every single dime I have in the massive bank account he set up in my name for just one more day together.

But, with all the change I am slowly unfolding in my life, this is the one I cannot alter, no matter how much I wish differently. So I try to let him go, only to fail completely each time. Bernie tries talking to me about it, in her roundabout cryptic ways, but it doesn't help. Keeping myself busy does. Confronting and changing the things I can control does.

So when Jocko insists I come with him on one of his assignments, I shock everyone by not being overly thrilled. We'll be heading down into Salt Lake City, which is nearly a five-hour drive. This in itself isn't so bad; it's that I'll be doing it with just Jocko, the least chatty person I have ever met. Getting him to shoot the breeze is like yanking teeth out of a *Velociraptor*. It just ain't gonna happen without a fight. Plus, I'll admit I balked at the whole concept of the trip in general. Having been intimately acquainted with death in the past, I want little to do with it now. But here I am, sitting next to Jocko as we pull into a dimly lit parking garage.

A glance at the clock shows it is nearly two in the morning. Airplanes roar over our heads. I peer out the window, but I can see nothing other than cars and concrete.

"I'm glad to hear you've picked up an extra shift at the animal shelter," he tells me with that bland smile of his. "I've always wanted a dog."

The idea of Jocko with a dog makes me laugh out loud. "Seriously?"

"They seem like stellar companions. I suppose I am surprised you have not brought one home yet."

I twist my bottom lip to the side so I can bite the corner as I study him. Then I sigh. "I have a cat, you know." I look away. "Or had, I guess. He was blind and very sweet."

Jocko is silent as we wind up to the next level. When we pass the sign for Level 2, he says, "While I know you are thriving in your new environment, and it pleases me that you are making friends, Bernie tells me you are ... how shall I put it. Depressed at times?"

Oh, now he wants to address this? Months after he dumped me in the middle of Wyoming? "I'm fine," I tell him, but I refuse to meet his seeking eyes.

"I understand this has been hard in many ways for you—"

That's rich. "Oh, you do, do you?"

He's silent for a good ten seconds. "It could be worse, and you and I both know it."

I sigh. Could it? Sometimes I'm not so sure. Wait, that's not true. He's right. I'm making friends. I'm keeping myself busy. I'm finding ways to make myself and my money useful—and I *like* being useful. I like knowing I'm putting good into the world.

"You should know that a certain individual has remained ... quite focused on procuring that which he sees is rightfully his."

My head whips around so quickly, it's a surprise it doesn't snap right off. Jocko is finally telling me something?

"This has caused a great deal of dissension, naturally," he continues, as if this is a common enough conversation. "As your friend and protector, I cannot fail to tell you it is more important than ever to remain vigilant in our quest to assure your safety, if you disagree with this person's assessments."

I sputter out something that sounds suspiciously close to gibberish.

"Steps are constantly being taken to assure your well-being. It is not like you are the only to make sacrifices. If you were to know the words said, the deeds done in your name."

My heart skips in my chest. "Then tell me," I plead. "Tell me anything about—"

Jocko lays a hand on my arm moments before he pulls into a parking space. "I cannot. As much as I have grown fond of you, I am beholden to the vows I took when I agreed to be your protector. However, as Bernadette has been right to point out on numerous occasions, I have been negligent toward your feelings in this matter. For that, I apologize. I am ... not good at understanding such matters, Maddy. It is not in my nature. I have been solely focused on your safety. Bernie informs me that, while this has been well and good, perhaps I need to look after your emotional well-being, too. Thus, after much consideration, I have decided that I will present a peace offering to you tonight, as long as you agree to a few rules beforehand."

He offers me something in the parking garage of the Salt Lake City airport? I'm immediately dubious. "What kind of peace offering?"

"One to help answer questions, and hopefully soothe heart. But only you will be able to decide if those are the outcomes. Will you agree to my terms?"

I must admit, I'm intrigued. "Name them."

"You will be allowed to witness a series of events that normally go unnoticed," he tells me, his dark eyes flat yet probing. "It will be crucial for me to cloak you and place you at a distance where there is no chance of your discovery. Furthermore, by my hand, you will be silenced. It is imperative that you remain hidden to any and all sets of eyes here tonight, Maddy. All except mine."

The parking lot is dim and quiet. From my vantage point, the only eyes around are those within this car. "What are the terms?"

"There may come a point when you might try to find your voice or move from your location. It will only be natural for you to do so, even in multiple moments. If you were to do so, you would be uncovered. And I cannot have that, Maddy. You must give me your word that if I allow you to witness tonight's events, you will become one of the statues you used to create. There will be no movement, no sound, no anything that could give you away."

Something to soothe my heart ... in a garage, no less. From Death. Huh. I'll admit it. I'm intrigued enough to agree to his terms. Death binds me to my oath by cutting my hand with a scythe he pulls out of the back seat—it's embarrassing, but I jump when I see it—and smearing my blood on the blade. Within seconds, the blade cleans itself and is spotless once more. He passes me an old-fashioned handkerchief to wrap my hand in.

Too bad my hand doesn't heal as fast as Hermes' did.

Minutes later, we're out of the car and across the level. Jocko positions me into a sitting position on the ground next to a beige minivan. "This may sting," he tells me, and it does when he lays the flat edge of the scythe over my head. A veil of darkness drapes over me, heavy and sticky. It makes me tired, and my eyes fight to stay open. But open they remain, because if Jocko went to all this trouble to get me here, I know I have to see whatever it is he wants me to.

It feels like forever, but a man and a woman appear at the end of the row, suitcases in hand. They are talking softly to one another—arguing, by the looks of it, and completely oblivious to Jocko. The words grow progressively louder until they reach a small red compact; there, the words escalate until they become shouts. They are so wrapped up in these hateful, angry barbs that they do not notice another man quietly step out from behind a white van. I watch in perverse horror from behind the black veil as he approaches them, gun tucked in the back of his black jeans. A tattoo covers the side of his neck, one of a phoenix. Other than that, he is clean cut in a dress shirt with the sleeves rolled up and nice shoes.

"Excuse me," he says, and it has to be repeated until the couple ceases their argument. "Just got back from Chicago and found my tire flat. Can you believe it? Just my luck. Any chance you have a tire changing kit in your trunk?"

The woman tut-tuts sympathetically, glancing over at the van, which, sure enough, has a flat tire. Her companion is more leery until she encourages him to help. He digs a rolled, black package out of the back of his car, and the three of them head back towards the van.

"Never used it before myself," the kit owner says. "I sure hope you know how to change a tire, because I'll be of no help, unfortunately."

The woman smacks his arm lightly and laughs, as if this is delightful and they had not just been caught arguing viciously with one another. He grins sheepishly at her and passes the kit over to Phoenix.

Phoenix smiles and takes it. And then, so fast it stuns me, his gun is out, and threats are issued. There are tears, and pleading, and so many awful things that include useless bargaining, and my screams are voiceless when Phoenix shoots the man first, right between his eyes, and the woman second, twice in her chest. There is a silencer on his gun, and the sounds are small puffs of pushed air—loud enough for me to hear, but not strong enough that anyone on any other level might discover. Keys are removed from the dead man's pocket, and money and suitcases and a purse are checked before Phoenix drives off in the compact.

I am horrified. I am beyond horrified. I have killed many a person in my long life, and yet I have never witnessed such an act of vicious brutality face to face. I want to scream, to cry, to run over to these people and check on them, help them, but the veil is so heavy, so sticky, that any small motion from me burns like wildfire in my veins.

Silence, Jocko had made me swear with my blood. *Stillness*.

Jocko appears by their bodies, his long scythe at attention next to him. He looks down at their forms, so still and surprisingly free of massive bloodshed, with an expression that is nothing more than mild interest. There is no revulsion on his face, no distraught. I try to reason with myself; this is Death, and he has seen every kind of loss of life there is to experience. Me, though? I want to rail against the unfairness of it all. They were young.

217

They had futures. It's all gone now, and done so in a matter of seconds.

Jocko taps the scythe a few times on the ground, reminding me of the way Bernie wields her cane. Did she know this is what he wanted to show me tonight? And, stars above, did he really think *this* would make me feel better? What was his rationale? That I have it better off than these poor souls?

But then Jocko looks up from the bodies, down toward the end of the aisle past me, and smiles that bland smile of his, as if there weren't two people dead at his feet with bullets in their heads and chests. "Ah. Wasn't sure if you were going to make it."

I cannot turn to see whom he is talking to, but I don't need to, not when a voice so dear to me answers. "After receiving your strongly worded encouragement to personally ferry these souls? Tell me, old friend. What is it about tonight's deaths that require my presence?"

My heart slams hard in my chest. Hermes is here. *My Hermes is here.* Jocko didn't bring me here to see these poor people die. He brought me here so I could see Hermes. Elation I haven't felt in months surges through me.

"I haven't seen you in a while," Jocko says, and Hermes finally steps into view. He is everything I remember and even more. He is beautiful and so achingly familiar that my fingers yearn to reach out and touch him. But they are frozen, just like the rest of me, trapped behind this veil.

And now he's walking right past me. I have never wanted to scream so loudly in my entire existence. To make myself known, if even for the tiniest of seconds. Can he not sense me? "If I remember correctly," Hermes says, and it's done sharply, "that's been by your choice, not mine."

"Necessary due to circumstances, as I'm sure you'll agree." Jocko doesn't look bothered in the least to be chastised by one of the gods.

Hermes glances down at the bodies below their feet. I wish I could see his face, but his back is to me. Does he see that this loss deserves his compassion? Or does he have the same look of carefully cultivated disinterest Death has?

Please let it be compassion. Please let him be the man I know him to be.

"How are things?" Jocko asks. "Last I heard, you've been having a go at it."

"That's certainly a nice way to put it." Hermes shoves his hands into his pockets. "It's nothing I can't handle, though. I have some new leads I'm following."

Jocko's head inclines. "Of course."

Hermes nods at the bodies on the ground. "They were so young." And I rejoice that he sounds truly sad.

"In love, too," Jocko says.

Hermes squats down and pushes a strand of the woman's brown hair out of her face. Jocko adds, "Many of their last words to one another were done in anger. Pity, really."

"I cannot say for certain, but I have a feeling my uncle will judge them fairly, and they will find much time to rectify that." Hermes looks back up at Jocko. "I hate to do this to you, but I have a very busy schedule tonight—"

"Of course," Jocko says. "If you don't mind moving to the side, I will happily harvest their souls for you."

Hermes stands up and takes a few steps back. Jocko sticks out the scythe and angles it to his left; I can hear Hermes' amused sigh, but he shifts like he's asked to. And this finally gives me the chance to see his face. That face I love so much. The one I dream about every single night.

Jocko swings the scythe: once, twice. He cuts cleanly into each body; twin flashes of light follow. When I look to the bodies, I see nothing more than they were before—eyes wide open, bullet holes, marble skin. The only change is the woman's hair, now moved by my beloved's hand. I envy the dead, not for the first time in my life, and now not because they entered a stage in their existences that I wished for, but for a different reason. I envy her what I am denied, and it's just a simple movement of a hand against hair and skin.

"Old friend," Hermes says quietly, and I have to strain to hear his voice. "I ... I find myself ... I have to ask. You know I do."

My breath stills in my chest at the same time Jocko stills the shining blade. "By your own hand, I am sworn to silence. You know this."

"Yes, of course you are, and for that I am eternally grateful. But I still find that I cannot, in good conscience, leave without assuring myself that we are doing the right thing here."

Jocko inclines his head once more. "The gods always do what is right."

Hermes laughs at that and runs a hand through his wonderfully messy hair. "Oh, if only that were the case." Then the laughter dies away, and he takes a step closer to Death. Eyes serious, he places a hand over his heart. And here, in this garage, there is a powerful god silently demanding—pleading—an answer.

Jocko nods. Just once.

Hermes' eyes close for the briefest of moments, his head tilted toward the ceiling. Then he holds out the other hand. "I owe you everything."

Jocko lays his blade in Hermes' outstretched palm, and the shining dissipates into the god's flesh. He straightens his staff, the blade now dull. "Is there anything else, sir?"

Hermes drops his hand to his side. "Tell her, will you? That every thought ..." He shakes his head and laughs, rueful and embarrassed. "I'm a mess, aren't I? Like some kind of green lad who didn't know better. If only I was more like the way they say I am."

"If you were, you wouldn't be the one she loves," Jocko tells him.

A smile so gorgeous, so bright it nearly blinds me through the dark veil, breaks out across his face. "Then I am fortunate to be as I am and will never wish to be different again." He closes his fist and turns toward where he first arrived. Just before the rush of wings beat in the air, he calls out, "I will wish, however, that someday you will experience love for yourself. Love makes every misery, every struggle, every moment of life worth it."

I am crying when Jocko removes the veil. They're tears of happiness, though, because he was right. Despite how bittersweet this moment is, my heart, still aching, is indeed soothed.

Chapter Twenty-Three

"Did you clean out the cages in the back?"

I put a broom and dustpan into the closet and turn around. "Yep. I also hit up the kennels on the east side. The poor beagle out there is having a rough go of it lately, by the way."

Frank, the supervisor I work under at the local no-kill animal shelter, grins and pats my back. "You are a godsend, Maddy." If only he knew, I can't help but think. "Do you have a minute we can talk?"

I follow him back to his office and sit down on a worn chair. He sits on the edge of a desk that must have been built thirty years ago; unlike certain pieces that age well, this desk is in its death throes, kept together by duct tape and love. "The board of directors have been discussing shuffling some funds around here at the shelter so they can hire you on part-time. Everybody's been impressed with your work ethic over the last few months. What say you? Would you be interested in the job?"

I've been in Jackson half a year now, a number of those months spent working for free at this shelter. I glance around Frank's office, at the peeling paint, stained carpet, and dented file cabinet in the corner. It's not a hard decision. "I thank you for the offer, but I'm going to have to decline." He goes to protest, so I hold up my hand. "That said, I'd love to continue volunteering for you as I have in the past; if you need me to work more hours, I am more than happy to do that. I love it here."

I make myself a mental note to have Bernie cut us an anonymous check to the shelter immediately.

He squints at me in confusion. "Are you sure? You work so hard here. You deserve to get paid for it."

I also have more money than Midas in my bank account. Giving it away doesn't seem to lessen the numbers one bit; the next day, money reappears to replace it. Bernie has given up trying to rein my donations in; she's also in on finding good places for us to support on a daily basis. I've given to the shelter in the past, but not nearly enough—it shames me now. Tonight, at least seven figures will come their way.

"I work hard because I love it here," I assure him. "And you do pay me; what I get from these animals is priceless."

He sighs and then laughs. "All right, Maddy. We'll do it your way. But if you're willing to pick up an extra shift a week, we could really use the help."

"Of course." I stand up and hug him. Frank is a good man—a good father whose heart of gold does so much for the animals in this shelter and the community at large. I make another note to have new office furniture sent in, too. "I'm off now, though. Granny wants us to go see that new movie—the one with the robots fighting aliens?"

His eyes brighten. "Saw that one with my son just a few nights ago. It's good fun. Tell Bernie 'hi' for me."

"Will do." On my way out, I wave goodbye to the other volunteers, all of whom I'm slowly letting into my life. We talk—not just about superficial things, but *talk*. And while I'm still overwhelmed in large crowds at times, I've definitely begun to get used to them, too. At times, it's hard to believe that, a little over a year ago, I lived on a tiny island all by myself. Because now, here ... I am surrounded by life.

And it feels good.

"Ski season is coming," Bernie tells me as we walk out of the theatre, bellies full of popcorn and senses fully blown into overload from exploding robots.

"You've said that to me at least once a day for the last two weeks." I hook my arm through hers. "I think you must have been a ski bunny in the past. Be honest, Granny. Were you one of those girls on the slopes in a puffy sky blue jacket?"

"Hmph."

I laugh and take the car keys from her. "If it will make you happy, we can go skiing. I'll order us some season passes in the morning."

She stops at the passenger side of the Range Rover and hits the car with her cane. "I do not want to go skiing, missy. I want to sit in the comfortable lodge and drink some spiked cocoa while taking in some eye candy of fit men on the slopes."

I open her door for her, falling into giggles. "Well, by all means then. How can I deny you this? I will be more than happy to learn how to ski so you may have your share of eye candy."

She grunts as I help her into the car. "You've got a mouth on you, missy."

"You love me anyway."

She looks up at me just as I begin to shut the door. "That I do, child. That I do."

"Maddy. *Maddy.*"

I am not ready to wake up yet. I am currently on a balcony in Paris that oversees the Eiffel tower, and Hermes' mouth is doing something very wicked, but extremely welcome, on the back of my neck.

"Maddy. MADELINE."

I blink, jerking in my bed. Bernadette is standing in the darkness, the hall light filtering behind her. "You need to wake up. Jocko is downstairs; he needs to talk to you."

A bleary glance at my clock reveals it's four in the morning. "Can't this wait a few hours?"

"No, child. Hurry and meet us there." She leaves, but not before flicking on my overhead light. I dive right back under my covers, wondering how long it would take me to get back to Paris.

What can only be a cane thunders on a wall somewhere in the hallway. "MADELINE GREGORSON, YOU GET YOUR SCRAWNY BUTT DOWNSTAIRS IN THE NEXT FIVE MINUTES, DO YOU HEAR ME?"

Ugh. "Fine!" I throw the covers off and slide my feet into slippers. Then I grab my robe and trudge downstairs without bothering to comb my hair. I find Jocko and Bernie in the living room, both grave as they talk quietly to one another.

My heart leaps into my throat. "What ... has something happened? Did—they ruled, didn't they? On the petition?"

When Bernie turns toward me, all I see is fear. And that right there scares the crap out of me. "Maddy—"

"I am still not at liberty to discuss the situation with you, Maddy," Jocko says in that supremely flat voice of his. "However, I am under the opinion that we need to move you to a more secure location immediately."

Everything in the room ceases moving. They have ruled. Poseidon won. He won, and Jocko is going to hide me somewhere even more isolating that Jackson.

I swallow slowly, looking around me. This is my house. My home. The home I share with Bernadette. The one near my dojo, the animal shelter I work at, and my support group. The one near the town I've grown to love. *I am losing my home.* "Where?"

"I am still working that out." Jocko picks up the remote control for the flat screen hanging over the fireplace. "It will be somewhere inland, considering what's going on right now."

I stumble closer to where they're standing. "What's going on?"

He turns the television on and flips the channel until we hit a news outlet. To my horror, I watch as the newscaster talk about the unprecedented five storms barreling across three oceans toward terrified shores. Four of the storms have already hit hurricane strength winds. All five are expected to cause devastating damage. Governments are scrambling to respond, to get coastal areas ready for the storms' furies. Residents are urged to flee.

I reach out and grab Bernie. Five storms—FIVE—across three oceans.

"Jocko—" I struggle to find words to even convey the horror that's seeping into my reality. "Is this—is he—?"

"As I rarely interact with *him*," Jocko says calmly, "I cannot say for sure what set this off. But if I had to offer a guess, I would assume this is a sign of rage."

Rage, because the Assembly has ruled in his favor and he cannot find me? I stare at the television set in dismay. People are at risk. Not hundreds, not thousands, but *millions* of people are at risk from Poseidon's wrath.

"You need to go pack a bag," Bernie is saying. "Jocko must move you within the hour." One of her hands grips my arm. "Maddy, do you hear me?"

I turn toward her slowly. "Are you coming with me?"

She's silent. Jocko gives nothing away with his normal inscrutable expression.

So. Poseidon is threatening to kill countless mortals, wreak unimaginable havoc on the world's shores, and I am to go in hiding once more without even Bernadette? I turn back toward the television set. The news anchor is saying simultaneous hurricanes and tropical storms in the Pacific are unheard of. There are two more in the Atlantic and a typhoon in the Indian. The only ocean saved from any kind of maelstrom is the Artic, but even those waters, the weather forecasters warn, are in the midst of wicked storms.

Nobody knows what to think. They're blaming global warming, El Niño, La Niña—anything they can to explain the storms. Flights that crisscross the oceans have ceased. Cruises that had enough time to escape are docked; those who didn't are the subject of intense search and rescues. Fishing boats are disappearing at alarming rates, and in this country alone, the Coast Guard and Navy are exhausted from their unending missions.

Every second I watch the news track these storms, I am filled with horror. People are dying. Sea life is dying.

Poseidon is pissed off and is not afraid to let the world know about it.

I pull in a deep breath. I let it go slowly. I breathe just the way June tells me that I should when it becomes too hard to put one foot in front of the other and move on.

And then I tell these people who I've come to love so very deeply over the last half year, "I'm not going anywhere. If Poseidon wants me, he can come and get me. But nobody is dying today; not for me, at least."

And then I walk back up the stairs so I can change my clothes. Because when the Lord of the Seas comes to find me, I won't be in my pajamas.

"ARE YOU INSANE?" Bernie is slamming her cane around as I lean closer to the bathroom mirror. "HAVE YOU NOT HEARD A WORD WE'VE SAID TO YOU ALL THIS TIME? WHY WOULD YOU SAY HIS NAME?"

I finish touching up my mascara and get to work on pulling my hair into a ponytail. "I heard you." I offer her a wobbly smile. "In case you didn't notice, I purposely chose to say it."

"Why would you do that, Maddy?" I've never seen her so pissed. "You know he will be here at any moment!"

"Then it's best to let me finish getting dressed." I sidestep around her and slip on my boots. Jocko is in the doorway, saying nothing.

She hobbles after me. "I refuse to allow you to do this. You— you're not thinking clearly!"

I shrug into a sweater. "It is your prerogative to think that."

She whacks Jocko with her cane, but he still says nothing.

I scoot past him and head into the hallway. She follows behind, yelling at me, but my mind is made up. Nobody is dying today. These storms? I refuse to let me be the cost of any further deaths in this world. If I have to suffer so others can live, then so be it.

I won't lie. I'm scared shitless. But luckily, I'm digging deep and finding that strength I'd been cultivating for months. And it's a good thing, because when I jog down to the base of the stairs, the strong tang of saltwater hits me.

"Hello, pretty girl," Poseidon says. "I've been looking for you."

Chapter Twenty-Four

I'll give it to him—he's a looker. Black hair, now laced with so-phisticated, textured silver threads, haphazardly falls into his face in just the way that would drive most women crazy. A crisp white shirt, first few buttons undone, grazes over khaki linen shorts. His feet are bare and sandy, his skin bronzed. He looks like the epito-me of a beach bum.

I have never been so less attracted to a man in my entire life.

I pull air into my lungs and then slowly let it out. "Well," I say, grateful my voice is steady, "looks like you found me."

For once, the expression on his face is inscrutable. He mo-tions to the nearby couch, as if I'd just entered his house and he was trying to make me feel welcome. I skirt around the opposite side and sit on the end, right on the edge, my back locked straight. He sighs heavily, sitting down in a nearby chair. "Medusa, don't be like that. Please. Not after what I've gone through to finally find you."

Fury curls my fingers into fists. He has the audacity to talk about what *he's* been through? After everything he's ever put me and my loved ones through?

"Madeline, we are going to talk about—" Bernadette bursts into the room and then promptly shuts up as she sees who's sitting twenty feet away.

Poseidon's eyes narrow sharply. "Well, well. So this is where you've been hiding, Pemphredo."

Pemphredo? I jerk my eyes up toward the woman I've come to love as my real grandmother. Bernadette is ... *Pemphredo*? One of the Graeae, the three gray sisters who were accused of being witches?

A monster, like me?

"Fuck off," she hisses in a voice so terrifying that I reel back just as surely as I would had she directed those words at me. "Leave this house, never to return."

"Or what?" Poseidon leans forward in his chair. "Will you curse me, old woman?" He clucks his tongue. "No, I think not. Without your sisters, you are nothing. No wonder I didn't feel you when I came in. You're not even ..." His head turns thoughtfully to the side. "You're nothing now, are you?"

How *dare* he say those things about someone I love. "Don't talk about her like that. She is five thousands times the better person than you are."

The look he gives me is one of utmost hurt, like I've just betrayed him in the worst of ways by siding with Bernadette over him. "So, my brother forced you to hide with one of his neutered pets. What an incredibly amateurish move. I'm sorry you had to go slumming, pretty girl."

It's then Jocko steps into the room, instantly grabbing Poseidon's attention. He rises slowly from his chair. "Ah. I was mistaken." He wags his finger at me. "My brother is smarter than I thought. He sent you with Death." To Jocko, he says, "I'm curious, what did he promise you? You so rarely agree to intervene with any of us nowadays."

Jocko says nothing as he comes to stand behind me. Bernie joins him, her cane now held like a sword.

"Your services don't come cheap," Poseidon continues softly. "Nor do they come easily. In fact ... I can't think of the last time you agreed to purposely work with one of the gods." He's thoughtful for an unbearable moment. "No. Wait. It was ... you aided Hel and Anubis when they quarreled with my brother that one time ... when was it? Seven, eight thousand years back now?"

"As a matter of fact," Jocko says, his hand falling on my tense shoulder, "you are incorrect with your recollection of the situation with Anubis and Hel."

Poseidon reaches up and runs a hand through his dark hair. "I guess it doesn't really matter why. I have no quarrel with you, Death. I'm just here for my girl."

My hands are shaking. Everything in me screams to stand up and show off my new moves courtesy of my dojo. To snap kick him and send him sprawling. To lay a precise punch across his windpipe.

To hurt him like he's hurt me.

I am not his girl. But I swallow my rage and fear so I can pretend to say calmly, "If you stop your storms in the next five minutes, I will go with you willingly."

When Bernie shouts, "No!" a chunk of my heart breaks off.

This surprises the Lord of the Seas. Did he really think I'd just agree to go? "Medusa. Sweetheart. Don't be like this. Not after everything we've been through to finally be together."

I want to shout, *I'm not your sweetheart, asshole.* But I keep my mouth shut; I have to for him to agree to such terms.

"She will not be going with you," Bernie snarls. "She is under our protection, and you will not be—"

Poseidon's annoyance finally shows. "Honestly, Pemphredo. You need to butt out of what is not your business in the least."

"She is my granddaughter, so I'm making it my business," she hisses.

I didn't think I could love her anymore than I did five minutes before, and yet my heart grows even larger with these words.

"I don't want to hurt you," Poseidon says quietly. Evenly. Calmly. "But I will if you stand in the way of me and my happiness."

Even though Jocko says nothing, I notice he's clutching his

scythe in his other hand.

I stand up slowly. I take another of my cleansing breaths. And then I say, even though every inch of my body crawls at the very thought of it, "I will do ... *be* ... whoever you want, as long as you stop these storms and leave my family here alone."

His eyes widen. "Family?" He takes a step closer; now, we are only a few feet apart. "Ah, sweet girl. That my brother has you so brainwashed makes me sad. I am all the family you need. I'm all the family you've ever needed." He lifts his hand and touches my cheek gently.

I hate him. Loathe him. I pray I can keep the contents of my stomach down until we at least leave.

"Don't," Bernie says, grabbing my arm. "Don't do this Maddy. We will find a way—"

"But to let you know just how sincere I am with my intentions," Poseidon says to me, "I'm willing to make that promise for you." He moves toward the coffee table. "Let us strike this deal together. Another blood pact to bind us." He picks a bowl up off the table and smashes it until it is nothing but shards. One piece is selected and swiped across the palm of his hand. "Do you remember our first pact, Medusa?" He's smiling happily up at me, like his hand isn't dripping blood all over my floors, like he didn't brutally rape me against my will. "It was the blood from your virginity. You don't remember it, but I cut myself then, too. Bound our blood together."

I stare at him in horror. His blood ... in mine? I press a hand against my mouth.

"Don't," Bernie begs again. "Don't ... you will never—"

"Do not listen to her, pretty girl," Poseidon cajoles, his stormy blue eyes holding mine. A piece of ceramic is offered to me. "All you have to do is cut a line. Then I will stop the storms. I promise. Everyone will have their happily ever after."

"Don't," Jocko whispers from behind me. I should be spooked—when Death tells you it's a bad idea, that's a sign right there. I glance up at the television screen, still playing. People are terrified. *People will die.* And I will not be the reason, not any longer. My hand shaking, I reach out to take the shard.

But then the front door swings open, bringing with it strong winds. And there, standing in the frame, his hair askew and his breath coming out in hard burst, is Hermes.

"Don't," he says to me, his voice achingly familiar. "Dusa, do not bind yourself to him. Not before you hear what we have to say."

I am a statue, clutching a bloody shard in a living room filled with immortals. Hermes comes through my door, Hades directly on his heels.

Poseidon hisses upon seeing his brother; he reaches to grab me, but Jocko clamps down on my arms and drags me well out of the Lord of the Seas' reach. Bernie slaps the shard out of my hand, sending it skittering across the wooden floors.

I stare at it dumbly, marveling at how there is blood on my floor, much like that awful night Poseidon first tried to lay claim to me.

"You sonofabitch," Hades snarls. A black pitchfork appears in his hands. "You dare come here after the Assembly's decision?"

"The Assembly no longer speaks for me," Poseidon snarls right back.

Hermes sidesteps his uncles and darts around to where I am. Jocko lets go of me a split second before I slam into Hermes' arms. But I have no time to revel in this moment; a trident materializes in Poseidon's hands as he rounds on his brother.

"Get her out of here," Hades roars, and the house shakes in his fury.

Hermes tightens his grip and swings me around toward the kitchen entrance. But then, Poseidon says something I cannot ignore.

"Will you sentence the world to die, Medusa, just so you can go play house with Hermes? Have you forgotten our deal?"

A wave of responsibility crashes down over me. "I can't go,"

I tell Hermes. "I can't let him—"

"You will get my daughter out of this house right this minute, Hermes, or so help me, I will destroy you just as surely as I will my brother!" Hades shouts, rattling the house once more.

My entire reality shatters, just as surely as the windows around us, as one word comes at me a thousand miles per hour.

Daughter?

That voice of Hermes', the one I've dreamed about for months, says to me, "Love, I will explain everything, but we must—"

"NO." I skid to a halt right as we reach the kitchen door. "NO. I AM NOT GOING ANYWHERE UNTIL SOMEBODY TELLS ME WHAT IS GOING ON HERE."

In the confusion of my meltdown, Poseidon swings his trident at his brother; Hades barely manages to pull up his pitchfork in time to block the strike. The clang of metal against metal rocks the house so hard that pictures fall off the walls and lamps jolt off tables.

"You think you can disobey the Assembly, that you are above us?" Hades' voice fills the entire house. "You think, even if you had won, I would ever let you put your hands on my daughter again?"

My heart stops, jumps into my throat, and nearly suffocates me. He's once more called me his daughter.

Poseidon laughs, like the Lord of the Underworld's fury was merely a fly buzzing around his head. "What trick is this, brother? Your daughter? I knew you're fond of the girl, but—"

The pitchfork swings through the air, striking Poseidon so hard he's sent sprawling into my fireplace. Hermes shoves me to the ground, covering my body with his as stones rain through the air. We stay that way until my fireplace is nothing but a crater.

"Had you showed up at the final decision," Hades continues, stepping through the rubble to stand in front of where his brother lies, "you would have heard the truth finally come out." The prongs of the pitchfork stab into Poseidon's chest. "You know what other truth came out that I found very interesting, brother?"

He shoves the prongs until blood seeps through Poseidon's shirt, kicking the trident just out of reach. "The one where you and Athena have been lovers for ages. And how she thought she'd take out her competition one at a time by cursing those you cheated on her with. How Medusa wasn't the only one, just the only who managed to not go insane and die before we could reverse her unjust punishment."

WHAT? I look up at Hermes; is this truth? His eyes, so bright blue, tell me it is.

"You *knew* what Athena was doing," Hades says, voice terrifyingly low.

Poseidon swats at the pitchfork, but Hades doesn't budge. "I had no idea what she was doing until it was too late!"

"I will kill you for what you've done," Hades growls.

For a moment, nobody in the room even breathes. And then Poseidon throws his arms wide. "I'd like to see you try, brother."

"Do it."

Persephone is standing in the door, her long black dress whipping in the wind. "Do it," she says again, her voice hard and unforgiving. "Because if you don't, I will."

Poseidon moves to knock the pitchfork away, but Hades clomps a steel-toed boot right below the prongs. "You heard my wife. Goodbye, brother."

"It would be unwise for you to do that," comes another female voice.

Both Hades and Poseidon still, as if they're both calculating their odds. The Lord of the Seas speaks first. "What ... Demeter. What are you doing here? Come to fetch your daughter home?"

From behind Persephone comes a goddess I have only seen once, at the initial petition to reverse my curse. Tall and proud, the Goddess of the Harvest appears as merciless as one can come. "Let him up, Hades." Her green eyes flick toward where I'm standing, halfway hidden behind Hermes, and then back toward where Hades has Poseidon pinned.

"Fuck you, Demeter," Hades seethes. "I'm done listening to you."

Her voice is cool and controlled. "Yes, but the Seas is not. Come. Let him up so I may end this petty play for this girl once and for all."

Persephone spots me, and the next thing I know, I'm being wrenched out of Hermes' arms to be folded into hers. She's sobbing, running her hands up and down my arms, my back, up to my face. "Darling, are you okay? Has he done anything to you?"

I don't even know what to say. Think. *Do.*

She pulls me closer, until I almost can't breathe. "Pemphredo, is she okay? Is my daughter okay?"

Daughter.

Bernie shuffles over to where we're standing. "My lady, she is fine. Lord Hermes arrived just before she could complete a bond with the Seas."

"Thank the heavens for that." She looks up at Hermes. "Will you take her home until we—"

I pull out of her arms and step back, right into Hermes. "Nobody is taking me anywhere until I know what's going on." His hands come down on my shoulders, weighting me to the ground when all I want to do is step out of my body and float away. *"What is going on?"*

Demeter's smile is cold. "I see the little bitch is still causing problems. Can any of you finally understand why I sent her away? I knew this day would come, where she would try to rip the Assembly asunder. Nothing good can ever come from a union between the Harvest and the Underworld!"

Hades backhands his mother-in-law straight across the face in a move that would normally shatter a skull. But Demeter barely rocks on her feet.

Persephone steps in front of me, just as Hermes pulls me closer into the safety of his arm. "Mother, if you ever say such a thing again, I don't care what bargain we made years ago, I will never speak another word to you. Am I clear?"

Stars, I am so confused. What bargain?

Demeter rubs her face, her haughtiness unyielding. "Have I not complied enough this week, daughter? I have laid myself bare in trying to please you."

"You did it only because Hermes discovered the truth and forced you to admit your sins before the Assembly!" Persephone yells. "Had he not, I never would have known what had happened to my daughter!"

"Somebody better tell me what in the hell is going on," Poseidon barks. For once, I agree with the bastard.

So Demeter does.

Chapter Twenty-Five

Once upon a time, there was a very beautiful princess who, in most eyes, could want for nothing. She was the origin of every little girl's stereotypical fantasy: the belle of the ball, spoiled beyond measure, beloved by all, and a joy to behold. Her life was charmed.

She was exceptional in every way barring one thing: she felt hollow inside.

The princess knew it was most ungrateful to feel so. She was fully cognizant of the bounties her life provided and the absence of such in so many others'. And yet, there was still something missing inside, and it gnawed at her soul in the ugliest of ways. Made her feel horrid inside, as if she was a fraud.

But she was not one to rebel or to strike out against the hands that made her life comfortable; her heart, while troubled, was mostly soft towards those who loved her. So she endured this emptiness for years, all the while pasting a smile on her face that never let anyone know of what lay within, the vacuum no physical object could fill.

Then came the day the princess met a prince.

And it was not love at first sight.

This prince was not like the others who pursued her. In fact, he didn't pursue her at all, which made him—in the beginning—intriguing. He was dark, and introspective; more volatile than calm in those days, like black-gray clouds on the brink of disaster. Their initial meetings went badly, and each time, the princess swore to herself and anyone who would listen (including the prince) afterwards, "I hate him; I wish to never see him again."

The prince gave the princess no afterthoughts at all. She was nothing to him; not a temptation, not a ray of sun in his allegedly gloomy existence. He was content with his lot in life. And it was this that angered the princess. She puzzled over the prince more than she would admit to anyone. His life was filled with horrors, with more pain and sorrow than any joys. And yet, *he* was happy. *He* was content. *He* did not have a hole that ached, that could not be filled with trinkets and adorations. It seemed patently unfair to the spoiled princess. He, who had one of the worst hands dealt to him (in her opinion, despite his princely status), did not find his life lacking. She, who had everything, yearned for something, and it was a thorn in her foot that she could not figure it out.

As the years passed, the princess and the prince were put much into each other's spheres due to family and obligations. It burned her that he was never dazzled by her charms as others were, and she found herself acting out to claim his attention, just to prove she could. And then the princess's mother made notice of these actions, and cautioned her daughter against the prince. "He is not suited for you," she'd murmur to her beloved child. "He is dark, when you are light."

Yet, the more the princess contemplated this, the less she believed the words to be true. For she believed herself to be dark and hollow, and he the one filled with the light of self-acceptance. And the more this resonated within her, the more frantic her attempts to capture his attention became. She began to believe that she had to discover his secret or her life could not go on, charmed or no.

After much consideration and scheming, the princess finagled a circumstance in which she and the prince were alone. And when she did, she did not hesitate to corner him. "Why are you so happy?" she spat, anger and jealousy filling her soul.

This took the prince aback—for one, he was not used to such ire from anyone, as he was powerful and influential. But more importantly, this came from a princess who was nearly universally placed on a pedestal. While he had given her little thought prior, now he found himself intrigued. So he told her the truth. "I like who I am."

This knowledge ate at the princess, because she realized she did not like who she was. In truth, she didn't even know *who* she was, outside of what was beloved by all.

Her obsession with the prince intensified until he became all she could think of. She lived and breathed for the moments she saw him. She studied him. She memorized every last feature of his. She strove to be like him, to find the things that called to her. She threw herself in work and causes she'd deemed beneath her before, ones he'd embraced, and put her in the path of helping others, only to find they helped her fill the hole inside. But even these new endeavors weren't enough. When her obsession with the prince threatened to consume her, she realized she'd fallen in love with him. Not knowing what else to do, the princess went to her beloved mother to admit her feelings. "I have to have him," she told her mother. "I will only find true happiness if he is mine."

"He is not for you," her mother told her. "You are not suited in the least—he so dark, and you such a ray of light. Choose from any of your other admirers; they will bring you much more joy."

The princess did not believe this. The prince was the one filled with light; it was she who fought the darkness within. Her life before had been frivolous, but now she'd found ways to add meaning to it. So, she and her mother fought bitterly, yet no matter how many tears and tantrums ensued, the queen refused to kowtow to her daughter's foolish obsession. Eventually, worried about disobedience and a tarnishing of her daughter's legacy, the queen locked the princess away.

It took time and cunning, but the princess eventually escaped.

And then she ran straight to the prince who was, to say the least, surprised by this turn of events.

"You do not want me," he gently told the princess. "I'm no good for you."

So she kissed him.

And he changed his mind. Because, like in so many fairy-tales, a single kiss can make all the difference. The kiss the prince and princess shared was nothing like either had ever experienced. It changed them.

It melded them.

Months later, the queen discovered where the princess was hiding after disappearing, only to be dismayed to discover her precious daughter was content. And pregnant.

It was not to be tolerated. The queen had her daughter's life planned out before her. This prince, and their child, and his causes, were not to be in the cards. Politically, the queen needed to ensure there was no lingering connection between her daughter and the prince. In her mind, a child of those two houses would only complicate the kingdom's tremulous alliances. A much better alliance could be made with another prince. There was much arguing—even the king was drawn into the battle—and eventually, the queen reluctantly came to realize that, no matter what she said or wanted, the princess was never going to come back to fulfill her obligations without the prince. And the prince was not able to disregard his obligations, either. So a quagmire developed.

Now, the queen was clever—one of the cleverest beings to ever exist. While the existence of a baby complicated matters greatly, as it would be solid proof of an alliance she did not sanction, she also knew it was the greatest bargaining chip she had. So she laid out an offer: if the prince and princess handed over their baby and swore to never create another one, the princess would be sanctioned to live with the prince part of the year. The rest of the year, she would be required to fulfill her familial obligations and legacy.

The princess wept bitterly over this. The child growing within was precious to her. But so was the prince. As the king himself had sided with the queen, ordering her to do as the queen said or face grave punishment, she grew desperate. She wanted her child—desperately so—but she also knew she couldn't live without the prince and his love. Had the king not agreed with the queen, she would have risked everything. But with the king ordering her to obey, she had no other choice; neither did the prince. Although powerful in his own regard, he was also beholden to the king's wishes.

So they agreed.

Nine months she carried her child. Nine months of nurturing a baby, loving it, wanting it more than everything save one person. And then, after hours of labor, the princess birthed a baby she didn't even get to hold once.

The queen immediately whisked the child away, only to later inform the princess and her love that it'd died mere hours after.

The prince and princess grieved horribly. Holes grew in their hearts, ones that even the other person couldn't fill. The years passed, and they remained childless. The princess spent part of her life with the queen, as agreed upon, and her existence was hollow during those times. She knew where she belonged.

She belonged with her husband. But that never stopped her from wanting, more than anything, to hold her child. Just one time.

This was my parents' fairytale. Whether it had a happy ending or not was yet to be seen.

There was no remorse, no anything as Demeter recounted the events. It just simply was. And while she spoke, the room was still. *I* was still. She'd just told the story of my birth, and all I can do is simply stare at the woman who took me away from my parents.

Finally, Poseidon says, "You lie. I have never heard of this tale before today." And I hate to say it, but I can't help but think

Demeter lies, too.

She must.

My mother ... my mother is often said to be a primordial sea goddess, one who personified the dangers of the sea. Ceto, I believe—and how ironic would that have been if true. It was said I was one of three Gorgon sisters, the only mortal amongst immortals. But then, it was also said that Athena was in possession of my head, and that it'd been cut off by some fop who wanted to save a princess even more beautiful than I (not that I'm saying it wasn't okay for her to be beautiful or anything). History had it all wrong. My mother was a lady of high standing, married to a man of high standing in ancient Greece. She was an efficient wife and a cold nurturer who left my welfare and that of my younger siblings more often than not to slaves, though I did not ever resent her for this. I ... I had siblings—brothers and sisters—but other than my beauty, I'd been nothing, no one special. Not until I became a monster.

The mother I grew up with was named Eugeneia. She is long dead. I grieved for her years ago, even though I never got to pay my respects when she went. But Hermes told me. He'd been there. He'd been there for me.

I look to him now. I don't know what to expect from him—shame? Astonishment? Anger? Resignation?

What I get is assuredness. Steady, absolute assuredness.

Demeter appears to be sucking on lemons when she says flatly, "It is the truth, sworn before the entire Assembly. Zeus himself has ruled it as fact."

"If that is the case," Poseidon snaps, "then how did none of us sense she was one of our kind? How was it that Athena was able to curse her?"

Persephone begins crying again. Hades shakes in his rage. And Demeter ... she is a cool cucumber as she says, "It is complicated, but I found a way to temporarily bind her divinity when I passed her off to a mortal family. Had she gotten sick before the age of thirty, there was an excellent chance she would have died with them. Unfortunately, Athena's curse triggered the girl's immortality to reappear." Her glacial eyes sweep over me again. "Now that Athena's bungling has been lifted, her divinity is slowly returning."

I don't even know what to think of this. I look up at Hermes again and ask, "Did you know?"

He turns to face me fully, his hands gently holding onto my upper arms. "I uncovered the truth of your heritage just this week."

I am a goddess? Me? Ex-monster Medusa a *goddess?*

Demeter's icy voice hits me like a brick. "I will never forgive you for your meddling, Hermes. It was not your place to dredge up this painful past."

"If you think I care one tiny iota about your opinion," he says in return, eyes flashing with anger, "then you are sorely mistaken."

Arguing begins in the room anew. Hades and Persephone are yelling at both Demeter and Poseidon. Poseidon, now standing up, is yelling about how he believes this all to be a lie, that he would have known I was divine. Demeter yells about how Hermes has ruined everything. But I am looking up at the face of the person I love most in the entire world.

"I swore to you I would find a way," he says, a hand coming up to touch my cheek. "I did not leave a single rock unturned."

I lean into his hand. "Where did you learn this?"

"Believe it or not, the Underworld." He angles a sly grin over at Jocko, who in return winks. "Thanks to several hints our mutual friend let slip to me about how it might be helpful to visit your original Athenian family, I spent the last few months tracking your adoptive mother down in the Asphodel Meadows. She was reluctant, but she told me her tale of how she received you from a witch after praying to the gods for a baby. Finding the witch took forever, as she was in Tartarus. And then, before I could discover the truth, I had to sort through various curses that Demeter had placed on her so long ago." He looks over at Jocko again. "I owe you much for what you've done."

I leave Hermes' arms just long enough to hug Jocko. "You did this for me?"

My hug pleases him. "I have told you before that you have nothing to fear from me, Maddy. I am Death. I know the difference between an immortal and a mortal girl altered by the gods. But as parts of your true heritage have been hidden behind Demeter's now fading curses, I was not sure beyond immortal what you truly were. Furthermore, I have grown ... fond of you. I didn't want you to suffer any longer than you have. I merely nudged the Greek Messenger toward the right direction; all the rest of the work is his."

Somebody sniffling nearby grabs my attention. Granny—no, Bernadette—no Pemphredo, is crying. Today is truly a day of miracles. "Are you hurt?" I rush to her side. "Granny! Are you hurt?"

"Stupid child." She swats me away. "I am just happy, that's all."

Something in my own chest swells when Hermes joins us. I am surrounded by so many people I love. "Is it the truth? Are Hades and Persephone ... are they truly my parents? My real ones?"

His eyes, so icy blue moments before as he confronted Demeter, melt into green. "Sworn before the Assembly just last night."

The arguing around us falls silent when the door swings open once more. The mighty Zeus has come to join the fray.

"Brothers," he says, glancing around at the damaged room, "it appears we have a serious problem."

Realizing it would be entirely inappropriate to laugh at how this is the understatement of the year, I wisely keep silent.

"I can't have the Seas and the Underworld at open war with one another," the King of the Gods continues. He's furious. "Not now, when there is already so much strife in the world."

"Our fucking brother raped my daughter!" Hades roars. "And your bitch-spawn tortured her for millennia!" He slams his pitchfork into the floor, rattling the walls once more. "*I demand justice.* And if you stand in my way, I will be more than happy to go to war with you, too. I no longer give a flying fuck that you wear the crown." He shoves the pitchfork toward Zeus. "You allowed Demeter to take my daughter. To lie to me about her death!"

Zeus actually flinches at the vehemence of Hades' fury. "I vow to you that I believed the child to have died, too. Demeter informed me—"

"And this acquits you? Acquits her?" Hades swings his rage toward Demeter before refocusing on Zeus. "Acquits your vicious bitch of a daughter? How would you like it if I tortured your girl?"

Zeus holds up a hand. I'm shocked to my core to see him so shaken over Hades' wrath. "Brother, we have already begun the process of addressing Athena's punishment—"

"If you tell me one more time that she chose to castigate my daughter because love makes fools of us all, I will lose my mind," Hades seethes. "That is not a good enough reason for me. Do you understand that, Zeus?"

I've got to admit, I feel stupid for never seeing that one coming. All these years, I wracked my mind for reasons why Athena hated me, yet never once considered love was her reason.

"Long story short," Hermes whispers in my ear as Zeus assures Hades that he will do everything in his power to rectify the issue, "my insane sister has been in love with my psychotic uncle for years. They've been having an on-going affair, but he has refused to carry it further because he ..." He tenses in my arms. "Because he was obsessed with you."

I turn the tale over in my head before facing Poseidon. Rather than watching his brothers argue, his attention is fully, desperately on me.

Puzzle pieces finally slide together. "You ... she ...?"

"No," he tells me in that soft, rational sounding voice of his. "Pretty girl, I've never loved her. Not like I love you. She's been ... what we are ... it's nothing. Just physical, and it ended after I met you. I swear—"

Hades stops arguing with Zeus long enough to punch the Lord of the Seas, sending him sprawling once more. Even Zeus looks disgusted at his brother.

I say in wonder, "She hates me because she loves him." I turn to Hermes. "For two thousand years, I've tortured myself with that question. And now ... now the answer is so simple."

Hermes tells me gently, "I told you the gods do not sway easily in our emotions."

Which is something that now applies to me, too.

Poseidon grunts, pulling my attention back to where he's struggling to stand back up. His bright blue eyes are filled with panic.

He's scared? What is he scared of? But ... no. I don't care anymore. "There is no part of me that loves you, let alone *likes* you, Poseidon. There never has been. Any chance for that died the day you decided to selfishly take my choices away from me." My voice rings through the house. June would be proud that I'm finally getting my feelings out in the open. "You have made my life hell; because of your twisted love, I became a monster. I ... I killed people."

Persephone's weeping intensifies. Demeter reaches for her, but she shoves her mother's hand away.

"I tried to protect you," Poseidon says quietly. "I protected your shores. I watched over you. Caught more people from reaching you than ever got through. Ensured to the best of my ability that you stayed safe. Had I known Athena would have ..." He swallows. "I wouldn't have allowed her to do that to you. I didn't know how to get the curse reversed without leaving you vulnerable to her attentions. You must believe me."

I'm shaking. "You. Raped. Me. Is that one Athena's fault, too?"

"No—no, that was ... what we did, that was love. I wanted ... it was to make you mine—"

"I am not yours." My fists clench into balls. "Do you understand that? *I am not yours*. I belong to no one but myself. And I'm done with you having any control over me."

He takes a step toward me, the fear intensifying in the tempestuous blue of his eyes. Both Hermes and Hades go to block him, even as Poseidon says to me, "We—"

I let loose a roundhouse kick that would make Aphrodite proud. And that bastard drops straight to the ground.

In the end, Zeus forcibly orders Poseidon to call off the storms; he does so with no further comment. If I had a more sympathetic heart, I'd almost say he leaves my house, under Zeus' watch and with several Automaton escorts, a broken man. But I am not sympathetic toward him in the least.

In a small, weird way, though, I am toward Athena, despite never wishing to see her again. She acted out of love and desperation—horribly misguided, but nonetheless real.

Before they leave, though, Zeus says to me, "You and I have a lot to catch up on, granddaughter."

And it freaks me out a bit. Because if Zeus is Persephone's dad, and therefore my grandfather, and Hades' brother, making him my uncle, too ... And now—he's Hermes' dad, which makes the god I'm in love with my ... cousin? No. Wait. Uncle? Is he Persephone's half-brother?

It's all too confusing.

"Are you okay?" Hermes says to me as we watch two of the Three leave.

I press my face against his warm chest. "I was just thinking, I'm a goddess and you're ... my uncle?"

There's that delightful exhale of a laugh of his. "That's what you're thinking about? After everything that just happened? That you've learned?"

I can't hide my smile. "Are you?"

"If I am, it doesn't matter. The gods alter their genetic makeups for their children; it's the only way the Assembly can function and thrive, what with a small population to choose from as spouses. Since we are gods, our ... DNA, if you will, alters constantly. We have no single strand. So, yes. My father is Zeus. Yes, Persephone's father is Zeus, too. And yet, we share no blood, no genes that tie us together."

"You call her your aunt."

"I do." I fall in love all over again with his smile. "But that is something I *choose* to call her. It's the same with Aphrodite. She and I share no similar markers in our makeup, but we have chosen to embrace the relationship between us."

"And ... Athena?"

He sighs. "She is no longer my family. You do not need to fear her any longer; Zeus has promised me that she is forbidden from even saying your name, let alone from being in the same room with you. The same with Poseidon. I no longer claim them at all in any capacity. They are nothing to me."

"And ... me?"

His hands cup my face. "You are, as you have been since the moment I met you, the most important person in my existence."

And as I did with our first kiss so many months ago, I make the first move. My mouth is on his, and I'm finally, finally home.

Chapter Twenty-Six

Persephone makes it vehemently clear the moment that we get back to their home on Olympus that whatever agreement she and Hades made so very long ago with Demeter is now negated. "I am not going back with her," she rages as she alternates between pacing in front of me and Hades sitting together on the couch, and coming over to hug and kiss me. "Ever! This is my place. Here, with my real family. None of us are to have anything to do with her again, do you hear me? *Nothing*."

"How are you doing with all this?" Hades asks me gently, his large hand stroking my hair. It feels really good; his hands are warm. And they look like a father's ought to: bigger than mine, worn with age.

"It's a lot to take in," I admit. And it is. Despite everything that's gone on today, all the truths I've learned, it still feels like I'm in the midst of a dream while lying in my bed in Jackson.

Yet, this is real. These people here—these powerful gods that I fell in love with so very long ago—are truly my parents. *I have a family*.

Persephone comes back to the couch, wrapping her arm

around my shoulders so it can join Hades'. I've got my cat on my lap, purring contentedly. Stars, I'm glad to have this little guy back. All that's missing is Hermes, who was strongly encouraged by Persephone to give her and Hades at least a few hours with me alone. He agreed to go back to Wyoming and deal with loose ends with Bernie and Jocko.

I hate to say it, especially since I've only been back in Olympus for a little over two hours, but I already miss Jackson.

"Of course, of course," she murmurs. Her eyes are steeped with worry. Regret. More tears. "But ... whatever you need, darling. It's yours. If you want us to give you space to wrap your mind around all of this, we will. If you don't want us to leave any room you're in unless asked to, we'll do that, too. But just know, now that we have found you, the only thing we can't do is give you up again."

I'd heard their story, and get it—for the most part. Even still, I say softly, "But you did once."

Tears track down her cheeks. "I know, and I will never be able to say to you enough how much I wish I could turn the clock back and change that. I would, darling. All these years, your father and I have tortured ourselves with the What Ifs. What if we'd refused to go along with my mother's wishes? What if we'd stood up to Zeus, not caring we could be evicted from Olympus? What if we'd fought harder to keep you? We wish so much that we had, Medusa. More than you will ever know."

"I believe you," I tell her. And I do. I know her well enough by now to know that Persephone—no, my mother—would not lie to me.

"The things you've gone through," my father chokes out, his voice rough with emotion. "It makes me sick, makes me want to ..." He has to look away. "I promise you this: I will make sure that nothing, no one can ever harm you again. Not even my brothers. You will never need to fear anything."

They make these promises, these vows over and over again over the next few hours. Their sincerity and love, it strengthens me. I have a family now.

251

Speaking of ...

"Thank you for allowing Granny—I mean Bernie—" I sigh. It's only been half a year, but in my heart, Bernie will forever be my grandmother. How will I ever treat her differently? "Pemphredo to live here with us once she gets back from Jackson."

"Of course," my mother says. "We know how much she means to you; Pemphredo will be forever welcome in this house." She presses another kiss against my cheek. "Kore is upstairs waiting for you, too. I brought her back, just like you asked. She's been working here the whole time."

"Albeit fully knowing that we are watching her closely," Hades adds grudgingly, "and that if she dares betray our household again, she will receive no further reprieves."

This is most welcome news, and a further testament to the love they had for me even before learning I was their daughter. "I'm glad. Only, Kore isn't going to stay with me in my suite any longer. She obviously has her own room by now, right?"

Blank looks from my parents. "Why wouldn't Kore stay with you, darling?" Persephone asks. "She's your handmaiden."

I scratch Matia's head. "Weeelll ..." Hello, awkwardness. They must remember Hermes and I were basically living with one another, right? I quickly switch the subject. "Just out of curiosity, and not that I'm complaining, but why Pemphredo?"

Persephone laughs guilty, peeking over at Hades. He's predictably rolling his eyes. "When we decided you'd have to go into hiding, we realized you needed to be guarded by only the best. Your father and Hermes insisted on Death himself, and don't get me wrong—that was an excellent choice. Death does not break his word. But it wasn't good enough for me. Death is ... not a nurturer, if that makes sense. And I wanted somebody there who would love you, see to your wants and emotional needs."

I interrupt her. "Believe it or not, Jocko—I mean, Death really did do those things. There was this one time, when I was really ... depressed," I wince, "and he made it so I could see Hermes. Hermes couldn't see me, didn't know I was there, but Jocko knew that it would help me."

My parents are agog. After a moment of silence, my father mutters, "That tricky bugger."

"Anyway," my mother continues, mischief sparkling in her eyes, "I chose one of my loyal followers to guard you. Somebody that the rest of the Assembly had no idea was in my corner. Oh, they knew that she was in the Underworld, but none of them knew she was actively in my employ."

I think back to the stories I'd heard as a child about the Graeae, the Gray Sisters. The ones who sometimes look like swans, other times like crones, and yet other times beauties. Universally, though, they share a commonality: "She was one of the three who share an eye?"

"As well as a tooth. And darling, this was before I knew you were *my* daughter, of my blood and bone, but part of why I selected her was that she was a matriarch of the Gorgon clan."

I sit up. "Granny was ... is? She's really my family?"

Persephone places her palm against my cheek. "In truth, adopted great-great grandmother. I knew she would protect you to the end. Family means everything to her. It always has."

"So, when she told me to call her Granny, it was ... real," I marvel. All this time, all of her loyalty toward me ... it was genuine.

Love for Bernie fills me until it spills out in happy tears.

"Plus," Persephone continues, wiping my cheeks. "she was a minor sea deity before her powers were stripped away, and one who loathes Poseidon, to boot. She was perfect in every way to protect you."

Bernadette is my great-great grandma. I'd lamented losing everyone, and I'd actually had family with me the entire time.

"She was," I tell them. "I love her. I loved them both."

The door opens, and Hermes comes in. I take a good two seconds to drink in his sight, starting at the top of his golden head to the tips of his toes and then back up to his beautiful face. "I see you found our buddy," he tells me, reaching down to scratch Mátia's head.

Our. I like the sound of that very much.

I wish my parents would scoot over so he can sit with me, but as they refuse to budge, Hermes quickly kisses my cheek and sits on the couch across from us.

I don't think it's my imagination, but both Hades and Persephone glare at him. I love them, too, but I won't stand for that. So I get up, taking my cat with me, and choose to sit next to Hermes.

Hades coughs. "I know we've said it countless times in the last few days, but, Hermes, thank you for everything you've done for our daughter. For being there when we couldn't be. For believing in her when nobody else did. For bringing us into her life. You ... you'll always have our gratitude and support. You will never need to worry about allies in the Assembly."

Hermes looks down at me. I look up at him. Heat rises to the surface of my skin.

I wish my parents would find another room to be in for a little bit.

It's my mother's turn to clear her throat. "You'll come for dinner? To celebrate?"

Do they think I'm going to let him leave my sight anytime soon? Silly parents. "Yes," I answer for him. And then, ashamed that I'm so obvious, "Unless, you have other plans?"

"None," he says, and I melt in the brilliance of his smile. "I'm at your disposal."

Oh, I like the sound of that very much, too. I give him a goofy grin in return, and before long, my parents are shuffling their feet and clearing their throats repeatedly.

I figure I have a bit of leverage nowadays. So I stand up, pulling Hermes with me. "Let's go for a walk."

Persephone protests, but I pass over my cat for her to hold and lead Hermes out of the room. We bypass the patios and the groves and head directly to my old room. We don't say a word, don't kiss or touch other than holding hands the entire way. We let the anticipation between us build until it's nearly unbearable. So when we finally open the door to my suite, only to find Kore, I quickly cross the room to hug her. "Kore, I've missed you, I'm glad you're here, no—don't apologize, that's all water under the bridge, and don't take this the wrong way, but you are dismissed until tomorrow, effective immediately."

Bless that girl's heart, she leaves with a knowing smile on her face and without any protest.

The look Hermes gives me when I shut the door behind her makes my knees go weak, it's so hot.

"I think your parents would have a fit if they knew we were up here right now," he tells me in a low, sexy tone that sends shivers down my spine. "It's funny how, for months, they've known you are my one and only love, and have fought alongside me to bring you safely back to Olympus. But now that you are here, and I am too, I get the very distinct feeling they are no longer quite so welcoming of our relationship."

I reach behind me and lock the door. "You know what? I don't care. Because you are *my* one and only love, and I'm pretty sure they know we've done more than chastely kiss before."

And then he's here, right in front of me, his arms boxing me against the wood. "Stars, I've missed you, Medusa. Let's not do this separation thing again. It nearly killed me."

I twine my arms around his neck. "I couldn't have said it better." And then, as my hands reach up to pull his face toward mine, I say, "I am a goddess now, you know. Or, at least, I'm becoming one."

He knows what I mean. "Mortal, monster, or goddess," he says quietly, seriously, "or any combination there in between, I love you all the same." His mouth meets mine then, and half a year of missing and loving tear through the both of us. Our tongues tangle together as one of his hands slides down my side until it cups my bottom. My fingers twist in his hair only for a brief moment, because I need to be touching him, too. I place one hand above his heart (I love feeling it race when he touches me) and the other down to where he is already hard for me. I squeeze gently and I'm gifted with that moan of his that is the best sound in the entire world.

Six months of sexually frustrating dreams have me practically ripping his shirt off. He follows with my sweater and then my long sleeved t-shirt. I'm tugging down his jeans, he's working on mine, and clothes and shoes are flying. He picks me up; I hook my legs around his waist so he can carry me over to the bed. It doesn't take long before he's exactly where I want him—deep inside me, moving in a rhythm that has me panting and reaching and needing.

This is so much better than any of those dreams.

"I love you," I whisper as his mouth finds my breast. My back arches and drives him in me deeper. Stars above, he feels so good.

He lifts his head so his mouth can reclaim mine. "I love you," he whispers back.

These words, like no other, have the power to send me over the edge. I dig into his shoulders as my orgasm blooms; he follows me over the edge within a matter of moments. I'm okay with this rush; I needed this, him. Next time we'll go slow.

As I have in the past, I refuse to let him slide out just yet. Next time will be soon, if I have my way with him.

"I don't care if Poseidon brings an army against us," he murmurs, his breath heavy, yet soft against my cheek. "Or my father, or any other person in the world. We're never being parted again."

I kiss the side of his face, not bothered in the least by his sweaty hair. "I'm going to hold you to that."

His hand traces lazy patterns around my breasts, sparking renewed warmth between my legs. How he has the ability to do this to me so easily and quickly is a most welcome one. I instinctively arch my back up, only to twist my hips against his.

He lets out a gasp. "Also. Today? When you kicked the shit out of that bastard?"

My hands, tracing their own patterns on his back, still.

"That was incredibly hot."

I stare up into his eyes—bright green in this moment—as his hips begin their own gently rhythm. Thank the heavens, he is soft in me no longer.

My hands slide down to cup his buttocks. "Yeah?"

His lips graze my collarbone. "Yeah." He flips us, so I'm

straddling him. His hands lead my hips and before long, just as I predicted, we are slowly but surely on our way to the bliss once more.

Chapter Twenty-Seven

"Medusa ..."

Persephone is sitting next to me on a comfy couch in the villa's theatre as we watch a movie, her hand on top of mine. She is uncharacteristically nervous. It is so odd to think that this woman, who appears to be no older than twenty-five, is my mother. That she carried me for nine months, only to give me over to her own mother.

I have to stop thinking of it like that. She's here now. It may have taken us thousands of years to find one another, but my mother is here for me now. My father, too—although, at this very moment, he is downstairs in a meeting.

They've been hovering, which ... I get. But still, it's hovering and, frankly, annoying. Even if they're gods.

"Hmm?"

She taps my hand. "You and Hermes."

Oh, stars—is this what I think it's going to be about?

"I just want to know. Is this what you want? Because it feels like it's moving oh-so-fast."

"Two thousand years is not fast," I tell her dryly. "If you want to quibble about labels, you might want to get on him for taking his sweet time."

Of course, the same could be said for me, too.

She isn't amused. I try again. "Earlier in the year, you were delighted that he and I were ..." Just what were we? Are we? Boyfriend and girlfriend? That sounds so ridiculous, in light of our divine statuses. Do gods and goddesses even date? I screw my nose up, trying to find a proper word to use.

I don't. Instead, I just shrug and say, "Together."

One of the most defining traits of the gods I've determined is that anytime they look at you, it's done with an intensity no mortal can match. And this is the case now, what with my mother scrutinizing me within an inch of my immortal life. It's hard not to squirm like a youth would, especially considering I am no youth. "That was before I knew you were our daughter."

I turn to face her fully. "I truly appreciate your concern, Persephone, I do—"

"Darling, have I mentioned how good it would do my heart to hear you call me *mother?*"

I smile, flashing back to my arguments with Kore over the use of my name. It is another change in my life, one I am still learning to embrace. "Mom ... it's just ... I am no longer a little girl. I've been alive for thousands of years. I grew up a long time ago, all on my own—"

She chokes up, but I can't let the guilt she still needlessly carries distract me from this message. "And while I'm delighted that we are becoming a true family," I quickly lean forward to press a kiss against her cheek, "I also think it's important to remind you that my life and my choices are mine to make, including whom I love. I would hope that you, of all people, would understand this."

She knows what I mean. "I hardly see how our situations are the same—"

I say gently, "You mother told you that she knew what was best for you. You wanted Hades. You knew what was in your heart. You knew he was the one for you. Well, it's the same for me. I know what's in my heart. I love Hermes. Absolutely, unequivocally, am head-over-heels in love with him. And love for our kind is a forever thing, isn't it?" I squeeze her hand, and the surrealism of the situation is not lost on me. "Besides. Don't you normally think the sun rises and sets on him?"

A guilty flush steals across her porcelain skin. "Fine. Yes, I love him dearly, and know him to be the finest of characters. And I will forever be grateful to him for uncovering the truth about you. It's just ... it's different now. You're my daughter. I will always worry and wish for the best for you." And then her eyes roll toward the ceiling. "Do *not* tell your grandmother that, understand?"

I tease, "That shouldn't be a problem, as I thought I was banned from talking to her."

She laughs. "You most certainly are." And then, more soberly, "I just want you to be happy, darling."

"I am," I say, and the fantastic thing is, I really, truly am.

paris

Chapter Twenty-Eight

I close my eyes and turn my face up towards the sky. There is a fine mist coming down, all gloriously soft and drizzly, and it feels divine against my skin. I pity the people nearby who are hovering under umbrellas. Don't they know rain is magical?

"Happy?" Hermes asks me, his arm warm around my shoulders.

"I love Paris." The smile stretching across my face almost hurts, it's so big. Aphrodite threatened to come along so she and I could shop, but Hermes made her swear to stay at home.

"I knew you would." He kisses the side of my face, bringing it back down towards him. And then, mischievously: "Pemphredo tells me that your bedroom in Wyoming was quite Parisian."

I laugh. "It was." I turn into his embrace and spy the Eiffel Tower in the distance. It is sunset, and soon the Tower will be lit up in thousands of twinkling celestial lights. I'm reminded of another magical night filled with lights. How I thank the stars above that I was smart enough to steal a kiss from this man. "Is it weird that I miss it?"

The side of his face finds mine before his forehead slides

down my cheek so he can kiss the space where my chin meets my neck. "Do you mean the bedroom? You can still have it, you know. We can recreate it in Olympus, if you'd like, once our new house is finished being constructed. If you mean your house in Jackson, well ... love, it's still there, waiting for you for whenever you want to visit. Jackson will always be one of our homes."

We. Our. "I like the sound of that," I tell him. I shiver as his lips graze the line from my ear to my chin.

"You can have an actual Parisian bedroom, too," he says softly, placing one last, gentle kiss before pulling his head away far enough so he can look into my eyes. They're green again and oh-so-beautiful.

I cannot get rid of my grin. I must look like a blithering idiot, drunk on sheer happiness. "I like the sound of that, too."

"I had a talk with your father," he tells me, and it strikes me that lately, he's been referring to Hades as *your father*, instead of *my uncle*.

"Must we talk about my parents right now? I can think of some other things we ought to be talking about. Like ... where to find macarons. Or *chocolat chaud*."

His laugh is that wonderful exhale I've come to adore after so many years of knowing him. "I mention this talk, because it's important."

I groan. "We are having such a wonderful time. Do you really want to muck things up by bringing up my overprotective father?" I rest my hands against his chest. "If you tell me he forbade us from being with one another, I say we do as he did, and not as he says."

His eyes twinkle in the gloriously gloomy Parisian twilight. "It was a good talk. We came to an understanding."

Is he funning me? Because the last time my parents and I discussed me moving out with Hermes, my father raged over how I was much too young to even consider declaring myself in love with anyone, beloved nephew Hermes or not. "Explain."

He doesn't, of course. Instead, he leans forward and kisses me in such a hot, intimate way that I actually do forget, for several delightful, frustrating minutes, that we are in public. Because when we are together, like this, we really are alone. He and I. *Us.*

It's always been us.

I let out a whimper ... or is it a groan? Forget the macarons. Or the *chocolat chaud.* All I need is him. As his kisses once more turn me inside out, I try to stay coherent long enough to calculate how soon we can get back to our hotel. Even though we made love just hours before, I'm already ready to take him back to bed and work on our epilogue.

His mouth leaves mine and traces a scorching path down my neck. "Do you remember when you queried as to why I wasn't married yet? And how I told you that it was because I had yet to ask the woman who owns my heart? It's far past time I rectify that."

The hotel is, what, a ten-minute walk, and if we leave right— wait. *What?* I pull back at the same time he does.

"Nothing would make me happier than my best friend, whom I happen to be desperately in love with, agreeing to spend eternity with me. Dusa, love ... will you marry me?" He's already dropping to one knee, just like a scene out of a movie or a book. Like a human would do, not a god who could have anyone or anything he wants without asking, if he put his mind to it.

But then, that's what has always set Hermes apart. He isn't like the rest. He's the very best of both worlds.

He takes my hands and kisses them. People around us stop and stare, their umbrellas tilted so they can see us all the better. "You and me," he says, and his smile is sunshine against the soft gray of the dying day. "Forever."

"Yes." And then, again: "Yes!" Because there is no other answer I could ever give and not be true to my heart.

I am in his arms again, and we are twirling, and laughing, and life is so sweet, so perfect in this moment. There is clapping all around us, wolf whistles and cheering; this is the City of Love, after all. And we are most assuredly, deliriously, wonderfully in the throes of forever love.

This is my fairy tale. And it most definitely has a happy

ending.

If you or anyone you know is a victim of sexual assault, you do not need to suffer in silence. Contact the National Sexual Assault Hotline at 1-800-656-HOPE to speak with a counselor, visit the RAINN (Rape, Abuse & Incest National Network) website at http://rainn.org, and/or connect with an online counselor via RAINN's confidential Online Hotline at http://online.rainn.org/ to learn more about your options.

Glossary

Ægir—In Norse mythology, **Ægir** is the god of the ocean and king of the sea creatures.

Amund—Norse given name derived from *Agmundr,* an Old Norse name meaning *respectful protector*.

Andlát—Icelandic word for death.

Angelia—Minor Greek deity personifying greetings and proclamations.

Anubis—Egyptian jackal-headed god of mummification and the afterlife.

Asphodel Meadows—The area where ordinary people end up in the Underworld in Greek mythology.

Aphrodite—Greek goddess of love and beauty.

Apollo—Greek god of the sun, light, and truth.

Ares—Greek god of war.

Athena—Greek goddess of wisdom and warfare.

Automatons—Metal people and creatures created by Hephaestus in Greek mythology often used as protectors.

Ceto—Greek primordial sea goddess.

Demeter—Greek goddess of the harvest.

Elysian Fields—The area where the heroic and virtuous end up in the Underworld in Greek mythology.

Glykia mou—Greek endearment for *my sweetheart*.

Gorgons—In Greek mythology, female monsters who could turn people to stone.

Graeae—Three minor Greek deities who personified sea foam; also known as the Gray Sisters, they shared a tooth and an eye.

Hades—Greek god of the Underworld.

Hel—Norse goddess of the Underworld.

Hephaestus—Greek god of blacksmiths.

Hera—Queen of the Greek Gods and Goddesses

Hermes—Greek god of commerce, travelers, and athletes, as well as a guide to the Underworld; considered to be the messenger of the Greek pantheon.

Hestia—Greek goddess of the hearth.

Kardia mou—Greek endearment for *my heart*.

Matakia mou—Greek endearment for *my eyes*.

Medusa—Monster in Greek mythology known as a Gorgon; had snakes for hair and could turn people to stone by looking at them.

Minn hirra—Old Norse for *my lord*.

Nymph—Minor female nature deity in Greek mythology.

Olympus—Also known as Mount Olympus, a mountain range in Greece thought to be home to the Greek pantheon of gods and goddesses.

Pemphredo—One of the Graeae, Pemphredo is known as *alarm* or *she who guides the way*.

Persephone—Greek goddess of spring and vegetation; Queen of the Underworld.

Perseus—Hero in Greek mythology celebrated for slaying Medusa.

Poseidon—Greek god of the seas and storms.

Satyr—Half man, half goat creatures in Greek mythology.

Talos—A giant man made of bronze who served as a protector in Greek mythology.

Tartarus— The area where wicked people end up in the Underworld in Greek mythology.

Telesphorus—Greek demi-god of convalescence.

Yassou—Common Greek greeting comparable with *hello* or *health to you!*

Zeus—King of the Greek gods.

Acknowledgements

This book has been truly a labor of love to write, and there are so many people to thank for coming on this journey with me. Pam van Hylckama Vlieg, thanks for believing in Medusa's story so much. John Hansen, Laura Cummings, and Natasha Tomic, I truly appreciate the editorial work you put into this story. KP Simmon, thank you for all you've done for me and this book. Kelsey Patton, I am so grateful you've allowed me to use your beautiful art on the cover. Speaking of ... Carly Stevens, thanks for designing another beauty for me! Stacey Blake, thank you for your wonderful formatting skills. I am incredibly lucky to have such a talented team behind me.

To my amazing beta readers Tracy Cooper, Andrea Johnston, Vilma Gonzalez, and Megan O'Connell, I am forever grateful for all the time, suggestions, feedback, love, and encouragements you've given this story and characters. It's meant the world to me.

To my wonderful street team, I send you lots of love and gratitude for the support you gift me with. You guys are the best! Big shout-outs also go out to the following bloggers, all of whom I owe so much to for their continual support of me and my books: Natasha at Natasha is a Book Junkie, Vilma at Vilma's Book Blog, Cristina at Cristina's Book Reviews, Ana at The Book Hookup, Jessica at Lovin' Los Libros, Caitlin at The Road is You, Chelsea at Starbucks & Books Obsession, Maria at Reading the Alphabet, Meredith at Pandora's Books, Tricia at Romance Addict Book Blog, Kathryn at TSK TSK What to Read, Autumn at The Book Trollop, Megan at Paperbook Princess, and Sarah at Simply Sarah's Corner.

To my husband and three boys, I love you guys more than anything. I am so grateful you guys put up with my need to get these stories out of my head. I also send love and appreciation out to my parents and the rest of my friends and family who have supported me as I chase these dreams.

All the gratitude to you, too, sweet readers.

Also by Heather Lyons

The magical first book of the Fate series ...

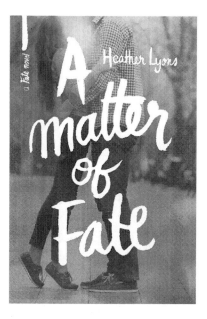

"Love, love, love this book! Such a fun and exciting premise. Full of teenage angst and heartache with a big helping of magic and enchantment. Can't wait to read the rest of this awesome series! Not to mention... TWO hot boys to swoon over." *–Elizabeth Lee, author of Where There's Smoke*

Chloe Lilywhite struggles with all the normal problems of a typical seventeen-year-old high school student. Only, Chloe isn't a normal teenage girl. She's a Magical, part of a secret race of beings who influence the universe. More importantly, she's a Creator, which means Fate mapped out her destiny long ago, from her college choice, to where she will live, to even her job. While her friends and relatives relish their future roles, Chloe resents the lack of say in her life, especially when she learns she's to be guarded against a vengeful group of beings bent on wiping out her kind. Their number one target? Chloe, of course.

That's nothing compared to the boy trouble she's gotten herself into. Because a guy she's literally dreamed of and loved her entire life, one she never knew truly existed, shows up in her math class, and with him comes a twin brother she finds herself inexplicably drawn to.

Chloe's once unyielding path now has a lot more choices than she ever thought possible.
Available as an eBook and paperback at book retailers

Follow Chloe's story in the rest of the Fate series books ...

"Heather Lyons' writing is an addiction...and like all addictions. I. Need. More."
--#1 New York Times Best Selling Author Rachel Van Dyken

"Enthralling fantasy with romance that will leave you breathless, the Fate Series is a must read!" *--Alyssa Rose Ivy, author of the Crescent Chronicles*

About the Author

photo @Regina Wamba of Mae I Design and Photography

Heather Lyons writes epic, heartfelt love stories and has always had a thing for words. In addition to writing, she's also been an archaeologist and a teacher. She and her husband and children live in sunny Southern California and are currently working their way through every cupcakery she can find.

Website: www.heatherlyons.net
Facebook: http://www.facebook.com/heatherlyonsbooks
Twitter: http://www.twitter.com/hymheather
Goodreads: http://www.goodreads.com/author/show/6552446.
Heather_Lyons

Made in the USA
Lexington, KY
10 December 2014